Three times the monster had jetted water. Now it enveloped them, capturing their vessel.

Above the steaming and bubbling, above the water's churning and the line of thin fire that reached upward, there was a fireball that exploded. Where the wire had touched living flesh there was a blaze of furious energy. It burned a hole ten feet wide and as many feet deep into the living mountain above him.

Not one minute after his bolt had struck the creature, it struck back.

Lucky's shocked and tortured senses told him that he was being driven down, down, down, in a turbulent jet of madly driving water. . . .

By Isaac Asimov

THE FOUNDATION SERIES:
 Prelude to Foundation
 Foundation
 Foundation and Empire
 Second Foundation
 Foundation's Edge

THE GALACTIC EMPIRE NOVELS:
 The Stars, Like Dust
 The Currents of Space
 Pebble in the Sky

THE ROBOT NOVELS:
 The Caves of Steel
 The Naked Sun
 I, Robot

The Gods Themselves

The End of Eternity

Nemesis

Fantastic Voyage

Fantastic Voyage II

THE LUCKY STARR ADVENTURES:
Writing as Paul French
 David Starr—Space Ranger & Lucky Starr and the
 Pirates of the Asteroids

Nightfall *with Robert Silverberg*

LUCKY STARR BOOK 2

LUCKY STARR AND THE OCEANS OF VENUS

&

LUCKY STARR AND THE BIG SUN OF MERCURY

ISAAC ASIMOV
writing as Paul French

SPECTRA

BANTAM BOOKS
NEW YORK · TORONTO · LONDON · SYDNEY · AUCKLAND

All the characters in this book are fictitious, and any resemblance
to actual persons living or dead is purely coincidental.

This edition contains the complete text
of the original hardcover edition.
NOT ONE WORD HAS BEEN OMITTED.

LUCKY STARR BOOK 2

A Bantam Spectra Book / by arrangement with Doubleday

PUBLISHING HISTORY

Lucky Starr and the Oceans of Venus
copyright © 1954 by Doubleday.
Lucky Starr and the Big Sun of Mercury
copyright © 1956 by Doubleday.

Bantam edition / May 1993

ISBN 0-553-56254-1

Published simultaneously in the United States and Canada

Bantam Books are published by Bantam Books, a division of Bantam
Doubleday Dell Publishing Group, Inc. Its trademark, consisting of the
words "Bantam Books" and the portrayal of a rooster, is Registered in
U.S. Patent and Trademark Office and in other countries. Marca
Registrada. Bantam Books, 1540 Broadway, New York, New York
10036.

PRINTED IN THE UNITED STATES OF AMERICA

RAD   0 9 8 7 6 5 4 3 2 1

LUCKY STARR
AND THE
OCEANS OF VENUS

DEDICATION

To Margaret Lesser
and all the girls in the department

CONTENTS

Preface

Back in the 1950s, I wrote a series of six derring-do novels about David "Lucky" Starr and his battles against malefactors within the Solar System. Each of the six took place in a different region of the system and in each case I made use of the astronomical facts—as they were then known.

LUCKY STARR AND THE OCEANS OF VENUS was written in 1953, at which time it was thought quite likely that there might be a great deal of liquid water on the planet.

On August 27, 1962, however, a probe, "Mariner II," was launched and it passed within 21,000 miles of Venus on December 14, 1962. Its measurements of radio-wave radiation from the planet showed that the surface temperature of Venus was far higher than the boiling point of water. All investigations since have backed this up—even the reports of devices actually landed on Venus's surface. There is therefore no world-wide ocean on Venus as described in this book. There is no ocean at all. The surface of the planet is absolutely dry and nearly red-hot. What's more, the atmosphere is about 95 times as dense as Earth's atmosphere and is almost all carbon dioxide. A most unpleasant world!

In 1964, radar beams bouncing off Venus's surface showed that it turned on its axis once in 243 days, and in the opposite direction from that in which other planets rotate. If I were writing the book today, I would have to take all these things into account.

I hope my Gentle Readers enjoy the book anyway, as an adventure story, despite the way scientific advance has outdated my—for that time—very conscientious descriptions.

ISAAC ASIMOV

1

Through the Clouds of Venus

Lucky Starr and John Bigman Jones kicked themselves up from the gravity-free Space Station No. 2 and drifted toward the planetary coaster that waited for them with its air lock open. Their movements had the grace of long practice under non-gravity conditions, despite the fact that their bodies seemed thick and grotesque in the space suits they wore.

Bigman arched his back as he moved upward and craned his head to stare once again at Venus. His voice sounded loudly in Lucky's ear through the suit's radio. "Space! Look at that rock, will you?" Every inch of Bigman's five-foot-two was tense with the thrill of the sight.

Bigman had been born and bred on Mars and had never in his life been so close to Venus. He was used to ruddy planets and rocky asteroids. He had even visited green and blue Earth. But here, now, was something that was pure gray and white.

Venus filled over half the sky. It was only two thousand miles away from the space station they were on. Another space station was on the opposite side of the planet. These two stations, acting as receiving depots for Venus-bound spaceships, streaked about the planet in a three-hour period of revolution, following one another's tracks like little puppies forever chasing their tails.

Yet from those space stations, close though they were to Venus, nothing could be seen of the planet's surface. No continents showed, no oceans, no deserts or mountains, no green valleys. Whiteness, only brilliant whiteness, interspersed with shifting lines of gray.

The whiteness was the turbulent cloud layer that hovered eternally over all of Venus, and the gray lines marked the boundaries where cloud masses met and clashed. Vapor moved downward at those boundaries, and below those gray lines, on Venus's invisible surface, it rained.

Lucky Starr said, "No use looking at Venus, Bigman. You'll be seeing plenty of it, close up, for a while. It's the sun you ought to be saying good-by to."

Bigman snorted. To his Mars-accustomed eyes, even Earth's sun seemed swollen and overbright. The sun, as seen from Venus's orbit, was a bloated monster. It was two and a quarter times as bright as Earth's sun, four times as bright as the familiar sun on Bigman's Mars. Personally, he was glad that Venus's clouds would hide its sun. He was glad that the space station always arranged its vanes in such a way as to block off the sunlight.

Lucky Starr said, "Well, you crazy Martian, are you getting in?"

Bigman had brought himself to a halt at the lip of the open lock by the casual pressure of one hand. He was still looking at Venus. The visible half was in the full glare of the sun, but at the eastern side the night shadow was creeping in, moving quickly as the space station raced on in its orbit.

Lucky, still moving upward, caught the lip of the lock

in his turn and brought his other space-suited hand flat against Bigman's seat. Under the gravity-free conditions, Bigman's little body went tumbling slowly inward, while Lucky's figure bobbed outward.

Lucky's arm muscle contracted, and he floated up and inward with an easy, flowing motion. Lucky had no cause for a light heart at the moment, but he was forced into a smile when he found Bigman spread-eagled in mid-air, with the tip of one gauntleted finger against the inner lock holding him steady. The outer lock closed as Lucky passed through.

Bigman said, "Listen, you wombug, someday I'm walking out on you and you can get yourself an-other———"

Air hissed into the small room, and the inner lock opened. Two men floated rapidly through, dodging Bigman's dangling feet. The one in the lead, a stocky fellow with dark hair and a surprisingly large mustache, said, "Is there any trouble, gentlemen?"

The second man, taller, thinner, and with lighter hair but a mustache just as large, said, "Can we help you?"

Bigman said loftily, "You can help us by giving us room and letting us get our suits off." He had flicked himself to the floor and was removing his suit as he spoke. Lucky had already shucked his.

The men went through the inner lock. It, too, closed behind them. The space suits, their outer surface cold with the cold of space, were frosting over as moisture from the warm air of the coaster congealed upon them. Bigman tossed them out of the coaster's warm, moist air on to the tiled racks, where the ice might melt.

The dark-haired man said, "Let's see, now. You two are William Williams and John Jones. Right?"

Lucky said, "I'm Williams." Using that alias under ordinary conditions was second nature to Lucky by now. It was customary for Council of Science members to shun publicity at all times. It was particularly advisable now with the situation on Venus as confused and uncertain as it was.

Lucky went on, "Our papers are in order, I believe, and our luggage is aboard."

"Everything's all right," the dark-haired one said, "I'm George Reval, pilot, and this is Tor Johnson, my co-pilot. We'll be taking off in a few minutes. If there's anything you want, let us know."

The two passengers were shown to their small cabin, and Lucky sighed inwardly. He was never thoroughly comfortable in space except on his own speed cruiser, the *Shooting Starr*, now at rest in the space station's hangar.

Tor Johnson said in a deep voice, "Let me warn you, by the way, that once we get out of the space station's orbit, we won't be in free fall any more. Gravity will start picking up. If you get space-sick———"

Bigman yelled, "Space-sick! You in-planet goop, I could take gravity changes when I was a baby that you couldn't take right now." He flicked his finger against the wall, turned a slow somersault, touched the wall again, and ended with his feet just a half-inch above the floor. "Try *that* someday when you feel real manly."

"Say," said the co-pilot, grinning, "you squeeze a lot of brash into half a pint, don't you?"

Bigman flushed instantly. "Half a pint! Why, you soup-straining cobber———" he screamed, but Lucky's hand was on his shoulder and he swallowed the rest of the sentence. "See you on Venus," the little Martian muttered darkly.

Tor was still grinning. He followed his chief into the control room toward the head of the ship.

Bigman, his anger gone at once, said to Lucky curiously, "Say, how about those mustaches? Never saw any so big."

Lucky said, "It's just a Venusian custom, Bigman. I think practically everybody grows them on Venus."

"That so?" Bigman fingered his lip, stroking its bareness. "Wonder how I'd look in one."

"With one that big?" smiled Lucky. "It would drown your whole face."

He dodged the punch Bigman threw at him just as the floor trembled lightly beneath their feet and the *Venus Marvel* lifted off the space station. The coaster turned its nose into the contracting spiral trajectory that would carry it "down" to Venus.

Lucky Starr felt the beginnings of a long-overdue relaxation flooding him as the coaster picked up speed. His brown eyes were thoughtful, and his keen, fine-featured face was in repose. He was tall and looked slim, but beneath that deceptive slimness were whipcord muscles.

Life had already given much to Lucky of both good and evil. He had lost his parents while still a child, lost them in a pirate attack near the very Venus he was now approaching. He had been brought up by his father's dearest friends, Hector Conway, now chief of the Council of Science, and Augustus Henree, section director of the same organization.

Lucky had been educated and trained with but one thought in mind: Someday he was to enter that very Council of Science, whose powers and functions made it the most important and yet least-known body in the galaxy.

It was only a year ago, upon his graduation from the academy, that he had entered into full membership and become dedicated to the advancement of man and the destruction of the enemies of civilization. He was the youngest member of the Council and probably would remain so for years.

Yet already he had won his first battles. On the deserts of Mars and among the dimlit rocks of the asteroid belt, he had met and triumphed over wrong-doing.

But the war against crime and evil is not a short-term conflict, and now it was Venus that was the setting for trouble, a trouble that was particularly disturbing since its details were misty.

Chief of the Council Hector Conway had pinched his lip and said, "I'm not sure whether it's a Sirian conspiracy against the Solar Confederation, or just petty racketeering. Our local men there tend to view it seriously."

Lucky said, "Have you sent any of our trouble shooters?" He was not long back from the asteroids, and he was listening to this with concern.

Conway said, "Yes: Evans."

"Lou Evans?" asked Lucky, his dark eyes lighting with pleasure. "He was one of my roommates at the academy. He's *good.*"

"Is he? The Venus office of the Council has requested his removal and investigation on the charge of corruption!"

"*What?*" Lucky was on his feet, horrified. "Uncle Hector, that's impossible."

"Want to go out there and look into it yourself?"

"Do I! Great stars and little asteroids! Bigman and I will take off just as soon as we get the *Shooting Starr* flight-ready."

And now Lucky watched out the porthole thoughtfully, on the last leg of his flight. The night shadow had crept over Venus, and for an hour there was only blackness to be seen. All the stars were hidden by Venus's huge bulk.

Then they were out in the sunlight again, but now the

viewpoint was only gray. They were too close to see the planet as a whole. They were even too close to see the clouds. They were actually inside the cloudy layer.

Bigman, having just finished a large chicken-salad sandwich, wiped his lips and said, "Space, I'd hate to have to pilot a ship through all this muck."

The coaster's wings had snapped out into extended position to take advantage of the atmosphere, and there was a definite difference in the quality of the ship's motion as a result. The buffeting of the winds could be felt and the plunging and lifting of the drafts that sink and rise.

Ships that navigate space are not suitable for the treachery of thick atmosphere. It is for that reason that planets like Earth and Venus, with deep layers of air enshrouding them, require space stations. To those space stations come the ships of deep space. From the stations planetary coasters with retractable wings ride the tricky air currents to the planet's surface.

Bigman, who could pilot a ship from Pluto to Mercury blindfolded, would have been lost at the first thickening wisp of an atmosphere. Even Lucky, who in his intensive training at the academy had piloted coasters, would not have cared to take on the job in the blanketing clouds that surrounded them now.

"Until the first explorers landed on Venus," Lucky said, "all mankind ever saw of the planet was the outer surface of these clouds. They had weird notions about the planet then."

Bigman didn't reply. He was looking into the celloplex container to make sure there wasn't another chicken-salad sandwich hiding there.

Lucky went on. "They couldn't tell how fast Venus was rotating or whether it was rotating at all. They weren't even sure about the composition of Venus's atmosphere. They knew it had carbon dioxide, but until the late 1900s astronomers thought Venus had no water. When ships began to land, mankind found that wasn't so."

He broke off. Despite himself, Lucky's mind returned once again to the coded spacegram he had received in mid-flight, with Earth ten million miles behind. It was from Lou Evans, his old roommate, to whom he had subethered that he was on his way.

The reply was short, blunt, and clear. It was, "Stay away!"

Just that! It was unlike Evans. To Lucky, a message like that meant trouble, big trouble, so he did not "stay away." Instead, he moved the micropile energy output up a notch and increased acceleration to the gasping point.

Bigman was saying, "Gives you a funny feeling, Lucky, when you think that once, long ago, people were all cooped up on Earth. Couldn't get off it no matter what they did. Didn't know anything about Mars or the moon or anywhere. It gives me the shivers."

It was just at that point that they pierced the cloud barrier, and even Lucky's gloomy thoughts vanished at the sight that met their eyes.

It was sudden. One moment they were surrounded by what seemed an eternal milkiness; the next, there was only transparent air about them. Everything below was bathed in a clear, pearly light. Above was the gray undersurface of the clouds.

Bigman said, "Hey, Lucky, look!"

Venus stretched out below them for miles in every direction, and it was a solid carpet of blue-green vegetation. There were no dips or rises in the surface. It was absolutely level, as though it had been planed down by a giant atomic slicer.

Nor was there anything to be seen that would have been normal in an Earthly scene. No roads or houses, no towns or streams. Just blue-green, unvarying, as far as could be seen.

Lucky said, "Carbon dioxide does it. It's the part of the air plants feed on. On Earth there's only three hundredths of one per cent in the air, but here almost ten per cent of the air is carbon dioxide."

Bigman, who had lived for years on the farms of Mars, knew about carbon dioxide. He said, "What makes it so light with all the clouds?"

Lucky smiled. "You're forgetting, Bigman. The sun is over twice as bright here as on Earth." Then as he looked out the port again, his smile thinned and vanished.

"Funny," he murmured.

Suddenly, he turned away from the window. "Bigman," he said, "come with me to the pilot room."

In two strides he was out the cabin. In two more, he was at the pilot room. The door wasn't locked. He pulled it open. Both pilots, George Reval and Tor Johnson, were at their places, eyes glued to the controls. Neither turned as they entered.

Lucky said, "Men———"

No response.

He touched Johnson's shoulder, and the co-pilot's arm twitched irritably, shaking off Lucky's grip.

The young Councilman seized Johnson by either shoulder and called, "Get the other one, Bigman!"

The little fellow was already at work on that very job, asking no questions, attacking with a bantam's fury.

Lucky hurled Johnson from him. Johnson staggered back, righted himself, and charged forward. Lucky ducked a wild blow and brought a straight-armed right to the side of the other's jaw. Johnson went down, cold. At nearly the same moment, Bigman, with a quick and skillful twist of George Reval's arm, flung him along the floor and knocked him breathless.

Bigman dragged both pilots outside the pilot room and closed the door on them. He came back to find Lucky handling the controls feverishly.

Only then did he ask for an explanation. "What happened?"

"We weren't leveling off," said Lucky grimly. "I watched the surface, and it was coming up too fast. It still is."

He strove desperately to find the particular control for the ailerons, those vanes that controlled the angle of flight. The blue surface of Venus was much closer. It was rushing at them.

Lucky's eyes were on the pressure gauge. It measured the weight of air above them. The higher it rose, the closer they were to the surface. It was climbing less quickly now. Lucky's fist closed more tightly on the duorod, squeezing the forks together. That must be it. He dared not exert force too rapidly or the ailerons might be whipped off altogether by the screaming gale that flung itself past their ship. Yet there was only five hundred feet to spare before zero altitude.

His nostrils flaring, the cords in his neck standing out, Lucky played those ailerons against the wind.

"We're leveling," breathed Bigman. "We're leveling———"

But there wasn't room enough. The blue-green came up and up till it filled all the view in the port. Then, with a speed that was too great and an angle that was also too great, the *Venus Marvel*, carrying Lucky Starr and Bigman Jones, struck the surface of the planet Venus.

2

Under the Sea Dome

Had the surface of Venus been what it seemed to be at first glance, the *Venus Marvel* would have smashed to scrap and burned to ash. The career of Lucky Starr would have ended at that moment.

Fortunately, the vegetation that had so thickly met the eye was neither grass nor shrubbery, but seaweed. The flat plain was no surface of soil and rock, but water, the top of an ocean that surrounded and covered all of Venus.

The *Venus Marvel*, even so, hit the ocean with a thunderous rattle, tore through the ropy weeds, and boiled its way into the depths. Lucky and Bigman were hurled against the walls.

An ordinary vessel might have been smashed, but the *Venus Marvel* had been designed for entering water at high speed. Its seams were tight; its form, streamlined. Its wings, which Lucky had neither time nor knowledge to retract, were torn loose, and its frame groaned under the shock, but it remained seaworthy.

Down, down it went into the green-black murk of the Venusian ocean. The cloud-diffused light from above was almost totally stopped by the tight weed cover. The ship's artificial lighting did not go on, its workings apparently put out of order by the shock of contact.

Lucky's senses were whirling. "Bigman," he called.

There was no answer, and he stretched out his arms, feeling. His hand touched Bigman's face.

"Bigman!" he called again. He felt the little Martian's chest, and the heart was beating regularly. Relief washed over Lucky.

He had no way of telling what was happening to the ship. He knew he could never find any way of controlling it in the complete darkness that enveloped them. He could only hope that the friction of the water would halt the ship before it struck bottom.

He felt for the pencil flash in his shirt pocket—a little plastic rod some six inches long that, on activation by thumb pressure, became a solid glow of light that streamed out forward, its beam broadening without seeming to weaken appreciably.

Lucky groped for Bigman again and examined him gently. There was a lump on the Martian's temple, but no broken bones so far as Lucky could tell.

Bigman's eyes fluttered. He groaned.

Lucky whispered, "Take it easy, Bigman. We'll be all right." He was far from sure of that as he stepped out into the corridor. The pilots would have to be alive and cooperative if the ship were ever to see home port again.

They were sitting up, blinking at Lucky's flash as he came through the door.

"What happened?" groaned Johnson. "One minute I was at the controls, and then———" There was no hostility, only pain and confusion, in his eyes.

The *Venus Marvel* was back to partial normality. It was limping badly, but its searchlights, fore and aft, had been restored to operation and the emergency batteries had been rigged up to supply them with all the power they would need for vital operations. The churning of the propeller could be dimly heard, and the planetary coaster was displaying, adequately enough, its third function. It was a vessel that could navigate, not only in space and in air, but under water as well.

George Reval stepped into the control room. He was downcast and obviously embarrassed. He had a gash on his cheek, which Lucky had washed, disinfected, and neatly sprayed with koagulum.

Reval said, "There are a few minor seepages, but I plugged them. The wings are gone, and the main batteries are all junked up. We'll need all sorts of repairs, but I guess we're lucky at that. You did a good job, Mr. Williams."

Lucky nodded briefly. "Suppose you tell me what happened."

Reval flushed. "I don't know. I hate to say it, but I don't know."

"How about you?" asked Lucky, addressing the other.

Tor Johnson, his large hands nursing the radio back to life, shook his head.

Reval said, "The last clear thoughts I can remember were while we were still inside the cloud layer. I remember nothing after that till I found myself staring at your flash."

Lucky said, "Do you or Johnson use drugs of any kind?"

Johnson looked up angrily. He rumbled, "No. Nothing."

"Then what made you blank out, and both at the same time, too?"

Reval said, "I wish I knew. Look, Mr. Williams, neither one of us is an amateur. Our records as coaster pilots are first class." He groaned. "Or at least we *were* first-class pilots. We'll probably be grounded after this."

"We'll see," said Lucky.

"Say, look," said Bigman, testily, "what's the use of talking about what's over and gone? Where are we now? That's what I want to know. Where are we going?"

Tor Johnson said, "We're 'way off our course. I can tell you that much. It will be five or six hours before we get out to Aphrodite."

"Fat Jupiter and little satellites!" said Bigman, staring at the blackness outside the port in disgust. "Five or six hours in *this* black mess?"

Aphrodite is the largest city on Venus, with a population of over a quarter of a million.

With the *Venus Marvel* still a mile away, the sea about it was lit into green translucence by Aphrodite's lights. In the eerie luminosity the dark, sleek shapes of the rescue vessels, which had been sent out to meet them after radio contact had been established, could be plainly made out. They slipped along, silent companions.

As for Lucky and Bigman, it was their first sight of one of Venus's underwater domed cities. They almost forgot the unpleasantness they had just passed through, in the amazement at the wonderful object before them.

From a distance it seemed an emerald-green, fairyland bubble, shimmering and quivering because of the water between them. Dimly they could make out buildings and the structural webbing of the beams that held up the city dome against the weight of water overhead.

It grew larger and glowed more brightly as they approached. The green grew lighter as the distance of water between them grew less. Aphrodite became less unreal, less fairylandish, but even more magnificent.

Finally they slid into a huge air lock, capable of holding a small fleet of freighters or a large battle cruiser, and waited while the water was pumped out. And when that was done, the *Venus Marvel* was floated out of the lock and into the city on a lift field.

Lucky and Bigman watched as their luggage was removed, shook hands gravely with Reval and Johnson, and took a skimmer to the Hotel Bellevue-Aphrodite.

Bigman looked out of the curved window as their skimmer, its gyro-wings revolving with stately dignity, moved lightly among the city's beams and over its rooftops.

He said, "So this is Venus. Don't know if it's worth going through so much for it, though. I'll never forget that ocean coming up at us!"

Lucky said, "I'm afraid that was just the beginning."

Bigman looked uneasily at his big friend. "You really think so?"

Lucky shrugged. "It depends. Let's see what Evans has to tell us."

The Green Room of the Hotel Bellevue-Aphrodite was just that. The quality of the lighting and the shimmer of it gave the tables and guests the appearance of being suspended beneath the sea. The ceiling was an inverted bowl, below which there turned slowly a large aquarium globe, supported by cunningly placed lift beams. The water in it was laced with strands of Venusian seaweed and in among it writhed colorful "sea ribbons," one of the most beautiful forms of animal life on the planet.

Bigman had come in first, intent on dinner. He was annoyed at the absence of a punch menu, disturbed by the presence of actual human waiters, and resentful over the fact that he was told that diners in the Green Room ate a meal supplied by the management and only that. He

was mollified, slightly, when the appetizer turned out to
be tasty and the soup, very good.

Then the music started, the domed ceiling gradually
came to glowing life, and the aquarium globe began its
gentle spinning.

Bigman's mouth fell open; his dinner was forgotten.

"Look at that," he said.

Lucky was looking. The sea ribbons were of different
lengths, varying from tiny threads two inches long to
broad and sinuous belts that stretched a yard or more
from end to end. They were all thin, thin as a sheet of
paper. They moved by wriggling their bodies into a series
of waves that rippled down their full length.

And each one fluoresced; each one sparkled with
colored light. It was a tremendous display. Down the
sides of each sea ribbon were little glowing spirals of
light: crimson, pink, and orange; a few blues and violets
scattered through; and one or two striking among the
larger specimens. All were overcast with the light-green
wash of the external light. As they swam, the lines of color
snapped and interlaced. To the dazzled eye they seemed
to be leaving rainbow trails that washed and sparkled in
the water, fading out only to be renewed in still brighter
tints.

Bigman turned his attention reluctantly to his dessert.
The waiter had called it "jelly seeds," and at first the little
fellow had regarded the dish suspiciously. The jelly seeds
were soft orange ovals, which clung together just a bit but
came up readily enough in the spoon. For a moment they
felt dry and tasteless to the tongue, but then, suddenly,
they melted into a thick, sirupy liquid that was sheer delight.

"Space!" said the astonished Bigman. "Have you tried
the dessert?"

"What?" asked Lucky absently.

"Taste the dessert, will you? It's like thick pineapple juice, only a million times better. . . . What's the matter?"

Lucky said, "We have company."

"Aw, go on." Bigman made a move to turn in his seat as though to inspect the other diners.

Lucky said quietly, "Take it easy," and that froze Bigman.

Bigman heard the soft steps of someone approaching their table. He tried to twist his eyes. His own blaster was in his room, but he had a force knife in his belt pocket. It looked like a watch fob, but it could slice a man in two, if necessary. He fingered it intensely.

A voice behind Bigman said, "May I join you, folks?"

Bigman turned in his seat, force knife palmed and ready for a quick, upward thrust. But the man looked anything but sinister. He was fat, but his clothes fit well. His face was round and his graying hair was carefully combed over the top of his head, though his baldness showed anyway. His eyes were little, blue, and full of what seemed like friendliness. Of course, he had a large, grizzled mustache of the true Venusian fashion.

Lucky said calmly, "Sit down, by all means." His attention seemed entirely centered on the cup of hot coffee that he held cradled in his right hand.

The fat man sat down. His hands rested upon the table. One wrist was exposed, slightly shaded by the palm of the other. For an instant, an oval spot on it darkened and turned black. Within it little yellow grains of light danced and flickered in the familiar patterns of the Big Dipper and of Orion. Then it disappeared, and there was only an innocent plump wrist and the smiling, round face of the fat man above it.

That identifying mark of the Council of Science could be neither forged nor imitated. The method of its controlled appearance by the exertion of will was just about the most closely guarded secret of the Council.

The fat man said, "My name is Mel Morriss."

Lucky said, "I rather thought you were. You've been described to me."

Bigman sat back and returned his force knife to its place. Mel Morriss was head of the Venusian section of the Council. Bigman had heard of him. In a way he was relieved, and in another way he was just a little disappointed. He had expected a fight—perhaps a quick dash of coffee into the fat man's face, the table overturned, and from then on, anything.

Lucky said, "Venus seems an unusual and beautiful place."

"You have observed our fluorescent aquarium?"

"It is very spectacular," said Lucky.

The Venusian councilman smiled and raised a finger. The waiter brought him a hot cup of coffee. Morriss let it cool for a moment, then said softly, "I believe you are disappointed to see me here. You expected other company, I think."

Lucky said coolly, "I had looked forward to an informal conversation with a friend."

"In fact," said Morriss, "you had sent a message to Councilman Evans to meet you here."

"I see you know that."

"Quite. Evans has been under close observation for quite a while. Communications to him are intercepted."

Their voices were low. Even Bigman had trouble hearing them as they faced one another, sipping coffee and allowing no trace of expression in their words.

Lucky said, "You are wrong to do this."

"You speak as his friend?"

"I do."

"And I suppose that, as your friend, he warned you to stay away from Venus."

"You know about that, too, I see?"

"Quite. And you had a near-fatal accident in landing on Venus. Am I right?"

"You are. You're implying that Evans feared some such event?"

"Feared it? Great space, Starr, your friend Evans *engineered* that accident."

3

Yeast!

Lucky's expression remained impassive. Not by so much as an eye flicker did he betray any concern. "Details, please," he said.

Morriss was smiling again, half his mouth hidden by his preposterous Venusian mustache. "Not here, I'm afraid."

"Name your place, then."

"One moment." Morris looked at his watch. "In just about a minute, the show will begin. There'll be dancing by sealight."

"Sealight?"

"The globe above will shine dim green. People will get up to dance. We will get up with them and quietly leave."

"You sound as though we are in danger at the moment."

Morriss said gravely, "You are. I assure you that since you entered Aphrodite, our men have never let you out of their sight."

A genial voice rang out suddenly. It seemed to come from the crystal centerpiece on the table. From the direction in which other diners turned their attention, it obviously came from the crystal centerpiece on every table.

It said, "Ladies and gentlemen, welcome to the Green Room. Have you eaten well? For your added pleasure, the management is proud to present the magnetonic rhythms of Tobe Tobias and his—"

As the voice spoke, the lights went out and the remainder of its words were drowned in a rising sigh of wonder that came from the assembled guests, most of whom were fresh from Earth. The aquarium globe in the ceiling was suddenly a luminous emerald green and the sea-ribbon glow was sharply brilliant. The globe assumed a faceted appearance so that, as it turned, drifting shadows circled the room in a soft, almost hypnotic fashion. The sound of music, drawn almost entirely from the weird, husky sound boxes of a variety of magnetonic instruments, grew louder. The notes were produced by rods of various shapes being moved in skillful patterns through the magnetic field that surrounded each instrument.

Men and women were rising to dance. There was the rustle of much motion and the sibilance of laughing whispers. A touch of Lucky's sleeve brought first him, and then Bigman, to their feet.

Lucky and Bigman followed Morriss silently. One by one, grim-faced figures fell in behind them. It was almost as though they were materializing out of the draperies. They remained far enough away to look innocent, but each, Lucky felt sure, had his hand near the butt of a blaster. No mistake about it. Mel Morriss of the Venusian section of the Council of Science took the situation very much in earnest.

Lucky looked about Morriss's apartment with approval. It was not lavish, although it was comfortable. Living in it, one could forget that a hundred yards above was a translucent dome beyond which was a hundred yards of shallow, carbonated ocean, followed by a hundred miles of alien, unbreathable atmosphere.

What actually pleased Lucky most was the collection of book films that overflowed one alcove.

He said, "You're a biophysicist, Dr. Morriss?" Automatically, he used the professional title.

Morriss said, "Yes."

"I did biophysical work myself at the academy," said Lucky.

"I know," said Morriss. "I read your paper. It was good work. May I call you David, by the way?"

"It's my first name," conceded the Earthman, "but everyone calls me Lucky."

Bigman, meanwhile, had opened one of the film holders, unreeled a bit of the film, and held it to the light. He shuddered and replaced it.

He said belligerently to Morriss, "You sure don't look like a scientist."

"I imagine not," said Morriss, unoffended. "That helps, you know."

Lucky knew what he meant. In these days, when science really permeated all human society and culture, scientists could no longer restrict themselves to their laboratories. It was for that reason that the Council of Science had been born. Originally it was intended only as an advisory body to help the government on matters of galactic importance, where only trained scientists could have sufficient information to make intelligent decisions. More and more it had become a crime-fighting agency, a counterespionage system. Into its own hands it was drawing more and more of the threads of government. Through its activities there might grow, someday, a great Empire of the Milky Way in which all men might live in peace and harmony.

So it came about that, as members of the Council had

to fulfill many duties far removed from pure science, it was better for their success if they didn't look particularly like scientists—as long, that is, as they had the brains of scientists.

Lucky said, "Would you begin, sir, by filling me in on the details of the troubles here?"

"How much were you told on Earth?"

"The barest sketch. I would prefer to trust the man on the scene for the rest."

Morriss smiled with more than a trace of irony. "Trust the man on the scene? That's not the usual attitude of the men in the central office. They send their own trouble shooters, and men such as Evans arrive."

"And myself, too," said Lucky.

"Your case is a little different. We all know of your accomplishments on Mars last year* and the good piece of work you've just finished in the asteroids."†

Bigman crowed, "You should have been *with* him if you think you know all about it."

Lucky reddened slightly. He said hastily, "Never mind now, Bigman. Let's not have any of your yarns."

They were all in large armchairs, Earth-manufactured, soft and comfortable. There was something about the reflected sound of their voices that, to Lucky's practiced ear, was good evidence that the apartment was insulated and spy-shielded.

Morriss lit a cigarette and offered one to the others but was refused. "How much do you know about Venus, Lucky?"

Lucky smiled. "The usual things one learns in school. Just to go over a few things quickly, it's the second closest planet to the sun and is about sixty-seven million miles

* See *David Starr, Space Ranger.*
† See *Lucky Starr and the Pirates of the Asteroids.*

from it. It's the closest world to Earth and can come to within twenty-six million miles of the home planet. It's just a little smaller than Earth, with a gravity about five sixths Earth-normal. It goes around the sun in about seven and a half months and its day is about thirty-six hours long. It's surface temperature is a little higher than Earth's but not much, because of the clouds. Also because of the clouds, it has no seasons to speak of. It is covered by ocean, which is, in turn, covered with seaweed. Its atmosphere is carbon dioxide and nitrogen and is unbreathable. How is that, Dr. Morriss?"

"You pass with high marks," said the biophysicist, "but I was asking about Venusian society rather than about the planet itself."

"Well, now, that's more difficult. I know, of course, that humans live in domed cities in the shallower parts of the ocean, and, as I can see for myself, Venusian city life is quite advanced—far beyond Martian city life, for instance."

Bigman yelled, "Hey!"

Morriss turned his little twinkling eyes on the Martian. "You disagree with your friend?"

Bigman hesitated. "Well, maybe not, but he doesn't have to say so."

Lucky smiled and went on, "Venus is a fairly developed planet. I think there are about fifty cities on it and a total population of six million. Your exports are dried seaweed, which I am told is excellent fertilizer, and dehydrated yeast bricks for animal food."

"Still fairly good," said Morriss. "How was your dinner at the Green Room, gentlemen?"

Lucky paused at the sudden change of topic, then said, "Very good. Why do you ask?"

"You'll see in a moment. What did you have?"

Lucky said, "I couldn't say, exactly. It was the house

meal. I should guess we had a kind of beef goulash with a rather interesting sauce and a vegetable I didn't recognize. There was a fruit salad, I believe, before that and a spicy variety of tomato soup."

Bigman broke in. "And jelly seeds for dessert."

Morriss laughed hootingly. "You're all wrong, you know," he said. "You had no beef, no fruit, no tomatoes. Not even coffee. You had only one thing to eat. Only one thing. Yeast!"

"What?" shrieked Bigman.

For a moment Lucky was startled also. His eye narrowed and he said, "Are you serious?"

"Of course. It's the Green Room's specialty. They never speak of it, or Earthmen would refuse to eat it. Later on, though, you would have been questioned thoroughly as to how you liked this dish or that, how you thought it might have been improved, and so on. The Green Room is Venus's most valuable experimental station."

Bigman screwed up his small face and yelled vehemently, "I'll have the law on them. I'll make a Council case of it. They can't feed me yeast without telling me, like I was a horse or cow—or a————"

He ended in a flurry of sputtering.

"I am guessing," said Lucky, "that yeast has some connection with the crime wave on Venus."

"Guessing, are you?" said Morriss, dryly. "Then you haven't read our official reports. I'm not surprised. Earth thinks we are exaggerating here. I assure you, however, we are not. And it isn't merely a crime wave. Yeast, Lucky, yeast! That is the nub and core of everything on this planet."

A self-propelled tender had rolled into the living room with a bubbling percolator and three cups of steaming coffee upon it. The tender stopped at Lucky first, then

Bigman. Morriss took the third cup, put his lips to it, then wiped his large mustache appreciatively.

"It will add cream and sugar if you wish, gentlemen," he said.

Bigman looked and sniffed. He said to Morriss with sharp suspicion, "Yeast?"

"No. Real coffee this time. I swear it."

For a moment they sipped in silence; then Morriss said, "Venus, Lucky, is an expensive world to keep up. Our cities must make oxygen out of water, and that takes huge electrolytic stations. Each city requires tremendous power beams to help support the domes against billions of tons of water. The city of Aphrodite uses as much energy in a year as the entire continent of South America, yet it has only a thousandth the population.

"We've got to earn that energy, naturally. We've got to export to Earth in order to obtain power plants, specialized machinery, atomic fuel, and so on. Venus's only product is seaweed, inexhaustible quantities of it. Some we export as fertilizer, but that is scarcely the answer to the problem. Most of our seaweed, however, we use as culture media for yeast, ten thousand and one varieties of yeast."

Bigman's lip curled. "Changing seaweed to yeast isn't much of an improvement."

"Did you find your last meal satisfactory?" asked Morriss.

"Please go on, Dr. Morriss," said Lucky.

Morriss said, "Of course, Mr. Jones is quite cor———"

"Call me Bigman!"

Morriss looked soberly at the small Martian and said, "If you wish. Bigman is quite correct in his low opinion of yeast in general. Our most important strains are suitable only for animal food. But even so, it's highly useful. Yeast-fed pork is cheaper and better than any other kind. The yeast is high in calories, proteins, minerals, and vitamins.

"We have other strains of higher quality, which are used in cases where food must be stored over long periods and with little available space. On long space journeys, for instance, so-called Y-rations are frequently taken.

"Finally, we have our top-quality strains, extremely expensive and fragile growths that go into the menus of the Green Room and with which we can imitate or improve upon ordinary food. None of these are in quantity production, but they will be someday. I imagine you see the whole point of all this, Lucky."

"I think I do."

"I don't," said Bigman belligerently.

Morriss was quick to explain. "Venus will have a monopoly on these luxury strains. No other world will possess them. Without Venus's experience in zymoculture———"

"In what?" asked Bigman.

"In yeast culture. Without Venus's experience in that, no other world could develop such yeasts or maintain them once they did obtain them. So you see that Venus could build a tremendously profitable trade in yeast strains as luxury items with all the galaxy. That would be important not only to Venus, but to Earth as well—to the entire Solar Confederation. We are the most overpopulated system in the Galaxy, being the oldest. If we could exchange a pound of yeast for a ton of grain, things would be well for us."

Lucky had been listening patiently to Morriss's lecture. He said, "For the same reason, it would be to the interest of a foreign power, which was anxious to weaken Earth, to ruin Venus's monopoly of yeast."

"You see that, do you? I wish I could persuade the rest

of the Council of this living and ever-present danger. If growing strains of yeast were stolen along with some of the knowledge of our developments in yeast culture, the results could be disastrous."

"Very well," said Lucky, "then we come to the important point: Have such thefts occurred?"

"Not yet," said Morriss grimly. "But for six months now we have had a rash of petty pilfering, odd accidents, and queer incidents. Some are merely annoying, or even funny, like the case of the old man who threw half-credit pieces to children and then went frantically to the police, insisting he had been robbed. When witnesses came forward to show that he had given the money away, he nearly went mad with fury, insisting that he had done no such thing. There are more serious accidents, too, like that in which a freight-roller operator released a half-ton bale of weed at the wrong time and killed two men. He insisted later that he had blacked out."

Bigman squealed excitedly, "Lucky! The pilots on the coaster claimed *they* blacked out."

Morriss nodded, "Yes, and I'm almost glad it happened as long as the two of you survived. The Council on Earth may be a bit readier to believe there is something behind all this."

"I suppose," said Lucky, "you suspect hypnotism."

Morriss drew his lips into a grim, humorless smile. "Hypnotism is a mild word, Lucky. Do you know of any hypnotist who can exert his influence at a distance over unwilling subjects? I tell you that some person or persons on Venus possesses the power of complete mental domination over others. They are exerting this power, practicing it, growing more adept in its use. With every day it will grow more difficult to fight them. Perhaps it is already too late!"

4

Councilman Accused!

Bigman's eyes sparkled. "It's never too late once Lucky gets going. Where do we start, Lucky?"

Lucky said quietly, "With Lou Evans. I've been waiting for you to mention him, Dr. Morriss."

Morriss's eyebrows drew together; his plump face contracted into a frown. "You're his friend. You want to defend him, I know. It's not a pleasant story. It wouldn't be if it involved any councilman at all—but a friend at that."

Lucky said, "I am not acting out of sentiment only, Dr. Morriss. I know Lou Evans as well as one man can know another. I know he is incapable of doing anything to harm the Council or Earth."

"Then listen, and judge for yourself. For most of Evans's tour of duty here on Venus, he accomplished nothing. A 'trouble shooter' they called him, which is a pretty word but means nothing."

"No offense, Dr. Morriss, but did you resent his arrival?"

"No, of course not. I just saw no point in it. We here have grown old on Venus. We have the experience. What do they expect a youngster, new from Earth, to accomplish?"

"A fresh approach is helpful sometimes."

"Nonsense. I tell you, Lucky, the trouble is that Earth headquarters don't consider our problem important. Their purpose in sending Evans was to have him give it a quick glance, whitewash it, and return to tell them it was nothing."

"I know the Council on Earth better than that. You do, too."

But the grumbling Venusian went on. "Anyway, three weeks ago, this man Evans asked to see some of the classified data concerning yeast-strain growth. The men in the industry objected."

"Objected?" said Lucky. "It was a councilman's request."

"True, but yeast-strain men are secretive. You don't make requests like that. Even councilmen don't. They asked Evans why he wanted the information. He refused to tell them. They forwarded his request to me, and I quashed it."

"On what grounds?" demanded Lucky.

"He wouldn't tell me his reasons either, and while I'm senior councilman on Venus, nobody in my organization will have secrets from me. But your friend Lou Evans then did something I had not expected. He stole the data. He used his position as councilman to get inside a restricted area in the yeast-research plants, and he left with microfilms inside his boot."

"Surely he had a good reason."

"He did," said Morriss, "he did. The microfilms dealt with the nutrient formulas required for the nourishment of a new and very tricky strain of yeast. Two days later a workman making up one component of that mixture introduced a trace of mercury salt. The yeast died, and six months' work was ruined. The workman swore he'd done no such thing, but he had. Our psychiatrists psychoprobed him. By now, you see, we had a pretty good notion of what to expect. He'd had a blackout period. The enemy still hasn't stolen the strain of yeast, but they're getting closer. Right?"

Lucky's brown eyes were hard. "I can see the obvious theory. Lou Evans had deserted to the enemy, whoever he is."

"Sirians," blurted Morriss. "I'm sure of it."

"Maybe," admitted Lucky. The inhabitants of the planets of Sirius had, for centuries now, been Earth's most fervent enemies. It was easy to blame them. "Maybe. Lou Evans deserted to them, let us say, and agreed to get data for them that would enable them to start trouble inside the yeast factories. Little troubles at first, which would pave the way for larger troubles."

"Yes, that's my theory. Can you propose any other? Couldn't Councilman Evans himself be under mental domination?"

"Not likely, Lucky. We have many cases in our files now. No one who has suffered from mental domination has blacked out for longer than half an hour, and all gave clear indication under the psychoprobe of periods of total amnesia. Evans would have had to be under mental domination for two days to have done what he did, and he gave no signs of amnesia."

"He was examined?"

"He certainly was. When a man is found with classified material in his possession—caught in the act, as it were—steps have to be taken. I wouldn't care if he were a hundred times a councilman. He was examined, and I, personally, put him on probation. When he broke it to send some message on his own equipment, we tapped his scrambler and made sure he'd do it no more—or, at least, not without our intercepting whatever he sent or received. The message he sent you was his last. We're through playing with him. He's under confinement now. I'm preparing my report for central headquarters, a thing I should have done before this, and I'm requesting his removal from office and trial for corruption, or, perhaps, for treason."

"Before you do that————" said Lucky.

"Yes?"

"Let me speak to him."

Morriss rose, smiling ironically. "You wish to? Certainly. I'll take you to him. He's in this building. In fact, I'd like to have you hear his defense."

They passed up a ramp, quiet guards snapping to attention and saluting.

Bigman stared at them curiously. "Is this a prison or what?"

"It's a kind of prison on these levels," said Morriss. "We make buildings serve many purposes on Venus."

They stepped into a small room, and suddenly, quite without warning, Bigman burst into loud laughter.

Lucky, unable to repress a smile, said, "What's the matter, Bigman?"

"No—nothing much," panted the little fellow, his eyes moist. "It's just that you look so funny, Lucky, standing there with your bare upper lip hanging out. After all those mustaches I've been watching, you look deformed. You look as though someone had taken a whiffgun and blown off the mustache you should have had."

Morriss smiled at that and brushed his own grizzled mustache with the back of his hand, self-consciously and a little proudly.

Lucky's smile expanded. "Funny," he said, "I was thinking exactly the same about you, Bigman."

Morriss said, "We'll wait here. They're bringing Evans

now." His finger moved away from a small pushbutton signal.

Lucky looked about the room. It was smaller than Morriss's own room, more impersonal. Its only furniture consisted of several upholstered chairs plus a sofa, a low table in the center of the room, and two higher tables near the false windows. Behind each of the false windows was a cleverly done seascape. On one of the two high tables was an aquarium; on the other, two dishes, one containing small dried peas and the other, a black, greasy substance.

Bigman's eyes automatically started following Lucky's about the room.

He said, suddenly, "Say, Lucky, what's this?"

He half-ran to the aquarium, bending low, peering into its depths. "Look at it, will you?"

"It's just one of the pet V-frogs the men keep about here," said Morriss. "It's a rather good specimen. Haven't you ever seen one?"

"No," said Lucky. He joined Bigman at the aquarium, which was two feet square and about three feet deep. The water in it was criss-crossed with feathery fronds of weed.

Bigman said, "It doesn't bite or anything, does it?" He was stirring the water with a forefinger and bending close to peer inside.

Lucky's head came down next to Bigman's. The V-frog stared back at them solemnly. It was a little creature, perhaps eight inches long, with a triangular head into which two bulging black eyes were set. It rested on six little padded feet drawn up close to its body. Each foot had three long toes in front and one behind. Its skin was green and froglike, and there were frilly fins, which vibrated rapidly, running down the center line of its back. In place of a mouth it had a beak, strong, curved and parrotlike.

As Lucky and Bigman watched, the V-frog started rising in the water. Its feet remained on the floor of the aquarium, but its legs stretched out like extendible stilts, as its numerous leg joints straightened. It stopped rising just as its head was about to pierce the surface.

Morriss, who had joined them and was staring fondly at the little beast, said, "It doesn't like to get out of the water. Too much oxygen in the air. They enjoy oxygen, but only in moderation. They're mild, pleasant little things."

Bigman was delighted. There was virtually no native animal life on Mars, and living creatures of this sort were a real novelty to him.

"Where do they live?" he asked.

Morriss put a finger down into the water and stroked the V-frog's head. The V-frog permitted it, closing its dark eyes in spasmodic motions that might have meant delight, for all they could guess.

Morriss said, "They congregate in the seaweed in fairly large numbers. They move around in it as though it were a forest. Their long toes can hold individual stems, and their beaks can tear the toughest fronds. They could probably make a mean dent in a man's finger, but I've never known one of them to bite. I'm amazed you haven't seen one yet. The hotel has a whole collection of them, real family groups, on display. You haven't seen it?"

"We've scarcely had the chance," said Lucky dryly.

Bigman stepped quickly to the other table, picked up a pea, dipped it into the black grease, and brought it back. He held it out temptingly, and with infinite care the V-frog's beak thrust out of the water and took the morsel from Bigman's fingers. Bigman crowed his delight.

"Did you see that?" he demanded.

Morris smiled fondly, as though at the tricks of a child. "The little imp. They'll eat that all day. Look at him gobble it."

The V-frog was crunching away. A small black droplet

leaked out of one side of its beak, and at once the little creature's legs folded up again as it moved down through the water. The beak opened and the little black droplet was caught.

"What is the stuff?" asked Lucky.

"Peas dipped in axle grease," said Morriss. "Grease is a great delicacy for them, like sugar for us. They hardly ever find pure hydrocarbon in their natural habitat. They love it so, I wouldn't be surprised if they let themselves be captured just to get it."

"How are they captured, by the way?"

"Why, when the seaweed trawlers gather up their seaweed, there are always V-frogs collected with it. Other animals, too."

Bigman was saying eagerly, "Hey, Lucky, let's you and I get one———"

He was interrupted by a pair of guards, who entered stiffly. Between them stood a lanky, blond young man.

Lucky sprang to his feet. "Lou! Lou, old man!" He held out his hand, smiling.

For a moment it seemed as though the other might respond. A flicker of joy rose to the newcomer's eyes.

It faded quickly. His arms remained stiffly and coldly at his side. He said flatly, "Hello, Starr."

Lucky's hand dropped reluctantly. He said, "I haven't seen you since we graduated." He paused. What could one say next to an old friend?

The blond councilman seemed aware of the incongruity of the situation. Nodding curtly to the flanking guards, he said with macabre humor, "There've been some changes made since then." Then, with a spasmodic tightening of his thin lips, he went on, "Why did you come? Why didn't you stay away? I asked you to."

"I can't stay away when a friend's in trouble, Lou."

"Wait till your help is asked for."

Morriss said, "I think you're wasting your time, Lucky. You're thinking of him as a councilman. I suggest that he's a renegade."

The plump Venusian said the word through clenched teeth, bringing it down like a lash. Evans reddened slowly but said nothing.

Lucky said, "I'll need proof to the last atom before I admit any such word in connection with Councilman Evans." His voice came down hard on the word "councilman."

Lucky sat down. For a long moment he regarded his friend soberly, and Evans looked away.

Lucky said, "Dr. Morriss, ask the guards to leave. I will be responsible for Evans's security."

Morriss lifted an eyebrow at Lucky, then after an instant's thought, gestured to the guards.

Lucky said, "If you don't mind, Bigman, just step into the next room, will you?"

Bigman nodded and left.

Lucky said gently, "Lou, there are only three of us here now. You, I, Dr. Morriss; that's all. Three men of the Council of Science. Suppose we start fresh. Did you remove classified data concerning yeast manufacture from their place in the files?"

Lou Evans said, "I did."

"Then you must have had a reason. What was it?"

"Now look. I stole the papers. I say *stole*. I admit that much. What more do you want? I had no reason for doing it. I just did it. Now drop it. Get away from me. Leave me alone." His lips were trembling.

Morriss said, "You wanted to hear his defense, Lucky. That's it. He has none."

Lucky said, "I suppose you know that there was an accident inside the yeast plants, shortly after you took those papers, involving just the strain of yeast the papers dealt with."

"I know all that," said Evans.

"How do you explain it?"

"I have no explanation."

Lucky was watching Evans closely, searching for some sign of the good-natured, fun-loving, steel-nerved youth he remembered so well at the academy. Except for a new mustache, grown according to Venusian fashion, the man Lucky saw now resembled the memory as far as mere physical appearance was concerned. The same long-boned limbs, the blond hair cut short, the angular, pointed chin, the flat-bellied, athletic body. But otherwise? Evans's eyes moved restlessly from spot to spot; his lips quivered dryly; his fingernails were bitten and ragged.

Lucky struggled with himself before he could put the next blunt question. It was a friend he was talking to, a man he had known well, a man whose loyalty he never had questioned, and on whose loyalty he would have staked his own life without thought.

He said, "Lou, have you sold out?"

Evans said in a dull, toneless voice, "No comment."

"Lou, I'm asking you again. First, I want you to know that I'm on your side no matter what you've done. If you've failed the Council, there must be a reason. Tell us that reason. If you've been drugged or forced, either physically or mentally, if you've been blackmailed or if someone close to you has been threatened, tell us. For Earth's sake, Lou, even if you've been tempted with offers of money or power, even if it's as crude as that, tell us. There's no error you can have made that can't be at least partially retrieved by frankness now. What about it?"

For a moment, Lou Evans seemed moved. His blue

eyes lifted in pain to his friend's face. "Lucky," he began, "I———"

Then the softness in him seemed to die, and he cried, "No comment, Starr, no comment."

Morriss, arms folded, said, "That's it, Lucky. That's his attitude. Only he has information and we want it, and, by Venus, we'll get it one way or another."

Lucky said, "Wait———"

Morriss said, "We can't wait. Get that through your head. There is no time. No time at all. These so-called accidents have been getting more serious as they get closer to their objective. We need to break this thing *now.*" And his pudgy fist slammed down on the arm of his chair, just as the communo shrilled its signal.

Morriss frowned. "Emergency signal! What in space———"

He flicked the circuit open, put the receiver to his ear.

"Morriss speaking. What is it? . . . *What?* . . . *WHAT?*"

He let the receiver fall, and his face, as it turned toward Lucky, was a doughy, unhealthy white.

"There's a hypnotized man at lock number twenty-three," he choked out.

Lucky's lithe body tightened like a steel spring. "What do you mean by 'lock'? Are you referring to the dome?"

Morriss nodded and managed to say, "I said the accidents are getting more serious. This time, the sea dome. That man may—at any moment—let the ocean into—Aphrodite!"

5

"Beware Water!"

From the speeding gyrocar, Lucky caught glimpses of the mighty dome overhead. A city built under water, he reflected, requires engineering miracles to be practical.

There were domed cities in many places in the solar system. The oldest and most famous were on Mars. But on Mars, gravity was only two fifths of Earth normal, and pressing down on the Martian domes was only a rarefied, wispy atmosphere.

Here on Venus, gravity was five sixths Earth normal, and the Venusian domes were topped with water. Even though the domes were built in shallow sea so that their tops nearly broke surface at low tide, it was still a matter of supporting millions of tons of water.

Lucky, like most Earthmen (and Venusians, too, for that matter), tended to take such achievements of mankind for granted. But now, with Lou Evans returned to confinement and the problem involving him momentarily dismissed, Lucky's agile mind was putting thoughts together and craving knowledge on this new matter.

He said, "How is the dome supported, Dr. Morriss?"

The fat Venusian had recovered some of his composure. The gyrocar he was driving hurtled toward the threatened sector. His words were still tight and grim.

He said, "Diamagnetic force fields in steel housings. It looks as though steel beams are supporting the dome, but that's not so. Steel just isn't strong enough. It's the force fields that do it."

Lucky looked down at the city streets below, filled with people and life. He said, "Have there ever been any accidents of this type before?"

Morriss groaned, "Great space, not like this. . . . We'll be there in five minutes."

"Are any precautions taken against accidents?" Lucky went on stolidly.

"Of course there are. We have a system of alarms and automatic field adjusters that are as foolproof as we can manage. And the whole city is built in segments. Any local failure in the dome brings down sections of transite, backed by subsidiary fields."

"Then the city won't be destroyed, even if the ocean is let in. Is that right? And this is well known to the populations?"

"Certainly. The people know they're protected, but still, man, a good part of the city will be ruined. There's bound to be some loss of life, and property damage will be terrific. Worse still, if men can be controlled into doing this once, they can be controlled into doing it again."

Bigman, the third man in the gyrocar, stared anxiously at Lucky. The tall Earthman was abstracted, and his brows were knit into a hard frown.

Then Morriss grunted, "Here we are!" The car decelerated rapidly to a jarring halt.

Bigman's watch said two-fifteen, but that meant nothing. Venus's night was eighteen hours long, and here under the dome there was neither day or night.

Artificial lights blossomed now as they always did. Buildings loomed clearly as always. If the city seemed different in any way, it was in the actions of its inhabitants. They were swirling out of the various sections of the city. News of the crisis had spread by the mysterious magic of word of mouth, and they were flocking to see the sight, morbidly curious, as though going to a show or a circus parade, or as men on Earth would flock for seats at a magnetonic concert.

Police held back the rumbling crowds and beat out a path for Morriss and the two with him. Already a thick partition of cloudy transite had moved down, blocking off the section of the city that was threatened by deluge.

Morriss shepherded Lucky and Bigman through a large door. The noise of the crowd muffled and faded behind them. Inside the building a man stepped hastily toward Morriss.

"Dr. Morriss———" he began.

Morriss looked up and snapped out hasty introductions. "Lyman Turner, chief engineer. David Starr of the Council. Bigman Jones."

Then, at some signal from another part of the room, he dashed off, his heavy body making surprising speed. He called out over his shoulder as he started, "Turner will take care of you two."

Turner yelled, "Just a minute, Dr. Morriss!" but the yell went unheard.

Lucky gestured to Bigman, and the little Martian raced after the Venusian councilman.

"Is he going to bring Dr. Morriss back?" asked Turner worriedly, stroking a rectangular box he carried suspended from a strap over one shoulder. He had a gaunt face and red-brown hair, a prominently hooked nose, a scattering of freckles, and a wide mouth. There was trouble in his face.

"No," said Lucky. "Morriss may be needed out there. I just gave my friend the high sign to stick closely to him."

"I don't know what good that will do," muttered the engineer. "I don't know what good anything will do." He put a cigarette to his mouth and absently held one out to Lucky. Lucky's refusal went unnoticed for a few moments, and Turner stood there, holding the plastic container of smokes at arm's length, lost in a thoughtful world of his own.

Lucky said, "They're evacuating the threatened sector, I suppose?"

Turner took back his cigarettes with a start, then puffed strongly at the one between his lips. He dropped it and pressed it out with the sole of his shoe.

"Thoy are," he said, "but I don't know . . ." and his voice faded out.

Lucky said, "The partition is safely across the city, isn't it?"

"Yes, yes," muttered the engineer.

Lucky waited a moment, then said, "But you're not satisfied. What is it you were trying to tell Dr. Morriss?"

The engineer looked hastily at Lucky, hitched at the black box he carried and said, "Nothing. Forget it."

They were off by themselves in a corner of the room. Men were entering now, dressed in pressure suits with the helmets removed, mopping perspiring foreheads. Parts of sentences drifted to their ears:

". . . not more than three thousand people left. We're using all the interlocks now . . ."

". . . can't get to him. Tried everything. His wife is on the etherics now, pleading with him . . ."

"Darn it, he's got the lever in his hand. All he has to do is pull it and we're . . ."

"If we could only get close enough to blast him down! If we were only sure he wouldn't see us first and . . ."

Turner seemed to listen to all of it with a grisly fascination, but he remained in the corner. He lit another cigarette and ground it out.

He burst out savagely, "Look at that crowd out there. It's fun to them. Excitement! I don't know what to do. I tell you, I don't." He hitched the black box he carried into a more comfortable position and held it close.

"What is that?" asked Lucky peremptorily.

Turner looked down, stared at the box as though he were seeing it for the first time, then said, "It's my computer. A special portable model I designed myself." For a moment pride drowned the worry in his voice. "There's not another one in the galaxy like it. I always carry it around. That's how I know———" And he stopped again.

Lucky said in a hard voice. "All right, Turner, what do you know? I want you to start talking. Now!"

The young councilman's hand came lightly to rest upon the engineer's shoulder, and then his grip began to tighten just a bit.

Turner looked up, startled, and the other's calm, brown eyes held him. "What's your name again?" he said.

"I'm David Starr."

Turner's eyes brightened. "The man they call 'Lucky' Starr?"

"That's right."

"All right, then, I'll tell you, but I can't talk loudly. It's dangerous."

He began whispering, and Lucky's head bent toward him. Both were completely disregarded by the busily hurrying men who entered and left the room.

Turner's low words flooded out now as though he were glad to be able to get rid of them. He said, "The walls of the city dome are double, see. Each wall is made of transite, which is the toughest, strongest silicone plastic known to science. And it's backed by force beams. It can stand immense pressures. It's completely insoluble. It doesn't etch. No form of life will grow on it. It won't change chemically as a result of anything in the Venusian ocean. In between the two parts of the double wall is compressed carbon dioxide. That serves to break the shock wave if the outer wall should give way, and of course the inner wall is strong enough to hold the water by itself. Finally, there's a honeycomb of partitions between the walls so that only small portions of the in-between will be flooded in case of any break."

"It's an elaborate system," said Lucky.

"Too elaborate," said Turner bitterly. "An earthquake, or a Venusquake, rather, might split the dome in two, but nothing else can touch it. And there are no Venusquakes in this part of the planet." He stopped to light still another cigarette. His hands were trembling. "What's more, every square foot of the dome is wired to instruments that continually measure the humidity between the walls. The slightest crack anywhere and the needles of those instruments jump. Even if the crack is microscopic and completely invisible, they jump. Then bells ring and sirens sound. Everyone yells, 'Beware water!' "

He grinned crookedly. "Beware water! That's a laugh. I've been on the job ten years, and in all that time the instruments registered only five times. In every case repairs took less than an hour. You pin a diving bell on the affected part of the dome, pump out the water, fuse the transite, add another gob of the stuff, let it cool. After that, the dome is stronger than before. Beware water! We've never had even a drop leak through."

Lucky said, "I get the picture. Now get to the point."

"The point is overconfidence, Mr. Starr. We've partitioned off the dangerous sector, but how strong is the partition? We always counted on the outer wall's going gradually, springing a small leak. The water would trickle in, and we always knew that we would have plenty of time to get ready for it. No one ever thought that someday a lock might be opened wide. The water will come in like a fat steel bar moving a mile a second. It will hit the sectional transite barrier like a spaceship at full acceleration."

"You mean it won't hold?"

"I mean no one has ever worked out the problem. No one has ever computed the forces involved—until half an hour ago. Then I did, just to occupy my time while all this is going on. I had my computer. I always have it with me. So I made a few assumptions and went to work."

"And it won't hold?"

"I'm not certain. I don't know how good some of my assumptions are, but I think it won't hold. I think it won't. So what do we do? If the barrier doesn't hold, Aphrodite is done. The whole city. You and I and a quarter of a million people. Everybody. Those crowds outside that are so excited and thrilled are doomed once that man's hand pulls downward on the switch it holds."

Lucky was staring at the man with horror. "How long have you known this?"

The engineer blurted in immediate self-defense, "Half an hour. *But what can I do?* We can't put subsea suits on a quarter of a million people! I was thinking of talking to Morriss and maybe getting some of the important people in town protected, or some of the women and children. I wouldn't know how to pick which ones to save, but maybe something should be done. What do you think?"

"I'm not sure."

The engineer went on, harrowed. "I thought maybe I

could put on a suit and get out of here. Get out of the city altogether. There won't be proper guards at the exits at a time like this."

Lucky backed away from the quivering engineer, his eyes narrowed. "Great Galaxy! I've been blind!"

And he turned and dashed out of the room, his mind tingled with a desperate thought.

6

Too Late!

Bigman felt dizzily helpless in the confusion. Hanging as closely as he could to the coattails of the restless Morriss, he found himself trotting from group to group, listening to breathless conversations which he did not always understand because of his ignorance about Venus.

Morriss had no opportunity to rest. Each new minute brought a new man, a new report, a new decision. It was only twenty minutes since Bigman had run off after Morriss, and already a dozen plans had been proposed and discarded.

One man, just returned from the threatened sector, was saying with pounding breath, "They've got the spy rays trained on him, and we can make him out. He's just sitting with the lever in his hand. We beamed his wife's voice in at him through the etherics, then through the public-address system, then through a loudspeaker from outside. I don't think he hears her. At least he doesn't move."

Bigman bit his lip. What would Lucky do if he were here? The first thought that had occurred to Bigman was to get behind the man—Poppnoe, his name was—and shoot him down. But that was the first thought everyone had had, and it had been instantly discarded. The man at the lever had closed himself off, and the dome-control chambers were carefully designed to prevent any form of tampering. Each entrance was thoroughly wired, the alarms being internally powered. That precaution was now working in reverse—to Aphrodite peril rather than its protection.

At the first clang, at the first signal gleam, Bigman was sure, the lever would be driven home and Venus's ocean would charge inward upon Aphrodite. It could not be risked while evacuation was incomplete.

Someone had suggested poison gas, but Morriss had shaken his head without explanations. Bigman thought he knew what the Venusian must be thinking. The man at the lever was not sick or mad or malevolent, but under mental control. That fact meant that there were two enemies. The man at the lever, considered by himself, might weaken from the gas past the point where he would be physically capable of pulling the lever, but before that the weakening would be reflected in his mind, and the men in control would work their tool's arm muscles quickly enough.

"What are they waiting for, anyway?" growled Morriss under his breath, while the perspiration rolled down his cheeks in streams. "If I could only train an atom cannon at the spot."

Bigman knew why that was impossible, too. An atom cannon trained to hit the man from the closest approach possible would require enough power to go through a quarter mile of architecture and would damage the dome enough to bring on the very danger they were trying to avoid.

He thought, Where *is* Lucky, anyway? Aloud he said, "If you can't get this fellow, what about the controls?"

"What do you mean?" said Morris.

"I mean, gimmick the lever. It takes power to open the lock, doesn't it? What if the power is cut?"

"Nice thought, Bigman. But each lock has its own emergency power generator on the spot."

"Can't it be closed off from anywhere?"

"How? He's closed off in there, with every cubic foot set off with alarms."

Bigman looked up and, in vision, seemed to see the mighty ocean that covered them. He said, "This is a closed-in city, like on Mars. We've got to pump air all over. Don't you do that, too?"

Morriss brought a handkerchief to his forehead and wiped it slowly. He stared at the little Martian. "The ventilating ducts?"

"Yes. There's got to be one to that place with the lock, doesn't there?"

"Of course."

"And isn't there someplace along the line where a wire can be wrenched loose or cut or *something*?"

"Wait a while. A microbomb shoved along the duct, instead of the poison gas we were talking about————"

"That's not sure enough," said Bigman impatiently. "Send a man. You need big ducts for an underwater city, don't you? Won't they hold a man?"

"They're not as big as all that," said Morriss.

Bigman swallowed painfully. It cost him a great deal to make the next statement. "I'm not as big as all that, either. Maybe I'll fit."

And Morriss, staring down wide-eyed at the pint-size Martian, said, "Venus! You might. You might! Come with me!"

From the appearance of the streets of Aphrodite, it seemed as though not a man or woman or child in the city was sleeping. Just outside the transite partition and surrounding the "rescue headquarters" building, people choked every avenue and turned them into black masses of chattering humanity. Chains had been set up, and behind them policemen with stunguns paced restlessly.

Lucky, having emerged from rescue headquarters at what amounted to a dead run, was brought up sharply by those chains. A hundred impressions burst in on him. There was the brilliant sign in lucite curlicues, set high in Aphrodite's sky with no visible support. It turned slowly and said: APHRODITE, BEAUTY SPOT OF VENUS, WELCOMES YOU.

Close by, a line of men were moving on in file. They were carrying odd objects—stuffed brief cases, jewel boxes, clothes slung over their arms. One by one, they were climbing into skimmers. It was obvious who and what they were: escapees from within the threatened zone, passing through the lock with whatever they could carry that seemed most important to them. The evacuation was obviously well under way. There were no women and children in the line.

Lucky shouted to a passing policeman, "Is there a skimmer I can use?"

The policeman looked up. "No, sir, all being used."

Lucky said impatiently, "Council business."

"Can't help it. Every skimmer in town is being used for those guys." His thumb jerked toward the moving file of men in the middle distance.

"It's important. I've got to get out of here."

"Then you'll have to walk," said the policeman.

Lucky gritted his teeth with vexation. There was no way of getting through the crowd on foot or on wheels. It had to be by air and it had to be *now*.

"Isn't there anything available I can use? Anything?" He was scarcely speaking to the policeman, more to his own impatient self, angry at having been so simply duped by the enemy.

But the policeman answered wryly, "Unless you want to use a hopper."

"A hopper? Where?" Lucky's eyes blazed.

"I was just joking," said the policeman.

"But *I'm* not. Where's the hopper?"

There were several in the basement of the building they had left. They were disassembled. Four men were impressed to help and the best-looking machine was assembled in the open. The nearest of the crowd watched curiously, and a few shouted jocularly, "Jump it, hopper!"

It was the old cry of the hopper races. Five years ago it had been a fad that had swept the solar system: races over broken, barrier-strewn courses. While the craze lasted, Venus was most enthusiastic. Probably half the houses in Aphrodite had had hoppers in the basement.

Lucky checked the micropile. It was active. He started the motor and set the gyroscope spinning. The hopper straightened immediately and stood stiffly upright on its single leg.

Hoppers are probably the most grotesque forms of transportation ever invented. They consist of a curved body, just large enough to hold a man at the controls. There was a four-bladed rotor above and a single metal leg, rubber-tipped, below. It looked like some giant wading bird gone to sleep with one leg folded under its body.

Lucky touched the leap knob and the hopper's leg retracted. Its body sank till it was scarcely seven feet from the ground while the leg moved up into the hollow tube that pierced the hopper just behind the control panel. The leg was released at the moment of maximum retraction with a loud click, and the hopper sprang thirty feet into the air.

The rotating blades above the hopper kept it hovering

for long seconds at the top of its jump. For those seconds, Lucky could get a view of the people now immediately below him. The crowd extended outward for half a mile, and that meant several hops. Lucky's lips tightened. Precious minutes would vanish.

The hopper was coming down now, its long leg extended. The crowd beneath the descending hopper tried to scatter, but they didn't have to. Four jets of compressed air blew men aside just sufficiently, and the leg hurtled down harmlessly to the ground.

The foot hit concrete and retracted. For a flash Lucky could see the startled faces of the people about him, and then the hopper was moving up again.

Lucky had to admit the excitement of hopper racing. As a youngster, he'd participated in several. The expert "hop rider" could twist his curious mount in unbelievable patterns, finding leg room where none seemed to exist. Here, in the domed cities of Venus, the races must have been tame compared to the bonebreakers in the vast, open arenas of rocky, broken ground on Earth.

In four hops Lucky had cleared the crowd. He cut the motors, and in a series of small, dribbling jumps the hopper came to a halt. Lucky leaped out. Air travel might still be impossible, but now he could commandeer some form of groundcar.

But more time would be lost.

Bigman panted and paused for a moment to get his breath. Things had happened quickly; he had been rushed along in a tide that was still whirling him onward.

Twenty minutes before, he had made his suggestion to Morriss. Now he was enclosed in a tube that tightened about his body and drenched him with darkness.

He inched along on his elbows again, working his way deeper. Momentarily he would stop to use the small flash whose pinpoint illumination showed him milky walls ahead, narrowing to nothing. In one sleeve, against his wrist, he held a hastily scrawled diagram.

Morriss had shaken his hand before Bigman had half-clambered, half-jumped, into the opening at one side of a pumping station. The rotors of the huge fan had been stilled, the air currents stopped.

Morriss had muttered, "I hope *that* doesn't set him off," and then he had shaken hands.

Bigman had grinned back after a fashion, and then he crawled his way into the darkness while the others left. No one felt it necessary to mention the obvious. Bigman was going to be on the wrong side of the transite barrier, the side from which the others were now retreating. If, at any time, the lever at the dome lock plunged down, the incoming water would crush the duct and the walls through which it ran as though they were all so much cardboard.

Bigman wondered, as he squirmed onward, whether he would hear a roar first, whether the surging water would make any hint of its presence known before striking him. He hoped not. He wanted not even a second of waiting. If the water came in, he wanted its work done quickly.

He felt the wall begin to curve. He stopped to consult his map, his small flash lighting the space about him with a cool gleam. It was the second curve shown in the map they had drawn for him, and now the duct would curve upward.

Bigman worked himself over to his side and bent around the curve to the damage of his temper and the bruising of his flesh.

"Sands of Mars!" he muttered. His thigh muscles ached as he forced his knees against either side of the duct to keep himself from slipping downward again. Inch by inch he clawed his way up the gentle slope.

Morriss had copied the map off the hieroglyphic charts held up before a visiphone transmitter in the Public Works Department of Aphrodite. He had followed the curving colored lines, asked for an interpretation of the markings and symbols.

Bigman reached one of the reinforcing struts that stretched diagonally across the duct. He almost welcomed it as something he could seize, close his hands about, use to take some of the pressure off his aching elbows and knees. He pressed his map back up his sleeve and held the strut with his left hand. His right hand turned his small flash end for end and placed the butt against one end of the strut.

The energy of the enclosed micropile, which ordinarily fed electricity through the small bulb of the flash and turned it into cold light, could also, at another setting of the control, set up a short-range force field through its opposite end. That force field would slice instantaneously through anything composed of mere matter that stood in its way. Bigman set that control and knew that one end of the strut now hung loose.

He switched hands. He worked his slicer to the other end of the strut. Another touch, and it was gone. The strut was loose in his fingers. Bigman worked it past his body, down to his feet, and let it go. It slid and clattered down the duct.

The water still held off. Bigman, panting and squirming, was distantly aware of that. He passed two more struts, another curve. Then the slope leveled off, and finally he reached a set of baffles plainly marked on the map. In all, the ground he had covered was probably less than two hundred yards, but how much time had it taken him?

And still the water held off.

The baffles, blades jutting alternately from either side of the duct to keep the air stream turbulent, were the last landmark. He sliced off each blade with a rapid sweep of his flash butt, and now he had to measure nine feet from the farthest blade. Again he used his flash. It was six inches long and he would have to lay it along the wall, end over end, eighteen times.

Twice it slipped, and twice he had to turn back to the slightly ragged marking of the last sheared baffle blade, scrambling backward and swearing "Sands of Mars!" in a whisper.

The third time the eighteenth measure landed truly. Bigman kept his finger on the spot. Morriss had said the desired place would be almost directly over his head. Bigman turned on his flash, ran his finger along the curved inner surface of the duct, twisted on to his back.

Using his slicer end and holding it, as nearly as he could judge in the dark, some quarter of an inch from actual contact (the force field must not slice in too far), he made a circle with it. Cleaved metal fell on him, and he pushed it to one side.

He turned his flash on the exposed wiring and studied it. Inches farther in would be the interior of a room not a hundred feet from where the man sat at the lock. Was he still sitting there? Obviously, he had not yet pulled the lever (what was he waiting for?) or Bigman would now be very water-logged, very dead. Had he been stopped then, somehow? Taken into custody, perhaps?

A wry grin forced itself onto Bigman's face as he thought that perhaps he was squirming through the interior of a metal worm for nothing.

He was following the wiring. Somewhere here should be a relay. Gently he pulled at the wires, first one, then another. One moved and a small, black, double cone came into view. Bigman sighed his relief. He gripped the flash with his teeth, freeing both hands.

Gingerly, very gingerly, he twisted the two halves of the cone in opposite directions. The magnoclasps yielded, and the two halves moved apart, exposing the contents. They consisted of a break relay: two gleaming contacts, one encased in its field selector and separated from the other by a nearly imperceptible gap. At an appropriate stimulus, such as the pulling of a small lever, the field selector set up the energies that would pull down the other contact, send energy streaming across the point of closure, and open a lock in the dome. It would all happen in a millionth of a second.

Bigman, sweating and half-expecting the final moment to come now, *now*, with his task a second from completion, fumbled in his vest pocket and withdrew a lump of insulating plastic. It was already soft from the warmth of his body. He kneaded it a moment and then brought it down delicately upon the point where the two contacts nearly met. He held it there while he counted three, then withdrew it.

The contacts might close now, but between them there would be a thin film of this plastic, and through it the flow of current could not pass.

The lever could be pulled now: the lock would not open.

Laughing, Bigman scrambled backward, made his way over the remnants of the baffle, passed the struts he had cut away, slid down the slopes. . . .

Bigman searched desperately for Lucky through the confusion that now flooded all the city. The man at the lever was in custody, the transite barrier had been lifted, and the population was flooding back (angry, for the most part, at the city administration for allowing the whole thing to happen) into the homes they had abandoned. To the crowds who had so ghoulishly waited for disaster, the removal of fear was the signal for a high holiday.

At the end Morriss appeared from nowhere and placed a hand on Bigman's sleeve. "Lucky's calling."

Bigman, startled, said, "Where from?"

"From my room in the Council offices. I've told him what you've done."

Bigman flushed with pleasure. Lucky would be proud! He said, "I want to talk to him."

But Lucky's face on the screen was grim. He said, "Congratulations, Bigman, I hear you were terrific."

"It was nothing," grinned Bigman. "But where've you been?"

Lucky said, "Is Dr. Morriss there? I don't see him."

Morriss squeezed his face into the viewer. "Here I am."

"You've captured the man at the lever, according to the news I hear."

"We did. We absolutely did, thanks to Bigman," said Morriss.

"Then let me make a guess. When you closed in on him, he did not try to pull the lever. He simply gave himself up."

"Yes," said Morris, frowning. "But what makes you guess that?"

"Because the whole incident at the lock was a smoke screen. The real damage was slated to happen at this end. When I realized that, I left. I tried to come back here. I had to use a hopper to get through the crowd and a groundcar the rest of the way."

"And?" asked Morriss anxiously.

"And I was too late!" said Lucky.

7

Questions

The day was over. The crowd had dispersed. The city had taken on a quiet, almost sleepy atmosphere, with only an occasional knot of two or three still discussing the events of the past several hours.

And Bigman was annoyed.

With Morriss he had left the scene of the recent danger and zoomed out to Council headquarters. There Morriss had had his conference with Lucky, a conference to which Bigman was not allowed entry and from which the Venusian had emerged looking grimly angry. Lucky remained calm but uncommunicative.

Even when they were alone again, Lucky said merely, "Let's get back to the hotel. I need sleep, and so do you after your own little game today."

He hummed the Council March under his breath, as he always did when he was completely abstracted, and signaled a passing tollcar. The car stopped automatically when the sight of his outstretched hand with fingers spread wide registered on its photoelectric scanners.

Lucky pushed Bigman in before him. He turned the dials to indicate the co-ordinate position of the Hotel

Bellevue-Aphrodite, put in the proper combination of coins, and let the machine's computer take over. With his foot he adjusted the speed lever to low.

The tollcar drifted forward with a pleasantly smooth motion. Bigman would have found it both comforting and restful if he had been in a less itchingly curious state of mind.

The little Martian flicked a glance at his large friend. Lucky seemed interested only in rest and thought. At least he leaned back on the upholstery and closed his eyes, letting the motion rock him while the hotel seemed to approach and then become a large mouth, which swallowed them as the tollcar automatically found the entrance to the receiving dock of the hotel's garage.

Only when they were in their own room did Bigman reach the point of explosion. He cried, "Lucky, what's it all about? I'm going nuts trying to figure it out."

Lucky stripped off his shirt and said, "Actually, it's only a matter of logic. What kind of accidents occurred as a result of men's being mentally dominated before today? What kind did Morriss mention? A man giving away money. A man dropping a bale of weed. A man placing poison in a nutrient mixture for yeast. In each case, the action was a small one, but it was an *action*. It was something *done*."

"Well?" said Bigman.

"All right, what did we have today? It wasn't something small at all; it was something big. But it wasn't action. It was exactly the opposite of action: A man put his hand on a dome-lock lever and then did nothing. Nothing!"

Lucky vanished into the bathroom and Bigman could hear the needle shower and Lucky's muffled gasps under its invigorating jets. Bigman followed at last, muttering savagely under his breath.

"Hey," he yelled.

Lucky, his muscled body drying in churning puffs of warm air, said, "Don't you get it?"

"Space, Lucky, don't be mysterious, will you? You know I hate that."

"But there's nothing mysterious. The mentalists have changed their entire style, and there must be a reason. Don't you see the reason for having a man sit at a dome-lock lever and do nothing?"

"I said I didn't."

"Well, what *was* accomplished by it?"

"Nothing."

"Nothing? Great galaxy! Nothing? They only get half the population of Aphrodite and practically every official out to the threatened sector in double-speed time. They get me out there and you and Morriss. Most of the city was left bare, including Council headquarters. And I was such a lunk that it was only when Turner, the city's chief engineer, mentioned how easy it would be to get out of the city with the police force disrupted that it occurred to me what was happening."

"I still don't see it. So help me, Lucky, I'm going to——"

"Hold it, boy," Lucky seized Bigman's threatening fists in one large palm. "Here it is: I got back to Council headquarters as fast as possible and found that Lou Evans had already gone."

"Where did they take him?"

"If you mean the Council, they didn't take him anywhere. He escaped. He knocked down a guard, seized a weapon, used his Council wrist-mark to get a subship and escaped to sea."

"Was *that* what they were really after?"

"Obviously. The threat to the city was strictly a feint. As soon as Evans was safely out into the ocean, the man at the lock was released from control and, naturally, he surrendered."

Bigman's mouth worked. "Sands of Mars! All that stuff in the ventilating duct was for nothing. I was fifty kinds of cobbered fool."

"No, Bigman, you weren't," said Lucky, gravely. "You did a good job, a terrific job, and the Council is going to hear about it."

The little Martian flushed, and for a moment pride left no room in him for anything else. Lucky took the opportunity to get into bed.

Then Bigman said, "But Lucky, that means————I mean, if Councilman Evans got away by a trick of the mentalists, then he's guilty, isn't he?"

"No," said Lucky vehemently, "he *isn't.*"

Bigman waited, but Lucky had nothing more to say on the subject and instinct told Bigman to let the matter die. It was only after he had burrowed into the cool plastex sheets, having undressed and washed in his turn, that he tried again.

"Lucky?"

"Yes, Bigman."

"What do we do next?"

"Go after Lou Evans."

"*We* do? What about Morriss?"

"I'm in charge of the project now. I had Chief Councilman Conway put that across all the way from Earth."

Bigman nodded in the darkness. That explained why he himself had not been able to attend the conference. Friend though he might be of Lucky Starr a dozen times over, he was not a member of the Council of Science. And, in a situation where Lucky would have to move in over a fellow councilman's head and call in the authority of Earth and central headquarters to back him, non-councilmen were strictly not wanted as witnesses.

But now the old lust for action was beginning to stir in him. It would be into an ocean now, the vastest, most alien ocean on the inner planets. He said excitedly, "How early do we leave?"

"As soon as the ship they're outfitting is ready. Only first we see Turner."

"The engineer? What for?"

"I have the records on the men involved in the various mentalist incidents in the city up to today, and I want to know about the man at the lock dome, too. Turner is the man who's likely to know most about him. But before we see Turner——"

"Yes?"

"Before that, you Martian peanut, we sleep. Now shut up."

Turner's dwelling place turned out to be a rather large apartment house that seemed suited for people high in the administrative scheme of things. Bigman whistled softly when they passed into the lobby, with its paneled walls and trimensional seascapes. Lucky led the way into a trundle and pressed Turner's apartment number.

The trundle lifted them five floors, then took to the horizontal, skittering along on directed force beams and stopping outside the back entrance to Turner's apartment. They stepped out, and the trundle went off with a whirr, disappearing behind a turn in the corridor.

Bigman watched it wonderingly. "Say, I never saw one of those before."

"It's a Venusian invention," said Lucky. "They're introducing them into new apartment houses on Earth now. You can't do anything about the old apartment houses, though, unless you redesign the building to give each apartment a special trundle-served entrance."

Lucky touched the indicator, which promptly turned

red. The door opened, and a woman looked out at them. She was slight of build, young and quite pretty, with blue eyes and blond hair drawn softly backward and over her ears in the Venusian fashion.

"Mr. Starr?"

"That's right, Mrs. Turner," said Lucky. He hesitated a trifle over the title; she was almost too young to be a housewife.

But she smiled at them in friendly fashion. "Won't you come in? My husband's expecting you, but he hasn't had more than two hours' sleep and he's not quite———"

They stepped in, and the door closed behind them.

Lucky said, "Sorry to have to trouble you so early, but it's an emergency, and I doubt that we'll bother Mr. Turner long."

"Oh, that's all right. I understand." She stepped fussily about the room, straightening objects that required no straightening.

Bigman looked about curiously. The apartment was completely feminine—colorful, frilly, almost fragile. Then, embarrassed to find his hostess's eyes upon him, he said clumsily, "It's a very nice place you have here, miss—uh —ma'am."

She dimpled and said, "Thank you. I don't think Lyman is very fond of the way I have it arranged, but he never objects, and I just love little doodads and whatnots. Don't you?"

Lucky spared Bigman the necessity of answering by saying, "Have you and Mr. Turner been living here very long?"

"Just since we got married. Less than a year. It's a darling apartment house, just about the nicest in Aphrodite. It's got completely independent utilities, its own coaster garage, a central communo. It even has chambers underneath. Imagine! Chambers! Not that anyone ever uses them. Even last night. At least I think no one did, but I can't say, because I just slept right through all the excitement. Can you imagine? I didn't even hear about it till Lyman came home."

"Perhaps that was best," said Lucky. "You missed a fright."

"I missed excitement, you mean," she protested. "Everyone in the apartment was out in the thick of it, and I slept. Slept all through it. No one woke me. I think that was terrible."

"What was terrible?" came a new voice, and Lyman Turner stepped into the room. His hair was rumpled; there were creases on his homely face and sleep in his eyes. He had his precious computer under his arm and put it down under the chair when he sat down.

"My missing the excitement," said his young wife. "How are you, Lyman?"

"All right, considering. And never mind missing the excitement. I'm glad you did. . . . Hello, Starr. Sorry to delay you."

"I've only been here a few moments," said Lucky.

Mrs. Turner flew to her husband and pecked quickly at his cheek. "I'd better leave you men alone now."

Turner patted his wife's shoulder, and his eyes followed her affectionately as she left. He said, "Well, gentlemen, sorry you find me as you do, but I've had a rough time of it in the last few hours."

"I quite realize that. What's the situation with the dome now?"

Turner rubbed his eyes. "We're doubling the men at each lock, and we're making the controls a little less self-contained. That rather reverses the engineering trend of the last century. We're running power lines to various spots in the city so that we can shut the power off from a distance just in case any such thing ever happens again.

And, of course, we will strengthen the transite barriers shielding the different sections of the city. . . . Does either of you smoke?"

"No," said Lucky, and Bigman shook his head.

Turner said, "Well, would you toss me a smoke from the dispenser, the thing that looks like a fish? That's right. It's one of my wife's notions. There's no holding her back when it comes to getting these ridiculous gadgets, but she enjoys it." He flushed a little. "I haven't been married long, and I still pamper her, I'm afraid."

Lucky looked curiously at the odd fish, carved out of a stonelike, green material, from whose mouth a lighted cigarette had appeared when he pressed a dorsal fin.

Turner seemed to relax as he smoked. His legs crossed, and one foot moved back and forth in slow rhythm over his computer case.

Lucky said, "Anything new on the man who started it all? The man at the lock?"

"He's under observation. A madman, obviously."

"Does he have a record of mental imbalance?"

"Not at all. It was one of the things I checked into. As chief engineer, you know, the dome personnel are under me."

"I know. It's why I came here to you."

"Well, I wish I could help, but the man was just an ordinary employee. He's been on our rolls for some seven months and never gave any trouble before. In fact, he had an excellent record; quiet, unassuming, diligent."

"Only seven months?"

"That's right."

"Is he an engineer?"

"He has a rating as engineer, but actually his work consisted largely of standing guard at the lock. After all, traffic passes in and out of the city. The lock must be opened and closed, bills of lading checked, records kept.

There's a lot more to managing the dome than just engineering."

"Did he have any actual engineering experience?"

"Just an elementary college course. This was his first job. He's quite a young man."

Lucky nodded. He said casually, "I understand there have been a whole series of queer accidents in the city lately."

"Have there?" Turner's weary eyes stared at Lucky, and he shrugged. "I rarely get a chance to look at the news-etheric tapes."

The communo buzzed. Turner lifted it and held it to his ear for a moment. "It's for you, Starr."

Lucky nodded. "I left word I'd be here." He took the communo but did not bother to activate the screen or to raise the sound above the ear-contact stage. He said, "Starr at this end."

Then he put it down and stood up. "We'll be going now, Turner."

Turner rose, too. "All right. If I can help you in the future, call on me any time."

"Thank you. Give our respects to your wife, will you?"

Outside the building Bigman said, "What's up?"

"Our ship is ready," said Lucky, flagging down a groundcar.

They got in, and again Bigman broke the silence. "Did you find out anything from Turner?"

"A thing or two," said Lucky curtly.

Bigman stirred uneasily and changed the subject. "I hope we find Evans."

"I hope so, too."

"Sands of Mars, he's in a spot. The more I think of it, the worse it seems. Guilty or not, it's rough having a request for removal on grounds of corruption sent in by a superior officer."

Lucky's head turned and he looked down at Bigman. "Morriss never sent any report on Evans to central headquarters. I thought you understood that from yesterday's conversation with him."

"He didn't?" said Bigman incredulously. "Then who did?"

"Great Galaxy!" said Lucky. "Surely it's obvious. Lou Evans sent that message himself, using Morriss's name."

8

Councilman Pursued!

Lucky handled the trim subsea craft with growing expertness as he learned the touch of the controls and began to get the feel of the sea about them.

The men who had turned the ship over to them had worriedly suggested a course of instruction as to its management, but Lucky had smiled and confined himself to a few questions while Bigman exclaimed with Bigmanian braggadocio, "There isn't anything that moves that Lucky and I can't handle." Braggadocio or not, it was very nearly true.

The ship, named the *Hilda*, drifted now with the engines cut off. It penetrated the inky blackness of the Venusian ocean with smooth ease. They were navigating blind. Not once had the ship's powerful beams been turned on. Radar, instead, plumbed the abyss ahead more delicately and more informatively than light possibly could.

Along with the radar pulses went the selected microwaves designed to attain maximum reflection from the metal alloy that formed the outer hull of a subship. Their range in the hundreds of miles, the microwaves plunged their probing fingers of energy this direction and that, seeking the particular design of metal that would send them careening back in their tracks.

So far, no reflecting message had come back, and the *Hilda* settled down in the ooze, half a mile of water above it, and motionless except for a slow rocking with the mighty sway of Venus's globe-girdling oceanic currents.

For the first hour Bigman had been scarcely aware of the microwaves and the object of their search. He had been lost in the spectacle to be seen from the portholes.

Venusian subsea life is phosphorescent, and the black ocean depths were dotted with colored lights thicker than the stars in space, larger, brighter, and most of all, *moving*. Bigman squashed his nose against the thick glass and stared, fascinated.

Some of the life forms were little round splotches, whose movement was a slow ripple. Others were darting lines. Still others were sea ribbons of the type Lucky and Bigman had seen in the Green Room.

Lucky joined him after a while. He said, "If I remember my xenozoology————"

"Your *what?*"

"That's the study of extraterrestrial animals, Bigman. I've just been looking through a book on Venusian life. I left it on your bunk in case you want to look at it."

"Never mind. I'll take it second hand from you."

"All right. We can start with those little objects. I think that represents a school of buttons."

"Buttons?" said Bigman. Then, "Sure, I see what you mean."

There were a whole series of yellow ovals of light moving across the black field visible through the porthole. Each had black markings on it in the form of two short parallel lines. They moved in brief spurts, settled down for a few moments, then moved again. The dozens in view all moved and rested simultaneously, so that Bigman had the queerly swimming sensation that the buttons weren't moving at all, but that every half minute or so the ship itself lurched.

Lucky said, "They're laying eggs, I think." He was silent for a long moment, then said, "Most of these things I can't make out. Wait! That must be a scarlet patch there. See it? The dark red thing with the irregular outline? It feeds on buttons. Watch it."

There was a scurrying among the yellow blotches of light as they became aware of the swooping predator, but a dozen buttons were blotted out by the angry red of the scarlet patch. Then the patch was the only source of light in the porthole's field of vision. On all sides of it, buttons had scattered away.

"The patch is shaped like a large pancake turned down at the edge," said Lucky, "according to the book. It's hardly anything but skin with a small brain in the center. It's only an inch thick. You can tear it through and through in a dozen places without bothering it. See how irregular the one we're watching is? Arrowfish probably chewed it up a bit."

The scarlet patch moved now, drifting out of sight. There was little left where it had been except for one or two faint, dying glimmers of yellow. Little by little, buttons began moving back again.

Lucky said, "The scarlet patch just settles down to the bottom, holding on to the ooze with its edges and digesting and absorbing whatever it covers. There's another species called the orange patch which is a lot more aggressive. It can shoot a jet of water with enough force to stagger a man, even though it's only a foot wide and not much more than paper thin. The big ones are a lot worse."

"How big do they get?" asked Bigman.

"I haven't the slightest idea. The book says there are occasional reports of tremendous monsters—arrowfish a mile long, and patches that can cover Aphrodite City. No authentic cases, though."

"A mile long! I'll *bet* there aren't any authentic cases."

Lucky's eyebrows lifted. "It's not as impossible as all that. These things here are only shallow-water specimens. The Venusian ocean is up to ten miles deep in spots. There's room in it for a lot of things."

Bigman looked at him doubtfully. "Listen, you're trying to sell me a bale of space dust." He turned abruptly and moved away. "I think I'll look at the book after all."

The *Hilda* moved on and took a new position, while the microwaves shot out, searching and searching. Then again it moved. And again. Slowly Lucky was screening the underwater plateau on which the city of Aphrodite stood.

He waited grimly at the instruments. Somewhere down here his friend Lou Evans *must* be. Evan's ship could navigate neither air nor space, nor any ocean depth of more than two miles, so he *must* be confined to the relatively shallow waters of the Aphrodite plateau.

The first answering flash caught his eye even as he repeated the *must* to himself for the second time. The microwave feedback froze the direction finder in place, and the return pip was brightening the entire receiving field.

Bigman's hand was on Lucky's shoulder instantly. "That's it! That's it!"

"Maybe," said Lucky. "And maybe it's some other ship, or maybe it's only a wreck."

"Get its position, Lucky. Sands of Mars, get its position!"

"I'm doing it, boy, and we're moving."

Bigman could feel the acceleration, hear the churning of the propeller.

Lucky leaned closely over the radio transmitter and its unscrambler, and his voice was urgent. "Lou! Lou Evans! Lucky Starr at this end! Acknowledge signals! Lou! Lou Evans!"

Over and over again, the words pushed out along the ether. The returning microwave pip grew brighter as the distance between the two ships grew less.

No answer.

Bigman said, "That ship we're pipping isn't moving, Lucky. Maybe it *is* a wreck. If it were the councilman, he'd either answer or try to get away from us, wouldn't he?"

"Sh!" said Lucky. His words were quiet and urgent as he spoke into the transmitter: "Lou! There's no point in trying to hide. I know the truth. I know why you sent the message to Earth in Morriss's name asking for your own recall. And I know who you think the enemy is. Lou Evans! Acknowledge————"

The receiver crackled, static-ridden. Sounds came through the unscrambler and turned into intelligible words: "Stay away. If you know that, stay away!"

Lucky grinned his relief. Bigman whooped.

"You've got him," shouted the little Martian.

"We're coming in to get you," said Lucky into the transmitter. "Hold on. We'll lick it, you and I."

Words came back slowly, "You don't—understand—I'm trying to————" Then, almost in a shriek, "For Earth's sake, Lucky, stay away! Don't get any closer!"

No more came through. The *Hilda* bored toward the position of Evan's ship relentlessly. Lucky leaned back, frowning. He murmured, "If he's *that* afraid, why doesn't he run?"

Bigman didn't hear. He was saying jubilantly, "Terrific, Lucky. That was terrific the way you bluffed him into talking."

"I wasn't bluffing, Bigman," said Lucky, grimly. "I know the key fact involved in this whole mess. So would you, if you stopped to think about it."

Bigman said shakily, "What are you getting at?"

"Do you remember when Dr. Morriss and you and I entered the small room to wait for Lou Evans to be brought to us? Do you remember the first thing that happened?"

"No."

"You started laughing. You said I looked queer and deformed without a mustache. And I felt exactly the same way about you. I said so. Remember?"

"Oh, sure. I remember."

"Did it occur to you to wonder why that was? We'd been watching men with mustaches for hours. Why was it that the thought suddenly occurred to both of us at that particular time?"

"I don't know."

"Suppose the thought had occurred to someone else who had telepathic powers. Suppose the sensation of surprise flooded from his mind to ours."

"You mean the mentalist, or one of them, was in the room with us?"

"Wouldn't that explain it?"

"But it's impossible. Dr. Morriss was the only other man———Lucky! You don't mean Dr. Morriss!"

"Morriss had been staring at us for hours. Why should he be suddenly amazed at our not having mustaches?"

"Well, then, was someone hiding?"

"Not hiding," said Lucky. "There was one other living creature in the room, and it was in plain view."

"No," cried Bigman. "Oh, no." He burst into laughter. "Sands of Mars, you can't mean the V-frog?"

"Why not?" said Lucky calmly. "We're probably the first men without mustaches it ever saw. It was surprised."

"But it's impossible."

"Is it? They're all over the city. People collect them, feed them, love them. Now do they really love V-frogs? Or do the V-frogs inspire love by mental control so as to get themselves fed and taken care of?"

"Space, Lucky!" said Bigman. "There's nothing surprising about people liking them. They're cute. People don't have to be hypnotized into thinking that."

"Did you like them spontaneously, Bigman? Nothing made you?"

"I'm sure nothing *made* me like them. I just liked them."

"You just liked them? Two minutes after you saw your first V-frog, you fed it. Remember that?"

"Nothing wrong with that, is there?"

"Ah, but what did you feed it?"

"What it liked. Peas dipped in axle g———" The little fellow's voice faded out.

"Exactly. That grease *smelled* like axle grease. There was no mistaking what it was. How did you come to dip the pea in it? Do you always feed axle grease to pet animals? Did you ever know any animal that ate axle grease?"

"Sands of Mars!" said Bigman weakly.

"Isn't it obvious that the V-frog wanted some, and that since you were handy it maneuvered you into delivering some—that you weren't quite your own master?"

Bigman muttered, "I never guessed. But it's so clear when you explain it. I feel terrible."

"Why?"

"It's a hateful thing, having an animal's thoughts rolling around inside your head. It seems unsanitary." His puckish little face screwed up in an expression of revulsion.

Lucky said, "Unfortunately, it's worse than unsanitary."

He turned back to the instruments.

The interval between pip and return disclosed the distance between the two ships to be less than half a mile when, with surprising suddenness, the radar screen showed, unmistakably, the shadow of Evans's ship.

Lucky's voice went out over the transmitter. "Evans, you're in sight now. Can you move? Is your ship disabled?"

The answer came back clearly in a voice torn with emotion. "Earth help me, Lucky, I did my best to warn you. You're trapped! Trapped as I'm trapped."

And as though to punctuate the councilman's wail, a blast of force struck the subship *Hilda*, knocking it to one side and jarring its main motors out of commission!

9

Out of the Deep

In Bigman's memory afterward, the events of the next hours were as though viewed through the reverse end of a telescope, a faraway nightmare of confused events.

Bigman had been slammed against the wall by the sudden thrust of force. For what seemed long moments, but was probably little more than a second in actuality, he lay spread-eagled and gasping.

Lucky, still at the controls, shouted, "The main generators are out."

Bigman was struggling to his feet against the crazy slope of the deck. "What happened?"

"We were hit. Obviously. But I don't know how badly."

Bigman said, "The lights are on."

"I know. The emergency generators have cut in."

"How about the main drive?"

"I'm not sure. It's what I'm trying to test."

The engines coughed hoarsely somewhere below and behind. The smooth purr was gone, and in its place a consumptive rattle sounded that set Bigman's teeth on edge.

The *Hilda* shook herself, like a hurt animal, and turned upright. The engines died again.

The radio receiver was echoing mournfully, and now Bigman gathered his senses sufficiently to try to reach it.

"Starr," it said. "Lucky Starr! Evans at this end. Acknowledge signals."

Lucky got there first. "Lucky speaking. What hit us?"

"It doesn't matter," came the tired voice. "It won't bother you any more. It will be satisfied to let you sit here and die. Why didn't you stay away? I asked you to."

"Is your ship disabled, Evans?"

"It's been stalled for twelve hours. No light, no power —just a little juice I can pump into the radio, and that's fading. Air purifiers are smashed, and the air supply is low. So long, Lucky."

"Can you get out?"

"The lock mechanism isn't working. I've got a subsea suit, but if I try to cut my way out, I'll be smashed."

Bigman knew what Lou Evans meant, and he shuddered. Locks on subsea vessels were designed to let water into the interlock chamber slowly, very slowly. To cut a lock open at the bottom of the sea in an attempt to get out of a ship would mean the entry of water under hundreds of tons of pressure. A human being, even inside a steel suit, would be crushed like an empty tin can under a pile driver.

Lucky said, "We can still navigate. I'm coming to get you. We'll join locks."

"Thanks, but why? If you move, you'll be hit again; and even if you aren't, what's the difference whether I die quickly here or a little more slowly in your ship?"

Lucky retorted angrily, "We'll die if we have to, but not one second *earlier* than we have to. Everyone has to die someday; there's no escaping that, but *quitting* isn't compulsory."

He turned to Bigman. "Get down into the engine room and check the damage. I want to know if it can be repaired."

In the engine room, fumbling with the "hot" micropile by means of long-distance manipulators, which luckily were still in order, Bigman could feel the ship inching painfully along the sea bottom and could hear the husky rasping of the motors. Once he heard a distant boom, followed by a groaning rattle through the framework of the *Hilda* as though a large projectile had hit sea bottom a hundred yards away.

He felt the ship stop, the motor noise drop to a hoarse rumble. In imagination, he could see the *Hilda's* lock extension bore out and close in on the other hull, welding itself tightly to it. He could sense the water between the ships being pumped out of that tube between them and, in actual fact, he saw the lights in the engine room dim as the energy drain on the emergency generators rose to dangerous heights. Lou Evans would be able to step from his ship to the *Hilda* through dry air with no need of artificial protection.

Bigman came up to the control room and found Lou Evans with Lucky. His face was drawn and worn under its blond stubble. He managed a shaky smile in Bigman's direction.

Lucky was saying, "Go on, Lou."

Evans said, "It was the wildest hunch at first, Lucky. I followed up each of the men to whom one of these queer accidents had happened. The one thing I could find in common was that each was a V-frog fancier. Everyone on Venus is, more or less, but each one of *these* fellows kept a houseful of the creatures. I didn't quite have the nerve to make a fool of myself advancing the theory without some facts. If I only had. . . . Anyway, I decided to try to trap the V-frogs into exhibiting knowledge of something that existed in my own mind and in as few others as possible."

Lucky said, "And you decided on the yeast data?"

"It was the obvious thing. I had to have something that wasn't general knowledge or how could I be even reasonably sure they got the information from me? Yeast data was ideal. When I couldn't get any legitimately, I stole some. I borrowed one of the V-frogs at headquarters, put it next to my table, and looked over the papers. I even read some of it aloud. When an accident happened in a yeast plant two days later involving the exact matter I had read about, I was positive the V-frogs were behind the mess. Only————"

"Only?" prompted Lucky.

"Only I hadn't been so smart," said Evans. "I'd let them into my mind. I'd laid down the red carpet and invited them in, and now I couldn't get them out again. Guards came looking for the papers. I was known to have been in the buildings, so a very polite agent was sent to question me. I returned the papers readily and tried to explain. I couldn't."

"You couldn't? What do you mean by that?"

"I *couldn't*. I was physically unable to. The proper words wouldn't come out. I was unable to say a word about the V-frogs. I even kept getting impulses to kill myself, but I fought them down. They couldn't get me to do something that far from my nature. I thought then: If I can only get off Venus, if I can only get far enough away from the V-frogs, I'd break their hold. So I did the one thing I thought would get me instantly recalled. I sent an accusation of corruption against myself and put Morriss's name to it."

"Yes," said Lucky grimly, "that much I had guessed."

"How?" Evans looked startled.

"Morriss told us his side of your story shortly after we

got to Aphrodite. He ended by saying that he was preparing his report to central headquarters. He didn't say he had sent one—only that he was preparing one. But a message had been sent; I knew that. Who else besides Morriss knew the Council code and the circumstances of the case? Only you yourself."

Evans nodded and said bitterly, "And instead of calling me home, they sent you. Is that it?"

"I insisted, Lou. I couldn't believe any charge of corruption against you."

Evans buried his head in his hands. "It was the worst thing you could have done, Lucky. When you subethered you were coming, I begged you to stay away, didn't I? I couldn't tell you why. I was physically incapable of that. But the V-frogs must have realized from my thoughts what a terrific character you were. They could read my opinion of your abilities and they set about having you killed."

"And nearly succeeded," murmured Lucky.

"And *will* succeed this time. For that I am heartily sorry, Lucky, but I couldn't help myself. When they paralyzed the man at the dome lock, I was unable to keep myself from following the impulse to escape, to get out to sea. And, of course, you followed. I was the bait and you were the victim. Again, I tried to keep you away, but I couldn't explain, I couldn't explain. . . ."

He drew a deep, shuddering breath. "I can speak about it now, though. They've lifted the block in my mind. I suppose we're not worth the mental energy they have to expend, because we're trapped, because we're as good as dead and they fear us no longer."

Bigman, having listened this far in increasing confusion, said, "Sands of Mars, what's going on? *Why* are we as good as dead?"

Evans, face still hidden in his hands, did not answer.

Lucky, frowning and thoughtful, said, "We're under an orange patch, a king-size orange patch out of the Venusian deeps."

"A patch big enough to cover the ship?"

"A patch two miles in diameter!" said Lucky. "Two miles across. What slapped the ship into almost a smashup and what nearly hit us a second time when we were making our way to Evans's ship was a jet of water. Just that! A jet of water with the force of a depth blast."

"But how could we get under it without seeing it?"

Lucky said, "Evans guesses that it's under V-frog mental control, and I think he's right. It could dim its fluorescence by contracting the photo cells in its skin. It could raise one edge of its cape to let us in; and now, here we sit."

"And if we move or try to blast our way out, the patch will let us have it again, and a patch never misses."

Lucky thought, then said suddenly, "But a patch *does* miss! It missed us when we were driving the *Hilda* toward your ship and then we were only going at quarter speed." He turned to Bigman, his eyes narrowed. "Bigman, can the main generators be patched?"

Bigman had almost forgotten the engines. He recovered and said, "Oh———The micropile alignment hasn't been knocked off, so it can be fixed if I can find all the equipment I need."

"How long will it take?"

"Hours, probably."

"Then get to work. I'm getting out into the sea."

Evans looked up, startled, "What do you mean?"

"I'm going after that patch." He was at the sea-suit locker already, checking to make certain the tiny forcefield linings were in order and well powered and that the oxygen cylinders were full.

• • •

It was deceptively restful to be out in the absolute dark. Danger seemed far away. Yet Lucky knew well enough that below him was the ocean bottom and that on every other side, up and all around, was a two-mile-wide inverted bowl of rubbery flesh.

His suit's pump jetted water downward, and he rose slowly with his weapon drawn and ready. He could not help but marvel at the subwater blaster he held. Inventive as man was on his home planet of Earth, it seemed that the necessity for adapting to the cruel environment of an alien planet multiplied his ingenuity a hundredfold.

Once the new continent of America had burst forth into a brilliance that the ancestral European homelands could never duplicate, and now Venus was showing *her* ability to Earth. There were the city domes, for instance. Nowhere on Earth could force fields have been woven into steel so cleverly. The very suit he wore could not resist the tons of water pressure for a moment without the microfields that webbed its interior braces (always provided those tons were introduced sufficiently slowly). In many other respects that suit was a marvel of engineering. Its jet device for underwater traveling, its efficient oxygen supply, its compact controls, were all admirable.

And the weapon he held!

But immediately his thoughts moved to the monster above. That was a Venusian invention, too. An invention of the planet's evolution. Could such things be on Earth? Not on land, certainly. Living tissue couldn't support the weight of more than forty tons against Earth's gravity. The giant brontosauri of Earth's Mesozoic Age had legs like treetrunks, yet had to remain in the marshes so that water could help buoy them up.

That was the answer: water's buoyancy. In the oceans any size of creature might exist. There were the whales of Earth, larger than any dinosaur that ever lived. But this monstrous patch above them must weigh two hundred million *tons*, he calculated. Two million large whales put together would scarcely weight that. Lucky wondered how old it was. How old would a thing have to be to grow as large as two million whales? A hundred years? A thousand years? Who could tell?

But size could be its undoing, too. Even under the ocean. The larger it grew, the slower its reactions. Nerve impulses took time to travel.

Evans thought the monster refrained from hitting them with another water jet because, having disabled them, it was indifferent to their further fate, or rather the V-frogs who manipulated the giant patch were. That might not be so! It might be rather that the monster needed time to suck its tremendous water sac full. It needed time to aim.

Furthermore, the monster could scarcely be at its best. It was adapted to the deeps, to layers of water six miles or more high above it. Here its efficiency must necessarily be cut down. It had missed the *Hilda* on its second try, probably because it had not fully recovered from the previous stroke.

But now it was waiting; its water sac was slowly filling; and as much as it could in the shallow water surrounding it, it was gathering its strength. He, Lucky, 190 pounds of man against two hundred million tons of monster, would have to stop it.

Lucky looked upward. He could see nothing. He pressed a contact on the inner lining in the left middle finger of the sheathed force-field-reinforced mitten that gauntleted his hand, and a jab of pure-white light poured out of the metal fingertip. It penetrated upward hazily and ended in nothingness. Was that the monster's flesh at the far end? Or just the petering out of the light beam?

Three times the monster had jetted water. Once and

Evâns's ship had been smashed. A second time and Lucky's ship had been mauled. (But not as badly; was the creature getting weaker?) A third time, prematurely, and the stroke had been a miss.

He raised his weapon. It was bulky, with a thick hand-grip. Within that grip was a hundred miles of wire and a tiny generator that could put out huge voltages. He pointed it upward and squeezed his fist.

For a moment, nothing—but he knew the hair-thin wire was squirting out and upward through the carbonated ocean water. . . .

Then it hit and Lucky saw the results. For in the moment that the wire made contact, a flash current of electricity screamed along it at the speed of light and flayed the obstruction with the force of a bolt of lightning. The hairlike wire gleamed brilliantly and vaporized steaming water into murky froth. It was more than steam, for the alien water writhed and bubbled horribly as the dissolved carbon dioxide gassed out. Lucky felt himself bobbing in the wild currents set up.

Above all that, above the steaming and bubbling, above the water's churning and the line of thin fire that reached upward, there was a fireball that exploded. Where the wire had touched living flesh there was a blaze of furious energy. It burned a hole ten feet wide and as many feet deep into the living mountain above him.

Lucky smiled grimly. That was only a pin prick in comparison to the monster's vast bulk, but the patch would feel it; or at least in ten minutes or so, it would feel it. The nerve impulses must first travel their slow way along the curve of its flesh. When the pain reached the creature's tiny brain, it would be distracted from the helpless ship on the ocean floor and turn upon its new tormentor.

But, Lucky thought grimly, the monster would not

find him. In ten minutes he would have changed position. In ten minutes, he———

Lucky never completed the thought. Not one minute after his bolt had struck the creature, it struck back.

Not one minute had passed when Lucky's shocked and tortured senses told him that he was being driven down, down, down, in a turbulent jet of madly driving water. . . .

10

The Mountain of Flesh

The shock sent Lucky's senses reeling. Any suit of ordinary metal would have bent and smashed. Any man of ordinary mettle would have been carried senseless down to the ocean floor, there to be smashed into concussion and death.

But Lucky fought desperately. Struggling against the mighty current, he brought his left arm up to his chest to check the dials that indicated the state of the suit machinery.

He groaned. The indicators were all lifeless things, their delicate workings jarred into uselessness. Still, his oxygen supply seemed unaffected (his lungs would have told him of any drop in pressure), and his suit obviously wasn't leaking. He could only hope that its jet action was still in order.

There was no use trying blindly to find his way out of the stream by main force. He almost certainly lacked the power. He would have to wait and gamble on one important thing: The stream of water lost velocity rapidly as it penetrated downward. Water against water was a high-friction action. At the rim of the jet, turbulence would grow and eat inward. A cutting stream five hundred feet across as it emerged from the creature's blowpipe might be only fifty feet wide when it hit bottom, depending upon its original velocity and the distance to the ocean floor.

And that original velocity would have slowed, too. That did not mean that the final velocity was anything to deride. Lucky had felt its force against the ship.

It all depended on how far from the center of the water gush he was, on how near a bull's-eye the creature scored.

The longer he waited, the better his chances—provided he did not wait too long. With his metal-gloved hand on the jet controls, Lucky let himself be flung downward, trying to wait calmly, striving to guess how close to solid bottom he was, expecting each moment the one last concussion he would never feel.

And then, when he had counted ten, he flung his suit's jets open. The small, high-speed propellers on either shoulder blade ground in harsh vibration as they threw out water at right angles to the main current. Lucky could feel his body take on a new direction of fall.

If he was dead center, it wouldn't help. The energy he could pump up would not suffice to overcome the mighty surge downward. If he was well off center, however, his velocity would, by now, have slowed considerably and the growing zone of turbulence might not be far off.

And as he thought that, he felt his body bob and yank with nauseating violence, and he knew he was safe.

He kept his own jets in operation, turning their force downward now and, as he did so, he turned his finger light in the direction of the ocean floor. He was just in time to see the ooze, some fifty feet below, explode and obscure everything with its muck.

He had made his way out of the stream with but seconds to spare.

He was hurrying upward now, as fast as the jet motors of his suit would carry him. He was in desperate haste. In the darkness within his helmet (darkness within darkness within darkness) his lips were pressed into a narrow line and his eyebrows pulled down low.

He was doing his best not to think. He had thought enough in those few seconds in the water spout. He had underestimated the enemy. He had assumed it was the gigantic patch that was aiming at him, and it wasn't. It was the V-frogs on the water's surface that controlled the patch's body through its mind! The V-frogs had aimed. They did not have to follow the patch's sensations in order to know it had been hit. They needed only to read Lucky's mind, and they needed only to aim at the source of Lucky's thoughts.

So it was no longer a matter of pin-pricking the monster into moving away from the *Hilda* and lumbering down the long underwater declivity to the deeps that had spawned it. The monster had to be killed outright.

And quickly!

If the *Hilda* would not take another direct blow, neither would Lucky's own suit. The indicators were gone already; the controls might go next. Or the liquid-oxygen containers might suffer damage to their tiny force-field generators.

Up and still up went Lucky, up to the only place of safety. Although he had never seen the monster's blowpipe, it stood to reason that it must be an extensible and flexible tube that could point this way and that. But the monster could scarcely point it at its own undersurface. For one thing, it would do itself damage. For another, the force of the water it expelled would prevent that blowpipe from bending at so great an angle.

Lucky had to move up then, close to the animal's undersurface, to where its weapon of water could not reach; and he had to do it before the monster could fill its water sac for another blow.

Lucky flashed his light upward. He was reluctant to do so, feeling instinctively that the light would make him an easy target. His mind told him his instinct was wrong. The sense that was responsible for the monster's rapid response to his attack was not sight.

Fifty feet or less above, the light ended on a rough, grayish surface, streaked with deep corrugations. Lucky scarcely attempted to brake his rush. The monster's skin was rubbery and his own suit hard. Even as he thought that, he collided, pressing upward and feeling the alien flesh give.

For a long moment, Lucky drew deep gasps of relief. For the first time since leaving the ship, he felt moderately safe. The relaxation did not last, however. At any time the creature could turn its attack (or the small mindmaster that controlled it could) on the ship. That must not be allowed to happen.

Lucky played his finger flash about his surroundings with a mixture of wonder and nausea.

Here and there in the undersurface of the monster were holes some six feet across into which, as Lucky could see by the flow of bubbles and solid particles, water was rushing. At greater intervals were slits, which opened occasionally into ten-foot-long fissures that emitted frothing gushes of water.

Apparently this was the way the monster fed. It poured digestive juices into the portion of the ocean trapped beneath its bulk, then sucked in water by the cubic yard to extract the nutriment it contained, and still later expelled water, debris, and its own wastes.

Obviously, it could not stay too long over any one spot

of the ocean or the accumulation of its own waste products would make its environment unhealthy. Of its own account it would not have lingered here so long, but with the .V-frogs driving it———

Lucky moved jerkily through no action of his own and, in surprise, turned the beam of light on a spot closer to himself. In a moment of stricken horror, he realized the purposes of those deep corrugations he had noticed in the monster's undersurface. One such was forming directly to one side of him and was sucking inward, into the creature's substance. The two sides of the corrugation rubbed against one another, and the monster broke up and shredded particles of food too large to be handled directly by its intake pores.

Lucky did not wait. He could not risk his battered suit against the fantastic strength of the monster's muscles. The walls of his suit might hold, but portions of the delicate working mechanisms might not.

He swung his shoulder so as to turn the suit's jets directly against the flesh of the monster and gave them full energy. He came loose with a sharp smacking sound, then veered round and back.

He did not touch the skin again, but hovered near it and traveled along it, following the direction against gravity, mounting upward, away from the outer edges of the thing, toward its center.

He came suddenly to a point where the creature's undersurface turned down again in a wall of flesh that extended as far as his light would reach on either side. That wall quivered and was obviously composed of thinner tissue.

It was the blowpipe.

Lucky was sure that was what it was—a gigantic cavern a hundred yards across, out of which the fury of rushing water emerged. Cautiously Lucky circled it. Undoubtedly this was the safest place one could be, here at the very base of the blowpipe, and yet he picked his way gingerly.

He knew what he was looking for, however, and he left the blowpipe. He moved away in the direction in which the monster's flesh mounted still higher, until he was at the peak of the inverted bowl, and there it was!

At first, Lucky was aware only of a long-drawn-out rumble, almost too deep to hear. In fact, it was vibration that attracted his attention, rather than any sound. Then he spied the swelling in the monster's flesh. It writhed and beat; a huge mass, hanging thirty feet downward and perhaps as big around as the blowpipe.

That *must* be the center of the organism; its heart, or whatever passed for its heart, must be there. That heart must beat in powerful strokes, and Lucky felt dizzy as he tried to picture it. Those heartbeats must last five minutes at a time, during which thousands of cubic yards of blood (or whatever the creature used) must be forced through blood vessels large enough to hold the *Hilda*. That heartbeat must suffice to drive the blood a mile and back.

What a mechanism it must be, thought Lucky. If one could only capture such a thing alive and study its physiology!

Somewhere in that swelling must also be what brain the monster might have. Brain? Perhaps what passed for its brain was only a small clot of nerve cells without which the monster could live quite well.

Perhaps! But it couldn't live without its heart. The heart had completed one beat. The central swelling had contracted to almost nothing. Now the heart was relaxing for another beat five minutes or more from now, and the swelling was expanding and dilating as blood rushed into it.

Lucky raised his weapon and with his light beam full

on that giant heart, he let himself sink down. It might be best not to be too close. On the other hand, he dared not miss.

For a moment a twinge of regret swept him. From a scientific standpoint it was almost a crime to kill this mightiest of nature's creatures.

Was that one of his own thoughts or a thought imposed upon him by the V-frogs on the ocean surface?

He dared wait no longer. He squeezed the handgrip of his weapon. The wire shot out. It made contact, and Lucky's eyes were blinded by the flash of light in which the near wall of the monster's heart was burnt through.

For minutes the water boiled with the death throes of the mountain of flesh. Its entire mass convulsed in its gigantic writhings. Lucky, thrown this way and that, was helpless.

He tried to call the *Hilda,* but the answer consisted of erratic gasps, and it was quite obvious that the ship, too, was being flung madly about.

But death, when it comes, must finally penetrate the last ounce of even a hundred-million-ton life. Eventually a stillness came upon the water.

And Lucky moved downward slowly, slowly, weary nearly to death.

He called the *Hilda* again. "It's dead," he said. "Send out the directional pulse and let me follow it down."

Lucky let Bigman remove his sea suit and managed a smile as the little Martian looked worriedly up at him.

"I never thought I'd see you again, Lucky," said Bigman, gulping noisily.

"If you're going to cry," said Lucky, "turn your head away. I didn't get in out of the ocean just to get all wet in here. How are the main generators coming along?"

"They'll be all right," put in Evans, "but it will still

take time. The knocking around just at the end there ruined one of the welding jobs."

"Well," said Lucky, "we'll just have to get on with it." He sat down with a weary sigh. "Things didn't go quite as I expected."

"In what way?" demanded Evans.

"It was my notion," said Lucky, "to pin-prick the monster into moving off us. That didn't work, and I had to kill him. The result is that its dead body has settled down around the *Hilda* like a collapsed tent."

11

To the Surface?

"**Y**ou mean we're trapped?" said Bigman, with horror.

"You can put it that way," said Lucky coolly. "You can also say that we're safe, if you want to. Certainly we're safer here than anywhere on Venus. Nobody can do anything to us physically with that mountain of dead meat over us. And when the generators are repaired, we'll just force our way out. Bigman, get at those generators; and Evans, let's pour ourselves some coffee and talk this thing over. There might not be another chance for a quiet chat."

Lucky welcomed this respite, this moment when there was nothing to be done but talk and think.

Evans, however, was upset. His china-blue eyes crinkled at the corners.

Lucky said, "You look worried?"

"I am worried. What in space and time do we do?"

Lucky said, "I've been thinking about that. It seems to me that all we can do is get the V-frog story to someone who's safe from any mental control by them."

"And who's that?"

"No one on Venus. That's for sure."

Evans stared at his friend. "Are you trying to tell me that everyone on Venus is under control?"

"No, but anyone *might* be. After all, there are different ways in which the human mind can be manipulated by these creatures." Lucky rested one arm over the back of the pilot swivel and crossed his legs. "In the first place, complete control can be taken for a short period of time over a man's mind. *Complete* control! During that interval a human being can be made to do things contrary to his own nature, things that endanger his own life and others': the pilots on the coaster, for instance, when Bigman and I first landed on Venus."

Evans said grimly, "That type of thing hasn't been *my* trouble."

"I know. That's what Morriss failed to realize. He was sure you weren't under control simply because you showed no signs of amnesia. But there's a second type of control that you suffered from. It's less intense, so a person retains his memory. However, just because it's less intense, a person cannot be forced to do anything against his own nature; you couldn't be forced to commit suicide, for instance. Still, the power lasts longer—days rather than hours. The V-frogs make up in time what they lose in intensity. Well, there must be still a third kind of control."

"And that is?"

"A control that is still less intense than the second type. A control that is so mild the victim isn't even aware of it, yet strong enough so that the victim's mind can be rifled and picked of its information. For instance, there's Lyman Turner."

"The chief engineer on Aphrodite?"

"That's right. He's a case in point. Can you see that? Consider that there was a man at the dome lock yesterday who sat there with a lever in his hand, endangering the whole city, yet he was so tightly protected all around, so netted about with alarms that no one could approach him without warning until Bigman forced a passage through a ventilator shaft. Isn't that odd?"

"No. Why it is odd?"

"The man had only been on the job a matter of months. He wasn't even a real engineer. His work was more like that of a clerk or an office boy. Where did he get the information to protect himself so? How could he possibly know the force and power system in that section of the dome so thoroughly?"

Evans pursed his lips and whistled soundlessly. "Hey, that *is* a point."

"The point didn't strike Turner. I interviewed him on just that matter before getting on the *Hilda.* I didn't tell him what I was after, of course. He himself told me about the fellow's inexperience, but the incongruity of the matter never struck him. Yet who *would* have the necessary information? Who but the chief engineer? Who better than he?"

"Right. Right."

"Well, then, suppose Turner was under very gentle control. The information could be lifted out of his brain. He could be very gently soothed into not seeing anything out of the way in the situation. Do you see what I mean? And then Morriss————"

"Morriss, too?" said Evans, shocked.

"Possibly. He's convinced it's a matter of Sirians after yeast. He can see it as nothing else. Is that a legitimate misjudgment or is he being subtly persuaded? He was ready to suspect you, Lou—a little too ready. One councilman ought to be a little less prepared to suspect another."

"Space! Then who's safe, Lucky?"

Lucky stared at his empty coffee cup and said, "No

one on Venus. That's my point. We've got to get the story and the truth somewhere else."

"And how can we?"

"A good point. How can we?" Lucky Starr brooded over that.

Evans said, "We can't leave physically. The *Hilda* is designed for nothing but ocean. It can't navigate the air, let alone space. And if we go back to the city to get something more suitable, we'd never leave it again."

"I think you're right," said Lucky, "but we don't have to leave Venus in the flesh. Our information is all that has to leave."

"If you mean ship's radio," said Evans, "that's out, too. The set we've got on this tub is strictly intra-Venus. It's not a subetheric, so it can't reach Earth. Down here, as a matter of fact, the instrument won't reach above the ocean. Its carrier waves are designed to be reflected down from the ocean surface so that they can get distance. Besides that, even if we could transmit straight up, we couldn't reach Earth."

"I don't see that we have to," said Lucky. "There's something between here and Earth that would do just as well."

For a moment, Evans was mystified. Then he said, "You mean the space stations?"

"Surely. Two space stations circle Venus. Earth may be anywhere from thirty to fifty million miles away, but the stations may be as close as two thousand miles to this point. Yet there can't be V-frogs on the stations, I'm sure. Morriss said they dislike free oxygen, and one could scarcely rig up special carbon-dioxide chambers for V-frogs considering the economy with which space stations must be run. Now, if we could get a message out to the stations for relay to central headquarters on Earth, we'd have it."

"That's it, Lucky," said Evans, excitedly. "It's our way out. Their mental powers can't possibly reach two thousand miles across space to———" But then his face turned glum once more. "No, it won't do. The subship radio still can't reach past the ocean surface."

"Maybe not from here. But suppose we go up to the surface and transmit from there directly into the atmosphere."

"Up to the surface?"

"Well?"

"But *they* are there. The V-frogs."

"I know that."

"We'll be put under control."

"Will we?" said Lucky. "So far they've never tackled anyone who's known about them, known what to expect and made up his mind to resist it. Most of the victims were completely unsuspecting. In your case you actually invited them into your mind, to use your own phrase. Now I am not unsuspecting, and I don't propose to issue any invitations."

"You can't do it, I tell you. You don't know what it's like."

"Can you suggest an alternative?"

Before Evans could answer, Bigman entered, rolling down his sleeves. "All set," he said. "I guarantee the generators."

Lucky nodded and stepped to the controls, while Evans remained in his seat, his eyes clouded with uncertainty.

There was the churning of the motors again, rich and sweet. The muted sound was like a song, and there was that strange feeling of suspension and motion under one's feet that was never felt on a spaceship.

The *Hilda* moved through the bubble of water that

had been trapped under the collapsing body of the giant patch and built up speed.

Bigman said uneasily, "How much room do we have?"

"About half a mile," said Lucky.

"What if we don't make it?" muttered Bigman. "What if we just hit it and stick, like an ax in a tree stump?"

"Then we pull out and try again," said Lucky.

There was silence for a moment, and Evans said in a low voice, "Being closed in under here, under the patch —it's like being in a chamber." He was mumbling, half to himself.

"In a what?" said Lucky.

"In a chamber," said Evans, still abstracted. "They build them on Venus. They're little transite domes under sea-floor level, like cyclone cellars or bomb shelters on Earth. They're supposed to be protection against incoming water in case of a broken dome, say by Venusquake. I don't know that a chamber has ever been used, but the better apartment houses always advertise that they have chamber facilities in case of emergency."

Lucky listened to him, but said nothing.

The engine pitch rose higher.

"Hold on!" said Lucky.

Every inch of the *Hilda* trembled, and the sudden, almost irresistible deceleration forced Lucky hard against the instrument panel. Bigman's and Evans's knuckles went white and their wrists strained as they gripped the guard rails with all their strength.

The ship slowed but did not stop. With the motors straining and the generators protesting in a squeal that made Lucky wince in sympathy, the *Hilda* plowed through skin and flesh and sinew, through empty blood-vessels and useless nerves that must have resembled two-foot-thick cables. Lucky, jaw set and grim, kept the drive rod nailed at maximum against the tearing resistance.

The long minutes passed and then, in a long churn of triumphant engine, they were through—through the monster and out once more into the open sea.

Silently and smoothly the *Hilda* rose through the murky, carbon-dioxide-saturated water of Venus's ocean. Silence held the three, a silence that seemed enforced by the daring with which they were storming the very fortress of Venus's hostile life form. Evans had not said a word since the patch had been left behind. Lucky had locked ship's controls and now sat on the pilot swivel with fingers softly tapping his knee. Even the irrepressible Bigman had drifted glumly to the rear port with its bellying, wide-angle field of vision.

Suddenly Bigman called, "Lucky, look there."

Lucky strode to Bigman's side. Together they gazed in silence. Over half the field of the port there was only the starry light of small phosphorescent creatures, thick and soft, but in another direction there was a wall, a monstrous wall glowing in smears of shifting color.

"Do you suppose that's the patch, Lucky?" asked Bigman. "It wasn't shining that way when we came down here; and anyway, it wouldn't shine after it was dead, would it?"

Lucky said thoughtfully, "It is the patch in a way, Bigman. I think the whole ocean is gathering for the feast."

Bigman looked again and felt a little ill. Of course! There were hundreds of millions of tons of meat there for the taking, and the light they viewed must be the light of all the small creatures of the shallows feeding on the dead monster.

Creatures darted past the port, moving always in the same direction. They moved sternward, toward the mountainous carcass the *Hilda* had left behind.

Pre-eminent among them were arrow fish of all sizes. Each had a straight white line of phosphorescence that marked its backbone (it wasn't a backbone really, but merely an unjointed rod of horny substance). At one end of that white line was a pale yellow V that marked the head. To Bigman it looked indeed as though a countless swarm of animated arrows were swarming past the ship, but in imagination he could see their needle-rimmed jaws, cavernous and ravenous.

"Great Galaxy!" said Lucky.

"Sands of Mars!" murmured Bigman. "The ocean will be empty. Every blasted thing in the ocean is gathering to this one spot."

Lucky said, "At the rate those arrow fish must be gorging themselves, the thing will be gone in twelve hours."

Evans's voice sounded from behind them. "Lucky, I want to speak to you."

Lucky turned. "Sure. What is it, Lou?"

"When you first suggested going to the surface, you asked if I could propose an alternative."

"I know. You didn't answer."

"I can answer now. I'm holding it, in fact, and the answer is that we're going back to the city."

Bigman called, "Hey, what's the idea?"

Lucky had no need to ask that question. His nostrils flared, and inwardly he raged at himself for those minutes he had spent at the porthole when all his heart, mind, and soul should have been concentrated on the business at hand.

For in Evans's clenched fist, as it lifted from his side, was Lucky's own blaster, and in Evans's narrowed eyes, there was hard determination.

"We're going back to the city," repeated Evans.

12

To the City?

Lucky said, "What's wrong, Lou?"

Evans gestured impatiently with his blaster. "Put the engines in reverse, start bottomward, and turn the ship's bow toward the city. Not you, Lucky. You let Bigman go to those controls; then you get in line with him, so I can watch both of you and the controls, too."

Bigman had his hands half-upraised, and his eyes turned to look at Lucky. Lucky kept his hands at his side.

Lucky said flatly, "Suppose you tell me what's biting you?"

"Nothing's biting me," said Evans. "Nothing at all. It's what's biting you. You went out and killed the monster, then came back and started talking about going to the surface. Why?"

"I explained my reasons."

"I don't believe your reasons. If we surface, I know the V-frogs will take over our minds. I've had experience with them, and because of that I know the V-frogs have taken over *your* mind."

"*What?*" exploded Bigman. "Are you nuts?"

"I know what I'm doing," said Evans, watching Lucky

warily. "If you look at this thing coolly, Bigman, you'll see that Lucky must be under V-frog influence. Don't forget, he's my friend, too. I've known him longer than you have, Bigman, and it bothers me to have to do this, but there's no way out. It must be done."

Bigman stared uncertainly at both men, then said in a low voice, "Lucky, have the V-frogs really got you?"

"No," said Lucky.

"What do you expect him to say?" demanded Evans with heat. "Of course they have him. To kill the monster, he had to jet upward to its top. He must have gone fairly close to the surface where the V-frogs were waiting, close enough for them to snatch him. They let him kill the monster. Why not? They would be glad to trade control of the monster for control of Lucky, so Lucky came back babbling of the need to go to the surface, where we'll all be among them, all trapped—the only men who know the truth helpless."

"Lucky?" quavered Bigman, his tone pleading for reassurance.

Lucky Starr said calmly, "You're quite wrong, Lou. What you're doing now is only the result of your own captivity. You've been under control before, and the V-frogs know your mind. They can enter it at will. Maybe they've never entirely left it. You're doing only what you're being made to do."

Evans's grip on his blaster hardened. "Sorry, Lucky, but it won't do. Let's get the ship back to the city."

Lucky said, "If you're not under control, Lou—if you're mind-free—then you'll blast me down if I try to force us up to the surface, won't you?"

Evans did not answer.

Lucky said, "You'll have to. It will be your duty to the Council and to Mankind to do so. On the other hand, if you are under mental control, you may be forced to threaten me, to try to make me change ship's course, but I doubt that you can be forced to kill me. Actually murdering a friend and fellow councilman would be too much against your basic ways of thought. —So give me your blaster."

Lucky advanced toward the other, hand outstretched.

Bigman stared in horror.

Evans backed away. He said hoarsely, "I'm warning you, Lucky. I'll shoot."

"I say you won't shoot. You'll give me the blaster."

Evans was back against the wall. His voice rose crazily. "I'll shoot. I'll shoot!"

Bigman cried, "Lucky, stop!"

But Lucky had already stopped and was backing away. Slowly, very slowly, he backed.

The life had suddenly gone out of Evans's eyes, and he was standing now, a carved stone image, finger firm on trigger. Evans's voice was cold. "Back to the city."

Lucky said, "Get the ship on the city course, Bigman."

Bigman stepped quickly to the controls. He muttered, "He's really under now, isn't he?"

Lucky said, "I was afraid it might happen. They've shifted him to intense control to make sure he shoots. And he will, too; no question about it. He's in amnesia now. He won't remember this part afterward."

"Can he hear us?" Bigman remembered the pilots on the coaster in which they had landed on Venus and their apparent complete disregard of the external world about them.

"I don't think so," said Lucky, "but he's watching the controls and if we deviate from city-direction, he'll shoot. Make no mistake about that."

"Then what do we do?"

Words again issued from between Evans's pale, cold lips: "Back to the city. Quickly!"

Lucky, motionless, eyes fixed on the unwavering muzzle of his friend's blaster, spoke softly and quickly to Bigman.

Bigman acknowledged the words by the slightest of nods.

The *Hilda* moved back along the path it had come, back toward the city.

Lou Evans, councilman, stood against the wall, white-faced and stern, his pitiless eyes shifting from Lucky to Bigman to the controls. His body, frozen into utter obedience to those who controlled his mind, did not even feel the need of shifting the blaster from one hand to the other.

Lucky strained his ears to hear the low sound of Aphrodite's carrier beam as it sounded steadily on the *Hilda's* direction finder. The beam radiated in all directions on a definite wave length from the topmost point of Aphrodite's dome. The route back to the city became as obvious as though Aphrodite were in plain sight and a hundred feet away.

Lucky could tell by the exact pitch of the beam's low whine that they were not approaching the city directly. It was a small difference indeed, and one that was not at all obvious to the ear. To Evans's controlled ears, it might pass unnoticed. Fervently, Lucky hoped so.

Lucky tried to follow Evans's blank glare when his eyes rested on the controls. He was certain that it was the depth indicator that those eyes rested upon. It was a large dial, a simple one that measured the water pressure. At the distance Evans stood it was simple enough to tell that the *Hilda* was not nosing surfaceward.

Lucky felt certain that, should the depth-indicator needle vary in the wrong direction, Evans would blast without a moment's hesitation.

Try as he might to think as little as possible about the situation, to allow as few specific thoughts as possible to be picked up by the waiting V-frogs, he could not help but wonder why Evans did not shoot them out of hand. They had been marked for death under the giant patch, but now they were only being herded back to Aphrodite.

Or would Evans shoot them down just as soon as the V-frogs could overcome some last scruple in the captive's subjected mind?

The carrier beam moved a little further off pitch. Again Lucky's eyes flickered quickly in Evans's direction. Was he imagining it, or did a spark of something (not emotion, exactly, but something) show in Evans's eyes?

A split second later it was obviously more than imagination, for there was a definite tightening of Evans's biceps, a small lifting of his arm.

He was going to shoot!

And even as the thought passed quickly through Lucky's mind and his muscles tensed involuntarily and uselessly for the coming of the blast, the ship crashed. Evans, caught unaware, toppled backward. The blaster slithered from his sprawling fingers.

Lucky acted instantly. The same shock that threw Evans back threw him forward. He rode that shock and came down upon the other, clutching for his wrist and seizing it with steely fingers.

But Evans was anything but a pigmy, and he fought with the unearthly rage that was imposed upon him. He doubled his knees above him, caught Lucky in the thighs, and heaved. The still rocking ship fortuitously added its roll to the force of Evans's thrust and the captive councilman was on top.

Evans's fist pounded, but Lucky's shoulder fended the blow. He raised his own knees and caught Evans in an iron scissors hold just below the hips.

Evans's face distorted with pain. He twisted, but Lucky writhed with him and was on top once more. He sat up, his legs maintaining their hold, increasing it.

Lucky said, "I don't know if you can hear or understand me, Lou———"

Evans paid no regard. With one last contortion of his body, he flung himself and Lucky into the air, breaking Lucky's hold.

Lucky rolled as he hit the floor and came lithely to his feet. He caught Evans's arm as the latter rose and swung it over his shoulder. A heave and Evans came crashing down on his back. He lay still.

"Bigman!" said Lucky, breathing quickly and brushing back his hair with a quick motion of his hand.

"Here I am," said the little fellow, grinning and swinging Turner's blaster lightly. "I was all set, just in case."

"All right. Put that blaster away, Bigman, and look Lou over. Make sure there are no bones broken. Then tie him up."

Lucky was at the controls now, and with infinite caution he backed the *Hilda* off the remnants of the carcass of the giant patch he had killed hours before.

Lucky's gamble had worked. He had hoped that the V-frogs with their preoccupation with mentalities would have no real conception of the physical size of the patch, that with their lack of experience of subsea travel, they would not realize the significance of the slight off-course route Bigman had taken. The whole gamble had been in the quick phrase which Lucky had spoken to Bigman as the latter had turned the ship back to the city under the threat of Evans's blaster.

"Afoul of the patch," he had said.

· · ·

Again the *Hilda's* course changed. Its nose lifted upward.

Evans, bound to his bunk, stared with weary shame-facedness at Lucky. "Sorry."

"We understand, Lou. Don't brood about it," said Lucky lightly. "But we can't let you go for a while. You see that, don't you?"

"Sure. Space, put more knots on me. I deserve it. Believe me, Lucky, most of it I don't even remember."

"Look, you better get some sleep, fella," and Lucky's fist punched Evans lightly in the shoulder. "We'll wake you when we hit surface, if we have to."

To Bigman, a few minutes later, he said quietly, "Round up every blaster on the ship, Bigman, every weapon of every sort. Look through stores, the bunk lockers, everywhere."

"What are you going to do?"

"Dump them," said Lucky succinctly.

"What?"

"You heard me. You might go under. Or I might. If we do, I don't want anything with which we can expect a repetition of what has just happened. Against the V-frogs, physical weapons are useless, anyway."

One by one, two blasters, plus the electric whips from each sea suit, passed through the trash ejector. The ejector's hinged opening stood flush with the wall just next to the first-aid cupboard, and through it the weapons were puffed through one-way valves into the sea.

"It makes me feel naked," muttered Bigman, staring out through the port as though to catch sight of the vanished weapons. A dim phosphorescent streak flashed across, marking the passing of an arrow fish. That was all.

The water pressure needle dropped slowly. They had been twenty-eight hundred feet under to begin with. They were less than two thousand now.

Bigman continued peering intently out the port.

Lucky glanced at him. "What are you looking for?"

"I thought," said Bigman, "it would get lighter as we got up toward the top."

"I doubt it," said Lucky. "The seaweed blankets the surface tightly. It will stay black till we break through."

"Think we might meet up with a trawler, Lucky?"

"I hope not."

They were fifteen hundred feet under now.

Bigman said with an effort at lightness, a visible attempt to change the current of his own thoughts, "Say, Lucky, how come there's so much carbon dioxide in the air on Venus? I mean, with all these plants? Plants are supposed to turn carbon dioxide into oxygen, aren't they?"

"On Earth they are. However, if I remember my course in xenobotany, Venusian plant life has a trick all its own. Earth plants liberate their oxygen into the air; Venusian plants store theirs as high-oxygen compounds in their tissues." He talked absently as though he himself was also using speech as a guard against too-deep thinking. "That's why no Venusian animal breathes. They get all the oxygen they need in their food."

"What do you know?" said Bigman in astonishment.

"In fact, their food probably has too much oxygen for them, or they wouldn't be so fond of low-oxygen food, like the axle grease you fed the V-frog. At least, that's my theory."

They were only eight hundred feet from the surface now.

Lucky said, "Good navigation, by the way. I mean the way you rammed the patch, Bigman."

"It's nothing," said Bigman, but he flushed with pleasure at the approval in Lucky's words.

He looked at the pressure dial. It was five hundred feet to the surface.

Silence fell.

And then there came a grating and scraping sound from overhead, a sudden interruption in their smooth climb, a laboring of their engines, and then a quick lightening of the view outside the porthole, together with an eye-blinking vision of cloudy sky and rolling water surface oozing up between shreds and fibers of weed. The water was pockmarked with tiny splashings.

"It's raining," said Lucky. "And now, I'm afraid, we'll have to sit tight and wait till the V-frogs come for us."

Bigman said blankly, "Well—well——— Here they are!"

For moving into view just outside the porthole, staring solemnly into the ship out of dark, liquid eyes, its long legs folded tightly down and its dexterous toes clasping a seaweed stem in a firm grip, was a V-frog!

13

Minds Meet

The *Hilda* rode high in the tossing waters of the Venusian ocean. The splatter of strong, steady rain drummed its sound upon the outer hull in what was almost an Earthlike rhythm. To Bigman, with his Martian background, rain and ocean were alien, but to Lucky it brought memories of home.

Bigman said, "Look at the V-frog, Lucky. Look at it!"

"I see it," said Lucky calmly.

Bigman swept the glass with his sleeve and then found himself with his nose pressing against it for a better look.

Suddenly he thought, Hey, I better not get too close.

He sprang back, then deliberately put the little finger of each hand into the corners of his mouth and drew them apart. Sticking his tongue out, he crossed his eyes and wiggled his fingers.

The V-frog stared at him solemnly. It had not budged a muscle since it had first been sighted. It merely swayed solemnly with the wind. It did not seem to mind, or even to be aware of, the water that splashed about it and upon it.

Bigman contorted his face even more horribly and went "A-a-gh" at the creature.

Lucky's voice sounded over his shoulder. "What are you doing, Bigman?"

Bigman jumped, took his hands away, and let his face spring back into its own pixy-ish appearance. He said, grinning, "I was just showing that V-frog what I thought of it."

"And it was just showing you what it thought of you!"

Bigman's heart skipped a beat. He heard the clear disapproval in Lucky's voice. In such a crisis, at a time of such danger, he, Bigman, was making faces like a fool. Shame came over him.

He quavered, "I don't know what got into me, Lucky."

"*They* did," said Lucky, harshly. "Understand that. The V-frogs are feeling you out for weak points. However they can do it, they'll crawl into your mind, and once there they may remain past your ability to force them to leave. So don't follow any impulse until you've thought it out."

"Yes, Lucky," muttered Bigman.

"Now, what next?" Lucky looked about the ship. Evans was sleeping, tossing fitfully and breathing with difficulty. Lucky's eyes rested on him for a bare moment, then turned away.

Bigman said almost timidly, "Lucky?"

"Well."

"Aren't you going to call the space station?"

For a moment Lucky stared at his little partner without comprehension. Then slowly the lines between his eyes smoothed away and he whispered, "Great Galaxy! I'd forgotten. Bigman, I'd forgotten! I never once thought of it."

Bigman cocked a thumb over his shoulder, pointing at

the port into which the V-frog was still owlishly gazing. "You mean, it————?"

"I mean *they*. Space, there may be thousands of them out there!"

Half in shame Bigman admitted to himself the nature of his own feelings; he was almost glad that Lucky had been trapped by the creatures as well as he. It relieved him of some of the blame that might otherwise attach to him. In fact, Lucky had no right————

Bigman stopped his thoughts, appalled. He was working himself into a resentment against Lucky. That wasn't he. That was *they!*

Savagely he forced all thought from his mind and concentrated on Lucky, whose fingers were now on the transmitter, working them into the careful adjustment required to reach finely out into space.

And then Bigman's head snapped back at a sudden new and strange sound.

It was a voice, flat, without intonation. It said, "Do not tamper with your machine of far-reaching sound. We do not wish it."

Bigman turned. His mouth fell open and, for a moment, stayed so. He said, "Who said that? Where is it?"

Lucky said, "Easy, Bigman. It was inside your head."

"Not the V-frog!" said Bigman despairingly.

"Great Galaxy, what else can it be?"

And Bigman turned to stare out the port again, at the clouds, the rain, and the swaying V-frog.

Once before in his life Lucky had felt the minds of alien creatures impressing their thoughts upon him. That had been on the day he had met the immaterial-energy beings that dwelt within the hollow depths of Mars. There his mind had been laid open, but the entry of thought had been painless, even pleasant. He had known his own helplessness, yet he had also been deprived of all fear.

Now he faced something different. The mental fingers inside his skull had forced their way in and he felt them with pain, loathing, and resentment.

Lucky's hand had fallen away from the transmitter, and he felt no urge to return to it. He had forgotten it again.

The voice sounded a second time. "Make air vibrations with your mouth."

Lucky said, "You mean, speak? Can you hear our thoughts when we do not speak?"

"Only very dimly and vaguely. It is very difficult unless we have studied your mind well. When you speak, your thoughts are sharper and we can hear."

"We hear you without trouble," said Lucky.

"Yes. We can send our thoughts powerfully and with strength. You cannot."

"Have you heard all I've said so far?"

"Yes."

"What do you wish of me?"

"In your thoughts we have detected an organization of your fellow beings far off, beyond the end, on the other side of the sky. You call it the Council. We wish to know more about it."

Inwardly Lucky felt a small spark of satisfaction. One question, at least, was answered. As long as he represented only himself, as an individual, the enemy was content to kill him. But in recent hours the enemy had discovered he had penetrated too much of the truth, and they were concerned about it.

Would other members of the Council learn as easily? What was the nature of this Council?

Lucky could understand the curiosity of the enemy, the new caution, the sudden desire to learn a little more from Lucky before killing him. No wonder the enemy had forborne forcing Evans to kill him even when the blaster was pointed and Lucky was helpless, forborne just an instant too long.

But Lucky buried further thought on the subject. They might, as they said, be unable to clearly hear unspoken thoughts. Then again, they might be lying.

He said abruptly, "What do you have against my people?"

The flat, emotionless voice said, "We cannot say what is not so."

Lucky's jaw hardened at that. Had they picked up his last thought concerning their lying? He would have to be careful, very careful.

The voice continued. "We do not think well of your people. They end life. They eat meat. It is bad to be intelligent and to eat meat. One who eats meat must end life to live, and an intelligent meat eater does more harm than a mindless one since he can think of more ways to end life. You have little tubes that can end the lives of many at one time."

"But we do not kill V-frogs."

"You would if we let you. You even kill each other in large groups and small."

Lucky avoided comment on the last remark. He said, instead, "What is it you want of my people, then?"

"You grow numerous on Venus," said the voice. "You spread and take up room."

"We can take only so much," reasoned Lucky. "We can build cities only in the shallow waters. The deeps will always remain yours, and they form nine parts of the ocean's ten. Besides that, we can help you. If you have the knowledge of mind, we have the knowledge of matter. You have seen our cities and the machines of shining metal that go through air and water to worlds on the other side of the sky. With this power of ours, think how we can help you."

"There is nothing we need. We live and we think. We are not afraid and we do not hate. What more can we need? What should we do with your cities and your metal and your ships? How can it make life better for us?"

"Well, then, do you intend to kill us all?"

"We do not desire to end life. It is enough for us if we hold your minds so that we will know you will do no harm."

Lucky had a quick vision (his own? implanted?) of a race of men on Venus living and moving under the direction of the dominant natives, gradually being cut off from all connection with Earth, the generations growing more and more into complacent mental slaves.

He said, in words whose confidence he did not entirely feel, "Men cannot allow themselves to be controlled mentally."

"It is the only way, and you must help us."

"We will not."

"You have no choice. You must tell us of these lands beyond the sky, of the organization of your people, of what they will do against us, and how we may guard ourselves."

"There is no way you can make me do that."

"Is there not?" asked the voice. "Consider, then. If you will not speak the information we require, we will then ask you to descend back into the ocean in your machine of shining metal, and there at the bottom you will open your machine to the waters."

"And die?" said Lucky grimly.

"The end of your lives would be necessary. With your knowledge it would not be safe to allow you to mingle with your fellows. You might speak to them and cause them to attempt reprisals. That would not be good."

"Then I have nothing to lose by not telling you."

"You have much to lose. Should you refuse what we ask, we would have to delve into your mind by force. That is not efficient. We might miss much of value. To diminish that danger, we would have to take your mind apart bit by bit, and that would be unpleasant for you. It would be much better for us and for you if you were to help us freely."

"No." Lucky shook his head.

A pause. The voice began again: "Although your people are given to ending life, they fear having their own lives end. We will spare you that fear if you help us. When you descend into the ocean to your life's end, we will remove fear from your mind. If, however, you do not choose to help us, we will force you into life's end anyhow, but we will not remove fear. We will intensify it."

"No," said Lucky, more loudly.

Another pause, a longer one. Then the voice said, "We do not ask your knowledge out of fear for our own safety, but to make it unnecessary for ourselves to take measures of an unpleasant nature. If we are left with but uncertain knowledge as to how to guard ourselves against your people from the other side of the sky, then we will be forced to put an end to the threat by ending life for all your people on this world. We will let the ocean into their cities as we have already almost done to one of them. Life will end for your people like the quenching of a flame. It will be snuffed out, and life will burn no more."

Lucky laughed wildly. "Make me!" he said.

"Make you?"

"Make me speak. Make me dive the ship. Make me do *anything*."

"You think we cannot?"

"I know you cannot."

"Look about you, then, and see what we have already

accomplished. Your fellow creature who is bound is in our hands. Your fellow creature who stood at your side is in our hands."

Lucky whirled. In all this time, through all this conversation, he had not heard Bigman's voice once. It was as though he had completely forgotten Bigman's existence. And now he saw the little Martian lying twisted and crumpled at his feet.

Lucky dropped to his knees, a vast and fearful dismay parching his throat. "You've killed him?"

"No, he lives. He is not even badly hurt. But, you see, you are alone now. You have none to help you now. They could not withstand us, and neither can you."

White-faced, Lucky said, "No. You will not make me do anything."

"One last chance. Make your choice. Do you choose to help us, so that life may end peacefully and quietly for you? Or will you refuse to help us, so that it must end in pain and sorrow, to be followed, perhaps, by life's end for all your people in the cities below the ocean? Which is it to be? Come, your answer!"

The words echoed and re-echoed within Lucky's mind as he prepared to stand, alone and unfriended, against the buffets of a mental power he did not know how to fight save by an unbending stubbornness of will.

Minds Battle

How does one set up a barrier against mental attack? Lucky had the desire to resist, but there were no muscles he could flex, no guard he could throw up, no way he could return violence. He must merely remain as he was, resisting all those impulses that flooded his mind which he could not surely tell to be his own.

And how could he tell which were his own? What did he himself wish to do? What did he *himself* wish most to do?

Nothing entered his mind. It was blank. Surely there *had* to be something. He had not come up here without a plan.

Up here?

Then he had come up. Originally, he had been down.

Far down in the recesses of his mind, he thought, That's it.

He was in a ship. It had come up from the sea bottom. It was on the surface of the water now. Good. What next?

Why at the surface? Dimly he could remember it was safer underneath.

He bent his head with great difficulty, closed his eyes

and opened them again. His thoughts were very thick. He had to get word somewhere . . . somewhere . . . about something.

He had to get word.

Get word.

And he broke through! It was as though somewhere miles inside of himself he had put a straining shoulder to a door and it had burst open. There was a clear flash of purpose, and he remembered something he had forgotten.

Ship's radio and the space station, of course.

He said, huskily, "You haven't got me. Do you hear that? I remember, and I'll keep on remembering."

There was no answer.

He shouted aloud, incoherently. His mind was faintly occupied with the analogy of a man fighting an overdose of a sleeping drug. Keep the muscles active, he thought. Keep walking. Keep walking.

In his case, he had to keep his mind active, he had to keep the mental fibers working. Do something. Do something. Stop, and they'll get you.

He continued shouting, and sound became words, "I'll do it. I'll do it."

Do what? He could feel it slipping from him again.

Feverishly, he repeated to himself, "Radio to station . . . radio to station . . ." but the sounds were becoming meaningless.

He was moving now. His body turned clumsily as though his joints were wood and nailed in place, but it was turning. He faced the radio. He saw it clearly for a moment, then it wavered and became foggy. He bent his mind to the task, and it was clear again. He could see the transmitter, see the range-setting toggle and the frequency condensers. He could recall and understand its workings.

He took a dragging step toward it and a sensation as of red-hot spikes boring into his temples overwhelmed him.

He staggered and fell to his knees, then, in agony, rose again.

Through pain-hazed eyes, he could still make out the radio. First one of his legs moved, then another.

The radio seemed a hundred yards away, hazy, surrounded by a bloody mist. The pounding in Lucky's head increased with each step.

He fought to ignore the pain, to see only the radio, to think only of the radio. He forced his legs to move against a rubbery resistance that was entangling them and dragging him down.

Finally, he put out his arm, and when his fingers were still six inches away from the ultrawave, Lucky knew that his endurance was at an end. Try as he might, he could drive his exhausted body no closer. It was all over. It was ended.

The *Hilda* was a scene of paralysis. Evans lay unconscious on his cot; Bigman was crumpled on the floor; and though Lucky remained stubbornly upright, his trembling fingertips were the only sign of life in him.

The cold voice in Lucky's mind sounded once again in its even, inexorable monotone: "You are helpless, but you will not lose consciousness as did your companions. You will suffer this pain until you decide to submerge your ship, tell us what we wish to know, and end your life. We can wait patiently. There is no way you can resist us. There is no way you can fight us. No bribe! No threat!"

Lucky, through the endless torture, felt a striving within his sluggish, pain-soaked mind, the stirring of something new.

No bribe? No threat?

No bribe?

Even through the misty semiconsciousness, the spark in his mind caught fire.

He abandoned the radio, turned his thoughts away, and instantly the curtain of pain lifted a fraction. Lucky took a faltering step away from the radio, and it lifted a bit more. He turned away completely.

Lucky tried not to think. He tried to act automatically and without foreplanning. They were concentrating on preventing his reaching the radio. They must not realize the other danger they faced. The pitiless enemy must not deduce his intentions and try to stop him. He would have to act quickly. They must not stop him.

They *must* not!

He had reached the first-aid wall chest and flung open its door. He could not see clearly, and he lost precious seconds in fumbling.

The voice said, "What is your decision?" and the fierceness of pain began to clamp down upon the young councilman once more.

Lucky had it—a squat jar of bluish silicone. His fingers groped through what seemed deadening cotton for the little catch that would shut off the paramagnetic microfield that held the jar's lid closed and airtight.

He scarcely felt the little nudge as one fingernail caught the catch. He scarcely saw the lid move to one side and fall off. He scarcely heard it hit the floor with the sound of metastic against metal. Fuzzily, he could see that the jar was open, and hazily, he lifted his arm toward the trash ejector.

The pain had returned in all its fury.

His left arm had lifted the hinged opening of the ejector; his right arm tremblingly raised the precious jar to the six-inch opening.

His arm moved for an eternity. He could no longer see. A red haze covered everything.

He felt his arm and the jar it held strike the wall. He pushed, but it would move no farther. The fingers on his left hand inched down from where they held the opening of the trash ejector, and touched the jar.

He daren't drop it now. If he did, he would never in his life find the strength to pick it up again.

He had it in both hands, and together both hands pulled at it. It inched upward, while Lucky hovered closer and closer to the edge of unconsciousness.

And then the jar was gone!

A million miles away, it seemed, he could hear the whistle of compressed air, and he knew the jar had been ejected into the warm Venusian ocean.

For a moment the pain wavered and then, in one giant stroke, lifted completely.

Lucky righted himself carefully and stepped away from the wall. His face and body were drenched in perspiration, and his mind still reeled.

As fast as his still faltering steps could take him, he moved to the radio transmitter, and this time nothing stopped him.

Evans sat in a chair with his head buried in his arms. He had gulped thirstily at water and kept saying over and over again, "I don't remember a thing. I don't remember a thing."

Bigman, bare to the waist, was mopping at his head and chest with a damp cloth, and a shaky grin came to his face. "I do. I remember everything. One minute I was standing there listening to you talking to the voice, Lucky, and then with no warning I was flat on the floor. I couldn't feel a thing, I couldn't turn my head, I couldn't even blink my eyes, but I could hear everything that was going on. I could hear the voice and what you said, Lucky. I saw you start for the radio . . ."

He puffed his breath out and shook his head.

"I never made it that first time, you know," said Lucky quietly.

"I couldn't tell. You passed out of my field of vision, and after that all I could do was lie there and wait to hear you start sending. Nothing happened, and I kept thinking they must have you, too. In my mind, I could see all three of us lying in living death. It was all over, and I couldn't nudge a thumbnail. It was all I could do just to breathe. Then you moved back past my eyes again, and I wanted to laugh and cry and yell all at the same time, but all I could do was lie there. I could just about make you out, Lucky, clawing at the wall. I couldn't tell what on Venus you were doing, but a few minutes later it was all over. Wow!"

Evans said wearily, "And we're really heading back for Aphrodite now, Lucky? No mistake?"

"We're heading back unless the instruments are lying, and I don't think they are," said Lucky. "When we do get back and we can spare the time, we'll all of us get a little medical attention."

"Sleep!" insisted Bigman. "That's all I want. Just two days of solid sleep."

"You'll get that, too," said Lucky.

But Evans, more than the other two, was haunted by the experience. It showed quite plainly in the way he huddled in his own arms and slouched, almost cowered, in his chair. He said, "Aren't they interfering with us in any way at all any more?" There was the lightest emphasis on the word *they*.

"I can't guarantee that," said Lucky, "but the worst of the affair is over in a way. I reached the space station."

"You're sure? There's no mistake?"

"None at all. They even relayed me to Earth and I spoke to Conway directly. That part is settled."

"Then it's *all* settled," crowed Bigman joyously. "Earth is prepared. It knows the truth about the V-frogs."

Lucky smiled, but offered no comment.

Bigman said, "Just one thing, Lucky. Tell me what happened. How did you break their hold? Sands of Mars! What did you do?"

Lucky said, "Nothing that I ought not to have thought of long in advance and saved us all a great deal of needless trouble. The voice told us that all they needed in life was to live and to think. You recall that, Bigman? It said later on that we had no way of threatening them and no way of bribing them? It was only at the last moment that I realized you and I knew better."

"*I* know better?" said Bigman blankly.

"Certainly you do. You found out two minutes after you saw your first V-frog, that life and thought is *not* all they need. I told you on the way to the surface that Venusian plants stored oxygen so that Venusian animals got their oxygen from their food and didn't have to breathe. In fact, I said, they probably get too much oxygen and that's why they're so fond of low-oxygen food like hydrocarbons. Like axle grease, for instance. Don't you remember?"

Bigman's eyes were widening. "Sure."

"Just think how they must crave hydrocarbon. It must be like the craving of a child for candy."

Bigman said once again, "Sure."

"Now the V-frogs had us under mental control, but to maintain us under such control they had to concentrate. What I had to do was distract them, at least to distract those that were nearest the ship, and whose power over us was strongest. So I threw out the obvious thing."

"But what? Don't play cute, Lucky."

"I threw out an open jar of petroleum jelly, which I got out of the medicine cabinet. It's pure hydrocarbon, of much higher grade than the axle grease. They couldn't resist. Even with so much at stake, they couldn't resist.

Those nearest to the jar dived for it. Others farther away were in mental rapport, and their minds turned instantly to hydrocarbon. They lost control of us, and I was able to put through the call. That was all."

"Well, then," said Evans, "we're through with them."

"If it comes to that," said Lucky, "I'm not at all certain. There are a few things————"

He turned away, frowning, his lips clamped shut, as though he had already spoken too much.

The dome glimmered gorgeously outside the port, and Bigman felt his heart lift at the sight. He had eaten, even napped a bit, and his ebullient spirits bubbled as ever now. Lou Evans had recovered considerably from his own despondency. Only Lucky had not lost his look of wariness.

Bigman said, "I tell you the V-frogs are demoralized, Lucky. Look here, we've come back through a hundred miles of ocean, nearly, and they haven't touched us once. Well, have they?"

Lucky said, "Right now, I'm wondering why we don't get an answer from the dome."

Evans frowned in his turn. "They shouldn't take this long."

Bigman looked from one to the other. "You don't think anything can be wrong inside the city, do you?"

Lucky waved his hand for silence. A voice came in over the receiver, low and rapid.

"Identification, please."

Lucky said, "This is the Council-chartered subship *Hilda*, out of Aphrodite, returning to Aphrodite. David Starr in charge and speaking."

"You will have to wait."

"For what reason, please?"

"The locks are all in operation at the moment."

Evans frowned and muttered, "That's impossible, Lucky."

Lucky said, "When will one be free? Give me its location, and direct me to its vicinity by ultrasignal."

"You will have to wait."

The connection remained open, but the man at the other end spoke no more.

Bigman said indignantly, "Get Councilman Morriss, Lucky. That'll get some action."

Evans said hesitantly, "Morris thinks I'm a traitor. Do you suppose he could have decided that you've thrown in with me, Lucky?"

"If so," said Lucky, "he'd be anxious to get us into the city. No, it's my thought that the man we've been speaking to is under mental control."

Evans said, "To stop us from getting in? Are you serious?"

"I'm serious."

"There's no way they can stop us from getting in in the long run unless they———" Evans paled and moved to the porthole in two rapid strides. "Lucky, you're right! They're bringing a cannon blaster to bear! They're going to blow us out of the water!"

Bigman was at the porthole, too. There was no mistake about it. A section of the dome had moved to one side, and through it, somewhat unreal as seen through water, was a squat tube.

Bigman watched the muzzle lower and center upon them, with fascinated horror. The *Hilda* was unarmed. It could never gain velocity fast enough to escape being blasted. There seemed no way out of instant death.

15

The Enemy?

But even as Bigman felt his stomach constrict at the prospect of imminent destruction, he could hear Lucky's even voice speaking forcefully into the transmitter:

"Subship *Hilda* arriving with cargo of petroleum . . . Subship *Hilda* arriving with cargo of petroleum . . . Subship *Hilda* arriving with cargo of petroleum . . . Subship *Hilda*———"

An agitated voice broke through from the other end. "Clement Heber at lock control at this end. What is wrong? Repeat. What is wrong? Clement Heber———"

Bigman yelled, "They're withdrawing the blaster, Lucky."

Lucky let out his breath in a puff, but only in that way did he show any sign of tension. He said into the transmitter, "Subship *Hilda* reporting for entrance to Aphrodite. Please assign lock. Repeat. Please assign lock."

"You may have lock number fifteen. Follow directional signal. There seems to be some confusion here."

Lucky rose and said to Evans, "Lou, take the controls and get the ship into the city as fast as you can." He motioned Bigman to follow him to the other room.

"What—what———" Bigman spluttered like a leaky popgun.

Lucky sighed and said, "I thought the V-frogs would try to arrange to have us kept out, so I was all set with the petroleum trick. But I didn't think things would get so bad they would point a cannon at us. That made it really tough. I wasn't as sure as all that that the petroleum notion would work."

"But how did it?"

"Hydrocarbon again. Petroleum is hydrocarbon. My words came over the open radio and the V-frogs who had the dome guards under control were distracted."

"How come they knew what petroleum was?"

"I pictured it in my mind, Bigman, with every bit of imagination I had. They can read minds when you sharpen the mental pictures by speaking, you know.

"But never mind all that." His voice dropped to a whisper. "If they're ready to blow us out of the ocean, if they're ready for something as crudely violent as that, they're desperate; and we're desperate, too. We've got to bring this to an end right away, and we've got to do the right thing. One mistake at this stage could be fatal."

From his shirt pocket Lucky had unclipped a scriber, and he was writing rapidly on a piece of foil.

He held it out to Bigman. "That's what you're to do when I give the word."

Bigman's eyes widened, "But Lucky———"

"Sh! Don't refer to any of this in words."

Bigman nodded, "But are you sure you're right?"

"I hope so." Lucky's handsome face was drawn with anxiety. "Earth knows about the V-frogs now, so they'll never win over humanity; but they may still do damage here on Venus. We've got to prevent that somehow. Now do you understand what you're to do?"

"Yes."

"In that case . . ." Lucky rolled the foil together and kneaded it with his strong fingers. The pellet that remained he returned to his shirt pocket.

Lou Evans called out, "We're in the lock, Lucky. In five minutes we'll be in the city."

Lucky said, "Good. Get Morriss on the radio."

They were in Council headquarters in Aphrodite again, the same room, Bigman thought, in which he had first met Lou Evans; the same room in which he had first seen a V-frog. He shuddered at the thought of those mental tendrils infiltrating his mind for the first time without his knowledge.

That was the one way in which the room was different now. The aquarium was gone; the dishes of peas and of axle grease were gone; the tall tables stood bare at the false window.

Morriss had pointed that out mutely as soon as they entered. His plump cheeks sagged and the lines of strain about his eyes were marked. His pudgy handshake was uncertain.

Carefully Bigman put what he was carrying on top of one of the tables. "Petroleum jelly," he said.

Lou Evans sat down. So did Lucky.

Morriss did not. He said, "I got rid of the V-frogs in this building. That was all I could do. I can't ask people to do away with their pets without a reason. And I couldn't give the reason, obviously."

"It will be enough," said Lucky. "Throughout this discussion, though, I want you to keep your eyes on the hydrocarbon. Keep its existence firmly in your mind."

"You think that will help?" asked Morriss.

"I think it will."

Morriss stopped his pacing immediately before Lucky. His voice was a sudden bluster. "Starr, I can't believe this. The V-frogs have been in the city for years. They've been here almost since the city was built."

"You've got to remember————" began Lucky.

"That I'm under their influence?" Morriss reddened. "That isn't so. I deny it."

"There's nothing to be ashamed of, Dr. Morriss," said Lucky, crisply. "Evans was under their control for days, and Bigman and I have been controlled, too. It is possible to be honestly unaware that your mind has been continuously picked."

"There's no proof of it, but never mind," said Morriss violently. "Suppose you're right. The question is, what can we do? How do we fight them? Sending men against them will be useless. If we bring in a fleet to bombard Venus from space, they may force the dome locks open and drown every city on Venus in revenge. We could never kill every V-frog on Venus anyway. There are eight hundred million cubic miles of ocean for them to hide in, and they can multiply fast if they want to. Now your getting word to Earth was essential, I admit, but it still leaves us with many important problems."

"You're right," admitted Lucky, "but the point is, I didn't tell Earth everything. I couldn't until I was certain I knew the truth. I————"

The intercom signal flashed, and Morriss barked. "What is it?"

"Lyman Turner for his appointment, sir," was the answer.

"One second." The Venusian turned to Lucky and said in a low voice, "Are you sure we want him?"

"You had this appointment about strengthening the transite partitions within the city, didn't you?"

"Yes, but————"

"And Turner is a victim. The evidence would seem to be clear there. He is the one highly-placed official beside ourselves who would definitely seem to be one. We would want to see him, I think."

Morriss said into the intercom, "Send him up."

Turner's gaunt face and hooked nose made up a mask of inquiry as he entered. The silence in the room and the way the others stared at him would have filled even a far less sensitive man with foreboding.

He swung his computer case to the floor and said, "Is anything wrong, gentlemen?"

Slowly, carefully, Lucky gave him the bare outline of the matter.

Turner's thin lips parted. He said, weakly, "You mean, *my* mind————"

"How else would the man at the lock have known the exact manner in which to keep out intruders? He was unskilled and untrained, yet he barricaded himself in with electronic perfection."

"I never thought of that. I never thought of that." Turner's voice was almost an incoherent mumble. "How could I have missed it?"

"They wanted you to miss it," said Lucky.

"It makes me ashamed."

"You have company in that, Turner. Myself, Dr. Morriss, Councilman Evans————"

"Then what do we do about it?"

Lucky said, "Exactly what Dr. Morriss was asking when you arrived. It will need all our thought. One of the reasons I suggested you be brought into this gathering is that we may require your computer."

"Oceans of Venus, I hope so," said Turner fervently. "If I could do something to make up for————" And he put his hand to his forehead as though half in fear that he had a strange head on his shoulders, one not his own.

He said, "Are we ourselves now?"

Evans put in, "We will be as long as we concentrate on that petroleum jelly."

"I don't get it. Why should that help?"

"It does. Never mind how for the moment," said Lucky. "I want to get on with what I was about to say when you arrived."

Bigman swung back to the wall and perched himself on the table where the aquarium once stood. He stared idly at the open jar on the other table as he listened.

Lucky said, "Are we sure the V-frogs are the real menace?"

"Why, that's your theory," said Morriss with surprise.

"Oh, they're the immediate means of controlling the minds of mankind, granted; but are they the real enemy? They're pitting their minds against the minds of Earthmen and proving formidable opponents, yet individual V-frogs seem quite unintelligent."

"How so?"

"Well, the V-frog you had in this place did not have the good sense to keep out of our minds. He broadcast his surprise at our being without mustaches. He ordered Bigman to get him peas dipped in axle grease. Was that intelligent? He gave himself away immediately."

Morriss shrugged. "Maybe not all V-frogs are intelligent."

"It goes deeper than that. We were helpless in their mental grip out on the ocean surface. Still, because I guessed certain things, I tried a jar of petroleum jelly on them, and it worked. It scattered them. Mind you, their entire campaign was at stake. They had to keep us from informing Earth concerning them. Yet they ruined everything for one jar of petroleum jelly. Again, they almost had us when we were trying to re-enter Aphrodite. The cannon was coming to an aim when the mere mention of petroleum spoiled their plans."

Turner stirred in his seat. "I understand what you mean by the petroleum now, Starr. Everyone knows the V-frogs have a craving for grease of all sorts. The craving is just too strong for them."

"Too strong for beings sufficiently intelligent to battle Earthmen? Would you abandon a vital victory, Turner, for a steak or a wedge of chocolate cake?"

"Of course I wouldn't, but that doesn't prove a V-frog wouldn't."

"It doesn't, I grant you. The V-frog mind is alien to us and we can't suppose that what works with us must work with them. Still, the matter of their being diverted by hydrocarbon is suspicious. It makes me compare V-frogs with dogs rather than with men."

"In what way?" demanded Morriss.

"Think about it," said Lucky. "A dog can be trained to do many seemingly intelligent things. A creature who had never seen or heard of a dog before, watching a seeing-eye dog guide a blind master in the days before Son-O-Taps, would have wondered whether the dog or the man was the more intelligent. But if he passed by them with a meaty bone and noted that the dog's attention was instantly diverted, he would suspect the truth."

Turner said, his pale eyes nearly bulging, "Are you trying to say that V-frogs are just the tools of human beings?"

"Doesn't that sound probable, Turner? As Dr. Morriss said just a while ago the V-frogs have been in the city for years, but it's only a matter of the last few months that they've been making trouble. And then the trouble started with trivialities, like a man giving away money in the streets. It is almost as though some men learned how to use the V-frogs' natural capacity for telepathy as tools with which to inflict their thoughts and orders on human minds. It is as though they had to practice at first, learn the nature and limitations of their tools, develop their control, until the time came when they could do big things. Eventually, it would be not the yeast that they were after but something more; perhaps control of the Solar Confederation, even of the entire galaxy."

"I can't believe it," said Morriss.

"Then I'll give you another piece of evidence. When we were out in the ocean, a mental voice—presumably that of a V-frog—spoke to us. It tried to force us to give it some information and then commit suicide."

"Well?"

"The voice arrived via a V-frog, but it did not originate with one. It originated with a human being."

Lou Evans sat bolt upright and stared incredulously at Lucky.

Lucky smiled. "Even Lou doesn't believe that, but it's so. The voice made use of odd concepts such as 'machines of shining metal' instead of 'ships.' We were supposed to think that V-frogs were unfamiliar with such concepts, and the voice had to stimulate our minds into imagining we heard round-about expressions that meant the same thing. But then the voice forgot itself. I remember what I heard it say. I remember it word for word: 'Life will end for your people like the quenching of a flame. It will be snuffed out and life will burn no more.'"

Morriss stolidly said again, "Well?"

"You still don't see it? How could the V-frogs use a concept like the 'quenching of a flame' or 'life will burn no more'? If the voice pretends to be that of a V-frog with no concept of such a thing as a ship, how could it have one of fire?"

They all saw it, now, but Lucky drove on furiously. "The atmosphere of Venus is nitrogen and carbon dioxide. There is no oxygen. We all know that. Nothing can burn in Venus's atmosphere. There can be no flame. In a million years no V-frog could possibly have seen a fire, and none of them can know what it is. Even granted that some might have seen fire and flame within the city domes, they could have no understanding of its nature any more than they understood our ships. As I see it, the thoughts we received originated with no V-frog, but with a man who used the V-frog only as a channel to reach from his own mind to ours."

"But how could that be done?" asked Turner.

"I don't know," said Lucky. "I wish I did. Certainly it would take a brilliant mind to find a way. A man would have to know a great deal about the workings of a nervous system and about the electrical phenomena associated with it." Lucky looked coldly at Morriss. "It might take, for instance, a man who specialized in biophysics."

And all eyes turned on the Venusian councilman, from whose round face the blood was draining until his grizzled mustache seemed scarcely visible against his pale skin.

16

The Enemy!

Morriss managed to say, "Are you trying to———" and his voice ground hoarsely to a halt.

"I'm not making any definite statement," said Lucky smoothly. "I have merely made a suggestion."

Morriss looked helplessly about, turning from face to face of the four other men in the room, watching each pair of eyes meet his in fixed fascination.

He choked out, "This is mad, absolutely insane. I was the first to report all this—this—trouble on Venus. Find the original report in Council headquarters. My name is on it. Why should I call in the Council if I were——— And my motive? Eh? My motive?"

Councilman Evans seemed uneasy. From the quick glance he shot in Turner's direction, Bigman guessed that this form of inter-Council squabble in front of an outsider was not to his liking.

Still, Evans said, "It would explain the effort Dr. Morriss made to discredit me. I was an outsider, and I might stumble on the truth. I had found half of it, certainly."

Morriss was breathing heavily. "I deny that I ever did such a thing. All this is a conspiracy of some sort against me, and it will go hard in the end for any of you who join in this. I will have justice."

"Are you implying that you wish a Council trial?" asked Lucky. "Do you want to plead your case before a meeting of the assembled Central Committee of the Council?"

What Lucky was referring to, of course, was the procedure ordained for the trial of councilmen accused of high treason against the Council and the Solar Confederation. In all the history of the Council, not one man had ever had to stand such a trial.

At its mention, whatever shreds of control Morriss had used to restrain his feelings vanished. Roaring, he scrambled to his feet and hurtled blindly at Lucky.

Lucky rolled nimbly up and over the arm of the chair he occupied and, at the same time, gestured quickly at Bigman.

It was the signal that Bigman was waiting for. Bigman proceeded to follow the instructions Lucky had given him on board the *Hilda* when they were passing through the lock of Aphrodite's dome.

A blaster bolt shot out. It was at low intensity but its ionizing radiations produced the pungent odor of ozone in the air.

Matters remained so for a moment. All motion ceased. Morris, his head against the overturned chair, made no move to get up. Bigman remained standing, like a small statue, with his blaster still held against his hip as though he had been frozen in the act of shooting.

And the target of the blaster bolt lay destroyed and in ruins upon the floor.

Lou Evans found his breath first, but it was only for a sharp exclamation, "What in space————"

Lyman Turner whispered, "What have you done?"

Morriss, panting from his recent effort, could say nothing, but he rolled his eyes mutely at Bigman.

Lucky said, "Nice shot, Bigman," and Bigman grinned.

And in a hundred fragments Lyman Turner's black computer case lay smashed and, for the most part, disintegrated.

Turner's voice rose. "My computer! You *idiot!* What have you done?"

Lucky said sternly, "Only what he had to do, Turner. Now, everyone quiet."

He turned to Morriss, helped that plump personage to his feet, and said, "All my apologies, Dr. Morriss, but I had to make certain that Turner's attention was completely misdirected. I had to use you for that purpose."

Morriss said, "You mean you *don't* suspect me of— of———"

"Not for one minute," said Lucky. "I never did."

Morriss moved away, his eyes hot and angry, "Then suppose you explain, Starr."

Lucky said, "Before this conference, I never dared tell anyone that I thought some man was behind the V-frogs. I couldn't even state it in my message to Earth. It seemed obvious to me that if I were to do so, the real enemy might be desperate enough to take some action—such as actually flooding one of the cities—and hold the possibility of a repetition over the heads of all of us as blackmail. As long as he did not know that I went past the V-frog in my suspicions, I hoped he would hold off and play for time or, at most, try to kill only my friends and myself.

"At this conference I could speak of the matter because I believed the man in question to be present. However, I dared not take action against him without proper preparation for fear that he might place us under control despite the presence of the petroleum and for fear that his actions thereafter would be drastic. First I had to distract his attention thoroughly to make sure that, for a few seconds at least, he would be too absorbed in the surface activities of the group to detect, via his V-frog tools, the strong emotions that might be leaking out of Bigman's mind and mine. To be sure, there are no V-frogs in the building, but he might well be able to use the V-frogs in other parts of the city as he was able to use V-frogs out on the ocean's surface miles away from Aphrodite.

"To distract him then, I accused you, Dr. Morriss. I couldn't warn you in advance because I wanted your emotions to be authentic—and they were admirably so. Your attack on me was all that was needed."

Morriss withdrew a large handkerchief from a sleeve pocket and mopped his glistening forehead. "That was pretty drastic, Lucky, but I think I understand. Turner is the man, then?"

"He is," said Lucky.

Turner was on his knees, scrabbling among the fused and shattered shards of his instrument. He looked up with hate-filled eyes, "You've destroyed my computer."

"I doubt that it was a computer," said Lucky. "It was too inseparable a companion of yours. When I first met you, you had it with you. You stated you were using it to compute the strength of the inner barriers of the city against the threatened flood. Right now you have it with you presumably to help you if you should require new computations for your discussions with Dr. Morriss on the strength of those same inner barriers."

Lucky paused, then went on with a hard calmness in his voice. "But I came to see you in your apartment the morning after the threatened flood. I was merely planning to ask you some questions that involved no computing and you knew that. Yet you had your computer with you.

You could not bring yourself to leave it in the next room. It had to be with you, at your feet. Why?"

Turner said desperately. "It was my own construction. I was fond of it. I always carried it with me."

"I should judge it weighed some twenty-five pounds. Rather heavy, even for affection. Could it be that it was the device you used to maintain touch with the V-frogs at all times?"

"How do you intend to prove that?" flashed back Turner. "You said I myself was a victim. Everyone here is witness to that."

"Yes," said Lucky, "the man who, despite inexperience, so expertly barricaded himself at the dome lock, got his information from you. But was that information stolen from your mind or did you yourself donate it freely?"

Morriss said angrily, "Let me put the question directly, Lucky. Are you or are you not responsible for the epidemic of mental control, Turner?"

"Of course I'm not," cried Turner. "You can't do anything just on the say-so of a young fool who thinks he can make guesses and have them stick because he's on the Council."

Lucky said, "Tell me, Turner, do you remember that night when a man sat at one of the dome locks with a lever in his hand? Do you remember it well?"

"Quite well."

"Do you remember coming to me and telling me that if the locks were opened the inner transite barrier would not hold and that all of Aphrodite would be flooded? You were quite frightened. Almost panicky."

"All right. I was. I still am. It's something to be panicky about." He added, with his lip curling, "Unless you're the brave Lucky Starr."

Lucky ignored that. "Did you come to me with that information in order to add a little to the already existing confusion, to make sure that we were all disconcerted long enough for you to maneuver Lou Evans out of the city in order that he might be safely killed in the ocean? Evans was hard to handle, and he had learned too much concerning the V-frogs. Perhaps, also, you were trying to frighten me out of Aphrodite and off Venus."

Turner said, "This is all ridiculous. The inner barriers *are* inadequate. Ask Morriss. He's already seen my figures."

Morriss nodded reluctantly. "I'm afraid Turner is right there."

"No matter," said Lucky. "Let's consider that settled. There was a real danger, and Turner was justifiably panicked. . . . You are married, Turner."

Turner's eyes flicked uneasily to Lucky's face and away again. "So?"

"Your wife is pretty and considerably younger than yourself. You have been married for not quite a year."

"What is that intended to prove?"

"That you probably have a deep affection for her. Immediately after marriage you move into an expensive apartment to please her; you allow her to decorate it according to her tastes even though your own taste differs. Surely you wouldn't neglect her safety, would you?"

"I don't understand. What are you talking about?"

"I think you know. The one time I met your wife she told me that she had slept through the entire excitement the night before. She seemed quite disappointed that she had. She also told me what a fine apartment house she lived in. She said it even possessed 'chambers.' Unfortunately, that meant nothing to me at the time, or I might have seen the truth then and there. It was only later, at the bottom of the ocean, that Lou Evans casually mentioned chambers and told me what they were. 'Chambers' is a word used on Venus to denote special shelters built to withstand the full force of the ocean in case a quake breaks a city dome. Now do you know what I'm talking about?"

Turner was silent.

Lucky went on. "If you were so frightened of citywide catastrophe that night, why didn't you think of your wife? You spoke of rescuing people, of escaping the city. Did you never consider your wife's safety? There were chambers in the basement of her apartment house. Two minutes and she would have been safe. You had only to call her, give her one word of warning. But you didn't. You let her sleep."

Turner mumbled something.

Lucky said, "Don't say you forgot. That's completely unbelievable. You might have forgotten anything, but not your wife's safety. Let me suggest an alternative explanation. You were not worried about your wife because you knew she was in no real danger. You knew she was in no real danger because you knew the lock in the dome would never be opened." Lucky's voice was hard with anger. "You knew the lock in the dome would never be opened because you yourself were in mental control of the man at the lever. It was your very fondness for your wife that betrayed you. You could not bring yourself to disturb her sleep merely in order to make your phony act more plausible."

Turner said suddenly, "I'm not saying anything more without a lawyer. What you have isn't evidence."

Lucky said, "It's enough to warrant a full Council investigation, though. . . . Dr. Morriss, would you have him taken in custody in preparation for flight under guard to Earth? Bigman and I will go with him. We'll see that he gets there safely."

• • •

At the hotel again, Bigman said worriedly, "Sands of Mars, Lucky, I don't see how we're going to get proof against Turner. All your deductions sound convincing and all that, but it isn't legal proof."

Lucky, with a warm yeast dinner inside himself, was able to relax for the first time since he and Bigman had penetrated the cloud barrier that encircles Venus. He said, "I don't think the Council will be mainly interested in legal proof or in getting Turner executed."

"Lucky! Why not? That cobber————"

"I know. He's a murderer several times over. He definitely had dictatorial ambitions, so he's a traitor, too. But more important than either of those things is the fact that he created a work of genius."

Bigman said, "You mean his machine?"

"I certainly do. We destroyed the only one in existence, probably, and we'll need him to build another. There are many questions we'd like answered. How did Turner control the V-frogs? When he wanted Lou Evans killed, did he instruct the V-frogs in detail, tell them every step of the procedure, order them to bring up the giant patch? Or did he simply say, 'Kill Evans,' and allow the V-frogs to do their jobs like trained dogs in whatever way they thought best?

"Then, too, can you imagine the use to which an instrument such as that can be put? It may offer us an entirely new method of attack on mental diseases, a new way of combating criminal impulses. It may even, conceivably, be used to prevent wars in the future or to defeat the enemies of Earth quickly and bloodlessly if a war is forced upon us. Just as the machine was dangerous in the hands of one ambition-riddled man, it can be very useful and beneficial in the hands of the Council."

Bigman said, "Do you think the Council will argue him into building another machine?"

"I think so, and with proper safeguards, too. If we offer him pardon and rehabilitation, with an alternative of life imprisonment with no chance of ever seeing his wife again, I think he'll agree to help. And, of course, one of the first uses of the machine would be to investigate Turner's own mind, help cure it of his abnormal desire for power, and save for the service of humanity a first-class brain."

The next day they would be leaving Venus, heading once again for Earth. Lucky thought with pleasant nostalgia of the beautiful blue sky of his home planet, the open air, the natural foods, the space and scope of land life. He said, "Remember, Bigman, it is easy to 'protect society' by executing a criminal, but that will not bring back his victims. If one can cure him instead and use him to make life better and brighter for that society, how much more has been accomplished!"

LUCKY STARR
AND
THE BIG SUN OF MERCURY

TO ROBYN JOAN,
WHO DID HER BEST TO INTERFERE.

CONTENTS

Preface

Back in the 1950s, I wrote a series of six derring-do novels about David "Lucky" Starr and his battles against malefactors within the Solar System. Each of the six took place in a different region of the system, and in each case I made use of the astronomical facts—as they were then known.

LUCKY STARR AND THE BIG SUN OF MERCURY was written in 1955 and at that time, astronomers were convinced that Mercury presented only one face to the Sun, and that it rotated on its axis in 88 days, which was exactly the length of the year. I made that conviction a central part of the plot of the book.

In 1965, however, astronomers studied radar-beam reflections from the surface of Mercury and found, to their surprise, that this was not so. Mercury rotates on its axis in 59 days, so that there is no perpetual day-side or night-side.

Every part of the planet gets both day and night, and the Sun moves in a rather complicated path in Mercury's sky, growing larger and smaller, and backtracking on some occasions. If I were writing this book today, I would take all this into account.

I hope my Gentle Readers enjoy this book anyway, as an adventure story, but please don't forget that the advance of science can outdate even the most conscientious science-fiction writer and that my astronomical descriptions are no longer accurate in all respects.

ISAAC ASIMOV

1

The Ghosts of the Sun

Lucky Starr and his small friend, John Bigman Jones, followed the young engineer up the ramp toward the air lock that led to the surface of the planet Mercury.

Lucky thought: At least things are breaking fast.

He had been on Mercury only an hour. He had had scarcely time to do more than see his ship, the *Shooting Starr*, safely stowed in the underground hangar. He had met only the technicians who had handled the landing red tape and seen to his ship.

Those technicians, that is, and Scott Mindes, engineer in charge of Project Light. It had been almost as though the young man had been lying in wait. Almost at once he had suggested a trip to the surface.

To see some of the sights, he had explained.

Lucky did not believe that, of course. The engineer's small-chinned face had been haunted with trouble, and his mouth twitched as he spoke. His eyes slid away from Lucky's cool, level glance.

Yet Lucky agreed to visit the surface. As yet, all he knew of the troubles on Mercury was that they posed a ticklish problem for the Council of Science. He was willing to go along with Mindes and see where that led him.

As for Bigman Jones, he was always glad to follow Lucky anywhere and any time, for any reason and no reason.

But it was Bigman whose eyebrows lifted as all three were getting into their suits. He nodded almost unnoticeably toward the holster attachment on Mindes's suit.

Lucky nodded calmly in return. He, too, had noticed that protruding from the holster was the butt of a heavy-caliber blaster.

The young engineer stepped out onto the surface of the planet first. Lucky Starr followed and Bigman came last.

For the moment, they lost contact with one another in the nearly total darkness. Only the stars were visible, bright and hard in the cold airlessness.

Bigman recovered first. The gravity here on Mercury was almost exactly equal to that on his native Mars. The Martian nights were almost as dark. The stars in its night sky were almost as brilliant.

His treble voice sounded brightly in the receivers of the others. "Hey, I'm beginning to make things out."

So was Lucky, and the fact puzzled him. Surely starlight could not be *that* bright. There was a faint, luminous haze that lay over the tumbled landscape and touched its sharp crags with a pale milkiness.

Lucky had seen something of the sort on the Moon during its two-week-long night. There, also, was the completely barren landscape, rough and broken. Never, in millions of years, either there on the Moon or here on Mercury, had there been the softening touch of wind or rain. The bare rock, colder than imagination could picture, lay without a touch of frost in a waterless world.

And in the Moon's night, too, there had been this milkiness. But there, over half the Moon at least, there had been Earth-light. When Earth was full it shone with sixteen times the brightness of the full Moon as seen from Earth.

Here on Mercury, at the Solar Observatory at the North Pole, there was no near-by planet to account for the light.

"Is that starlight?" he finally asked, knowing it wasn't.

Scott Mindes said wearily, "That's the coronal glimmer."

"Great Galaxy," said Lucky with a light laugh. "The corona! Of course! I should have known!"

"Known what?" cried Bigman. "What's going on? Hey, Mindes, come on, give!"

Mindes said, "Turn around. You've got your back to it."

They all turned. Lucky whistled softly between his teeth; Bigman yelped with surprise. Mindes said nothing.

A section of the horizon was etched sharply against a pearly region of the sky. Every pointed irregularity of that part of the horizon was in keen focus. Above it, the sky was in a soft glow (fading with height) a third of the way to the zenith. The glow consisted of bright, curving streamers of pale light.

"That's the corona, Mr. Jones," said Mindes.

Even in his astonishment Bigman was not forgetful of his own conception of the proprieties. He growled, "Call me Bigman." Then he said, "You mean the corona around the Sun? I didn't think it was that big."

"It's a million miles deep or more," said Mindes, "and we're on Mercury, the planet closest to the Sun. We're only thirty million miles from the Sun right now. You're from Mars, aren't you?"

"Born and bred," said Bigman.

"Well, if you could see the Sun right now, you'd find it

was thirty-six times as big as it is when seen from Mars, and so's the corona. And thirty-six times as bright too."

Lucky nodded. Sun and corona would be nine times as large as seen from Earth. And the corona could not be seen at all on Earth, except during periods of total eclipse.

Well, Mindes had not altogether lied. There were sights to be seen on Mercury. He tried to fill out the corona, to imagine the Sun it surrounded which was now hidden just below the horizon. It would be a majestic sight!

Mindes went on, an unmistakable bitterness in his voice. "They call this light 'the white ghost of the Sun.'"

Lucky said, "I like that. A rather good phrase."

"Rather good?" said Mindes savagely. "I don't think so. There's too much talk about ghosts on this planet. This planet's all jinx. Nothing ever goes right on it. The mines failed . . ." His voice trailed off.

Lucky thought: We'll let that simmer.

Aloud he said, "Where is this phenomenon we were to see, Mindes?"

"Oh yes. We'll have to walk a bit. Not far, considering the gravity, but watch your footing. We don't have roads here, and the coronal glimmer can be awfully confusing. I suggest the helmet lights."

He clicked his on as he spoke, and a shaft of light sprang out from above the face-plate, turning the ground into a rough patchwork of yellow and black. Two other lights flashed on, and the three figures moved forward on their thickly insulated boots. They made no sound in the vacuum, but each could sense the soft vibrations set up by each footfall in the air within their suits.

Mindes seemed to be brooding about the planet as he walked. He said in a low, tense voice, "I hate Mercury. I've been here six months, two Mercurian years, and I'm sick of it. I didn't think I'd be here more than six months to begin with, and here the time's up and nothing's done. Nothing. Everything about this place is wrong. It's the smallest planet. It's the closest to the Sun. Only one side faces the Sun. Over there"—and his arm swung in the direction of the corona's gleam—"is the Sun-side, where it gets hot enough in places to melt lead and boil sulfur. Over there in the other direction"—again his arm swung —"is the one planetary surface in the whole Solar System that never sees the Sun. Everything about the place is miserable."

He paused to jump over a shallow, six-foot-wide rift in the surface, a reminder of some eons-old Mercury-quake, perhaps, which could not heal over without wind and weather. He made the jump clumsily, the picture of an Earthman who, even on Mercury, stayed close to the artificial gravity of the Observatory Dome.

Bigman clicked his tongue disapprovingly at the sight. He and Lucky negotiated the jump with scarcely anything more than a lengthening of stride.

A quarter mile farther on, Mindes said abruptly, "We can see it from here, and just in time too."

He stopped, teetering forward, with arms outflung for balance. Bigman and Lucky halted with a small hop which kicked up a spurt of gravel.

Mindes's helmet flash went out. He was pointing. Lucky and Bigman put out their own lights and there, in the darkness, where Mindes had pointed, was a small, irregular splotch of white.

It was brilliant, a more burning sunshine than Lucky had ever seen on Earth.

"This is the best angle for seeing it," said Mindes. "It's the top of Black and White Mountain."

"Is that its name?" asked Bigman.

"That's right. You see why, don't you? It stands just far

enough nightward of the Terminator——That's the boundary between the dark-side and the Sun-side."

"I know that," said Bigman indignantly. "You think I'm ignorant?"

"I'm just explaining. There's this little spot around the North Pole, and another around the South Pole, where the Terminator doesn't move much as Mercury circles the sun. Down at the Equator, now, the Terminator moves seven hundred miles in one direction for forty-four days and then seven hundred miles back in the next forty-four. Here it just moves half a mile or so altogether, which is why this is a good place for an observatory. The Sun and the stars stand still.

"Anyway, Black and White Mountain is just far enough away so that only the top half of it is lit up at most. Then, as the Sun creeps away, the light moves up the mountain slopes."

"And now," interposed Lucky, "only the peak is lit up."

"Only the top foot or two maybe, and that will be gone soon. It will be all dark for an Earth-day or two, and then the light starts coming back."

Even as he spoke the white splotch shrank to a dot that burned like a bright star.

The three men waited.

"Look away," advised Mindes, "so that your eyes get accustomed to darkness."

And after slow minutes he said, "All right, look back."

Lucky and Bigman did so and for a while saw nothing.

And then it was as though the landscape had turned bloody. Or a piece of it had, at any rate. First there was just the sensation of redness. Then it could be made out, a rugged mountain climbing up to a peak. The peak was brightly red now, the red deepening and fading as the eye traveled downward until all was black.

"What is it?" asked Bigman.

"The Sun," said Mindes, "has sunk just low enough now so that, from the mountain peak, all that remains above the horizon is the corona and the prominences. The prominences are jets of hydrogen gas that lift thousands of miles above the Sun's surface, and they're a bright red in color. Their light is there all the time, but ordinary sunlight drowns it out."

Again Lucky nodded. The prominences were again something which on Earth could be seen only during a total eclipse or with special instruments, thanks to the atmosphere.

"In fact," added Mindes in a low voice, "they call this 'the red ghost of the Sun.'"

"That's two ghosts," said Lucky suddenly, "a white one and a red one. Is it because of the ghosts that you carry a blaster, Mr. Mindes?"

Mindes shouted, "What?" Then, wildly, "What are you talking about?"

"I'm saying," said Lucky, "that it's time you told us why you really brought us out here. Not just for the sights, I'm sure, or you wouldn't carry a blaster on an empty, desolate planet."

It took a while for Mindes to answer. When he did, he said, "You're David Starr, aren't you?"

"That's right," said Lucky patiently.

"You're a member of the Council of Science. You're the man they call Lucky Starr."

Members of the Council of Science shunned publicity, and it was with a certain reluctance that Lucky said again, "That's right."

"Then I'm not wrong. You're one of their ace investigators, and you're here to investigate Project Light."

Lucky's lips thinned as they pressed together. He would much rather that were not so easily known. He said, "Maybe that's true, maybe it isn't. Why did you bring me here?"

"I know it's true, and I brought you here"—Mindes was panting—"to tell you the truth before the others could fill you—full of—lies."

"About what?"

"About the failures that have been haunting—I hate that word—the failures in Project Light."

"But you might have told me what you wanted to back at the Dome. Why bring me here?"

"For two reasons," said the engineer. His breathing continued rapid and difficult. "In the first place, they all think it's my fault. They think I can't pull the project through, that I'm wasting tax money. I wanted to get you away from them. Understand? I wanted to keep you from listening to them first."

"Why should they think it's your fault?"

"They think I'm too young."

"How old are you?"

"Twenty-two."

Lucky Starr, who wasn't very much older, said, "And your second reason?"

"I wanted you to get the feeling of Mercury. I wanted you to absorb the—the———" He fell silent.

Lucky's suited figure stood straight and tall on Mercury's forbidding surface, and the metal of one shoulder caught and reflected the milky light of the corona, "the white ghost of the Sun."

He said, "Very well, Mindes, suppose I accept your statement that you are not responsible for failures in the project. Who is?"

The engineer's voice was a vague mutter at first. It coalesced gradually into words. "I don't know——— At least———"

"I don't understand you," said Lucky.

"Look," said Mindes desperately, "I've investigated. I spent waking and sleeping periods trying to pinpoint the blame. I watched everybody's movements. I noted times when accidents took place, when there were breaks in the cables or when conversion plates were smashed. And one thing I'm sure of———"

"Which is?"

"That nobody at the Dome can be directly responsible. Nobody. There are only about fifty people in the Dome, fifty-two to be exact, and the last six times something has gone wrong I've been able to account for each one. Nobody was anywhere near the scenes of the accidents." His voice had gone high-pitched.

Lucky said, "Then how do you account for the accidents? Mercury-quakes? Action of the Sun?"

"Ghosts!" cried the engineer wildly, flinging his arms about. "There's a white ghost and a red ghost. You've seen those. But there are two-legged ghosts too. I've seen them, but will anyone believe me?" He was almost incoherent. "I tell you——— I tell you———"

Bigman said, "Ghosts! Are you nuts?"

At once Mindes screamed, "You don't believe me either. But I'll prove it. I'll blast the ghost. I'll blast the fools who won't believe me. I'll blast everyone. Everyone!"

With a harsh screech of laughter he had drawn his blaster, and with frenzied speed, before Bigman could move to stop him, he had aimed it at Lucky at point-blank range and squeezed its trigger. Its invisible field of disruption lashed out———

2

Mad or Sane?

It would have been the end of Lucky if he and Mindes had been on Earth.

Lucky had not missed the gathering madness in Mindes's voice. He had been waiting carefully for some break, some action to suit the violence of the engineer's hard-breathed sentences. Yet he had not entirely expected an outright assault with the blaster.

When Mindes's hand flashed to his holster, Lucky leaped to one side. On Earth, that movement would have come too late.

On Mercury, however, matters were different. Mercury's gravity was two fifths that of Earth, and Lucky's contracting muscles threw his abnormally light body (even including the suit he wore) farther to one side. Mindes, unaccustomed to low gravity, stumbled as he turned too quickly in order that his blaster might follow Lucky's motion.

The blaster's energy, therefore, struck bare ground, inches from Lucky's sinking body. It gouged a foot-deep hole into the frigid rock.

Before Mindes could recover and aim again, Bigman

had struck him at the end of a long, low tackle carried through with the natural grace of a born Martian accustomed to low gravity.

Mindes went down. He shrieked wordlessly and then was silent, whether unconscious as the result of the fall or as the climax of his fevered emotions could not be told.

Bigman did not believe either possibility. "He's shamming," he cried passionately. "The dirty cobber is playing dead." He had wrenched the blaster from the fallen engineer's unresisting grip, and now he pointed it at the man's head.

Lucky said sharply, "None of that, Bigman."

Bigman hesitated. "He tried to kill you, Lucky." It was obvious that the little Martian would not have been half as angry if it had merely been himself who had been in danger of death. Yet he backed away.

Lucky was on his knees examining Mindes's face through the face-plate, shining his helmet light onto the other's pale, drawn features. He checked the pressure gauge of Mindes's suit, making sure the shock of the fall had not loosened any of its joints. Then, seizing the fallen figure by a wrist and ankle, he slung it across his shoulders and rose to his feet.

"Back to the Dome," he said, "and, I'm afraid, to a problem that's a little more complicated than the Chief thinks."

Bigman grunted and followed Lucky's long stride closely, his own smaller build forcing him into a gravity-lengthened half trot. He kept his blaster ready, maneuvering his position to enable him, in case of need, to strike at Mindes without blasting down Lucky.

The "Chief" was Hector Conway, head of the Council of Science. At more informal times he was called Uncle Hector by Lucky, since it was Hector Conway, along with

Augustus Henree, who were the guardians of the young
Lucky after the death of Lucky's parents as the result of a
pirate attack near the orbit of Venus.

A week earlier Conway had said to Lucky with a casual air, almost as though he were offering him a vacation,
"How would you like to go to Mercury, Lucky?"

"What's up, Uncle Hector?" asked Lucky.

"Nothing really," said Conway, frowning, "except
some cheap politics. We're supporting a rather expensive
project up at Mercury, one of those basic research things
that may come to nothing, you know, and, on the other
hand, may turn out to be quite revolutionary. It's a gamble. All those things are."

Lucky said, "Is it anything I know about?"

"I don't think so. It's quite recent. Anyway, Senator
Swenson has pounced on it as an example of how the
Council wastes taxpayers' money. You know the line. He's
pressing for an investigation, and one of his boys went out
to Mercury some months ago."

"Senator Swenson? I see." Lucky nodded. This was
nothing new. The Council of Science over the past de-
cades had slowly come to the fore of the fight against the
dangers to Earth from both within and without the Solar
System. In this age of Galactic civilization, with humanity
spread through all the planets of all the stars in the Milky
Way, only scientists could properly cope with mankind's
problems. In fact, only the specially trained scientists of
the Council were adequate.

Yet there were some men of Earth's government who
feared the growing power of this Council of Science and
others who used this suspicion to further their own ambitions. Senator Swenson was the foremost of the latter
group. His attacks, usually directed against the Council's
"wasteful" way of supporting research, were making him
famous.

Lucky said, "Who's the man in charge of the project on Mercury? Anyone I know?"

"It's called Project Light, by the way. And the man in charge is an engineer named Scott Mindes. A bright boy, but he's not the man to handle this. The most embarrassing thing is that since Swenson kicked up this fuss all sorts of things have been going wrong with Project Light."

"I'll look into it if you wish, Uncle Hector."

"Good. The accidents and bad breaks are nothing, I'm sure, but we don't want Swenson to maneuver us into some bad-looking spot. See what he's up to. And watch out for that man of his. Urteil is his name and he has a reputation of being a capable and dangerous fellow."

So that was all it started out as. Just a bit of investigation to forestall political difficulties. Nothing more.

Lucky landed on Mercury's North Pole expecting nothing more, and in two hours found himself at the wrong end of a blaster bolt.

Lucky thought as he slogged back to the Dome with Mindes over his shoulders: There's more than just a bit of politics here.

Dr. Karl Gardoma stepped out of the small hospital room and faced Lucky and Bigman somberly. He was wiping his strong hands on a pad of fluffy plastosorb, which he tossed into the disposal unit when he finished. His dark-complexioned face, almost brown, was disturbed, his heavy eyebrows lowering. Even his black hair, cut close so that it stood up stiffly in thick array, seemed to accentuate his troubled appearance.

"Well, Doctor?" said Lucky.

Dr. Gardoma said, "I've got him under sedation. He'll be all right when he wakes. I don't know if he'll remember clearly what happened."

"Has he had attacks like this before?"

"Not since he came to Mercury, Mr. Starr. I don't know what happened before then, but these last few months he's been under a great strain."

"Why?"

"He feels responsible for the accidents that have been interfering with the progress of Project Light."

"Is he responsible?"

"No, of course not. But you can see how he feels. He's sure everyone blames him. Project Light is vitally important. A great deal of money and effort has been put into it. Mindes is in charge of ten construction men, all five to ten years older than he is, and of an enormous amount of equipment."

"How does it happen he's so young?"

The doctor smiled grimly, but despite his grimness his white, even teeth made him look pleasant, even charming. He said, "Sub-etheric optics, Mr. Starr, is a completely new branch of science. Only young men, fresh out of school, know enough about it."

"You sound as though you know a bit about it yourself."

"Only what Mindes told me. We arrived on Mercury on the same ship, you know, and he fascinated me, quite won me over with what his project hopes to accomplish. Do you know about it?"

"Not a thing."

"Well, it involves hyperspace, that portion of space that lies outside the ordinary boundary of the space we know. The laws of nature that apply to ordinary space don't apply to hyperspace. For instance, in ordinary space it is impossible to move faster than the speed of light, so that it would take at least four years to reach the nearest star. In going through hyperspace any speed is possible————" The physician broke off with a sudden, apologetic smile. "You know all this, I'm sure."

"I suppose most people know that the discovery of hyperspatial flight made travel to the stars possible," said Lucky, "but what about Project Light?"

"Well," said Dr. Gardoma, "in ordinary space, light travels in straight lines in a vacuum. It can only be bent by large gravitational forces. In hyperspace, on the other hand, it can be bent as easily as if it were a cotton thread. It can be focused, dispersed, bent back upon itself. That's what the theory of hyperoptics says."

"And Scott Mindes, I suppose, is here to test that theory."

"That's right."

"Why here?" asked Lucky. "I mean, why on Mercury?"

"Because there's no other planetary surface in the Solar System where there is such a concentration of light over so large an area. The effects Mindes is looking for can be detected most easily here. It would be a hundred times as expensive to set up the project on Earth, and results would be a hundred times as uncertain. So Mindes tells me."

"Only now we're having these accidents."

Dr. Gardoma snorted. "They're no accidents. And, Mr. Starr, they have to be stopped. Do you know what the success of Project Light would mean?" He drove on, caught up in the vision. "Earth would no longer be the slave of the Sun. Space stations circling Earth could intercept sunlight, push it through hyperspace, and spread it evenly over the Earth. The desert heat and the polar cold would vanish. The seasons would be rearranged to our liking. We could control the weather by controlling the distribution of sunlight. We could have eternal sunlight where we wanted it; night of any length where we wanted it. Earth would be an air-conditioned paradise."

"It would take time, I imagine."

"A great deal of it, but this is the beginning. . . . Look, I may be out of order here, but aren't you the David Starr who cleared up the matter of the food poisonings on Mars?"

There was an edge to Lucky's voice as he answered, and his brows contracted slightly. "What makes you think so?"

Dr. Gardoma said, "I am a physician, after all. The poisonings seemed at first to be a disease epidemic, and I was much interested in it at the time. There were rumors about a young Councilman's having played the chief role in straightening the mystery, and names were mentioned."

Lucky said, "Suppose we let it go at that." He was displeased, as always, at any intimation that he was becoming well known. First Mindes, now Gardoma.

Dr. Gardoma said, "But if you are that Starr, you're here, I hope, to stop these so-called accidents."

Lucky did not seem to hear. He said, "When will I be able to talk to Scott Mindes, Dr. Gardoma?"

"Not for at least twelve hours."

"And will he be rational?"

"I'm certain of that."

A new guttural baritone voice broke in. "Are you, Gardoma? Is that because you know our boy Mindes was never irrational?"

Dr. Gardoma whirled at the sound and made no effort to hide the look of acute dislike on his face. "What are you doing here, Urteil?"

"Keeping my eyes and ears open, though I suppose you'd rather I kept them closed," the newcomer said.

Both Lucky and Bigman were staring at him curiously.

He was a large man; not tall, but broad of shoulder and thick-muscled. His cheeks were blue with stubble, and there was a rather unpleasant air of self-assurance about him.

Dr. Gardoma said, "I don't care what you do with your eyes and ears, but not in my office, if you don't mind."

"Why not in your office?" demanded Urteil. "You're a doctor. Patients have a right to come in. Maybe I'm a patient."

"What's your complaint?"

"How about these two? What are their complaints? Hormone deficiency, for one thing, I suppose." His eyes fell lazily on Bigman Jones as he said that.

There was a breathless interlude in which Bigman turned a deathly white and then seemed to swell. Slowly he rose from his seat, his eyes round and staring. His lips moved as though forming the words "hormone deficiency," as though he were trying to convince himself that he had actually heard the words and that it was no illusion.

Then, with the speed of a cobra striking, Bigman's five foot two of cord-whip muscle launched itself at the broad, sneering figure before him.

But Lucky moved faster. His hands shot downward, catching Bigman at each shoulder. "Easy, Bigman."

The small Martian struggled desperately. "You heard him, Lucky. You heard him."

"Not now, Bigman."

Urteil's laugh was a series of sharp barks. "Let him go, fella. I'll smear the little boy over the floor with my finger."

Bigman howled and writhed in Lucky's grip.

Lucky said, "I wouldn't say anything else, Urteil, or

you may be in a kind of trouble your senator friend won't be able to get you out of."

His eyes had become brown ice as he spoke and his voice was smooth steel.

Urteil's glance locked with Lucky's for a moment, then fell away. He mumbled something about joking. Bigman's harsh breathing calmed somewhat, and as Lucky slowly released his grip the Martian took his seat, still trembling with almost unbearable fury.

Dr. Gardoma, who had watched the bit of byplay tensely, said, "You know Urteil, Mr. Starr?"

"By reputation. He's Jonathan Urteil, Senator Swenson's roving investigator."

"Well, call it that," muttered the physician.

"And I know you too, David Starr, Lucky Starr, whatever you call yourself," said Urteil. "You're the roving wonder-boy for the Council of Science. Mars poisonings. Asteroid pirates. Venusian telepathy. Do I have the list correct?"

"You have," said Lucky tonelessly.

Urteil grinned triumphantly. "There isn't much the senator's office doesn't know about the Council of Science. And there isn't much I don't know about things happening here. For instance, I know about the attempt on your life, and I've come here to see you about it."

"Why?"

"To give you a little warning. Just a friendly little warning. I suppose the medic here has been telling you what a nice guy Mindes is. Just a momentary splash of unbearable strain, he's been telling you, I suppose. They're great friends, Mindes and he."

"I just said———" began Dr. Gardoma.

"Let *me* say," said Urteil. "Let me say this. Scott Mindes is about as harmless as a two-ton asteroid heading for a space-ship. He wasn't temporarily insane when he pointed a blaster at you. He knew what he was doing. He tried to kill you in cold blood, Starr, and if you don't watch out, he'll succeed next time. Because you can bet your small friend's Martian hip boots he'll try again."

3

Death Waits in a Room

The silence that followed seemed pleasant for no one but Urteil.

Then Lucky said, "Why? What's his motive?"

Urteil said calmly, "Because he's afraid. He's out here with millions of cash invested, cash that's been given him by a lax Council of Science, and he can't make his experiments work. He's calling his incompetence bad breaks. Eventually he'll go back to Earth and cry about Mercury's jinx. Then he'll get more money out of the Council, or, rather, out of the taxpayers, for some other fool scheme. Now you're coming to Mercury to investigate, and he's afraid that the Council, in spite of itself, may learn a little of the truth——— You take it from there."

Lucky said, "If this is the truth, you know it already."

"Yes, and I hope to prove it."

"But you're the danger to Mindes, then. By your reasoning, it is *you* he should try to kill."

Urteil grinned and his plump cheeks broadened until his jowly face looked wider than it was long. He said, "He *has* tried to kill me. True enough. But I've been through many tough sieges working for the senator. I can handle myself."

"Scott Mindes never tried to kill you or anybody," said Dr. Gardoma, his face pinched and white. "You know it, too."

Urteil made no direct answer. He spoke instead to Lucky. "And keep an eye on the good doctor too. As I said, he's great friends with Mindes. If I were you, I wouldn't let him treat me for as much as a headache. Pills and injections can————" He snapped his fingers with a sharp cracking noise.

Dr. Gardoma, words coming thickly, said, "Someday, someone will kill you for————"

Urteil said carelessly, "Yes? Are you planning on being the one?" He turned to go, then said over his shoulder, "Oh, I forgot. I hear that old man Peverale wants to see you. He's very disturbed at there being no official welcome. He's upset. So go see him and pat his poor old head for him———— And, Starr, another hint. After this, don't use any protective suits of any kind without checking them for leaks. Know what I mean?" With that, finally, he left.

Long moments passed before Gardoma was near normality again, before he could talk without choking. Then he said, "He riles me more every time I see him. He's a mean-mouthed, lying—"

"A mighty shrewd fellow," said Lucky dryly. "It seems obvious that one of his methods of attack is deliberately to say exactly what is calculated most to anger his opponent. An angry opponent is a half-helpless one. . . . And, Bigman, that goes for you. You can't just flail away at anyone who hints you're under six feet."

"Lucky," wailed the pint-sized Martian, "he said I was hormone-deficient."

"Then learn to wait for the appropriate moment to convince him otherwise."

Bigman grumbled rebelliously, and one clenched fist

beat softly against the tough plastic of his silver-and-vermilion hip boots (the colorfully designed hip boots that no one but a Martian farm boy would wear and which no Martian farm boy would be without. Bigman owned a dozen, each more glaring than the last).

Lucky said, "Well, we'll look up Dr. Peverale. He's the head of the Observatory, isn't he?"

"The head of the whole Dome," said the doctor. "Actually, he's getting old and he's lost touch. I'm glad to say that he hates Urteil as much as any of us do, but there's nothing he can do about it. He can't buck the senator. I wonder if the Council of Science can?" he ended gloomily.

Lucky said, "I think so. Now remember, I'll want to see Mindes when he wakes up."

"All right. Take care of yourself."

Lucky stared at him curiously. "Take care of myself? How do you mean?"

Dr. Gardoma flushed. "Just an expression. I always say it. I don't mean anything by it."

"I see. Well, then, we'll be meeting again. Come along, Bigman, and stop frowning."

Dr. Lance Peverale shook them both by the hand with a vigor that was surprising in a man so old. His dark eyes were lit with concern and appeared the darker for the white eyebrows that topped them. His hair, still abundant, retained a considerable amount of its original color and had not faded past an iron gray. His lined and leathery cheeks, above which sharp cheekbones stood out prominently, did most to give him the appearance of age.

He spoke slowly and gently. "I am sorry, gentlemen, most concerned that you should have had such a distressing experience so soon after arriving at the Observatory. I blame myself."

"You have no reason to, Dr. Peverale," said Lucky.

"The fault is mine, sir. Had I been here to greet you as I ought to have——— But there, we were following an important and quite anomalous prominence, and I'm afraid I allowed my profession to tempt me from the proper expression of hospitality."

"In any case, you are forgiven," said Lucky, and he glanced sidewise with some amusement at Bigman, who was listening, open-mouthed, to the old man's stately flow of words.

"I am past forgiveness," said the astronomer, "but it pleases me that you make the attempt. Meanwhile, I have ordered that quarters be placed at your disposal." He linked arms with both of them, urging them along the well-lit but narrow corridors of the Dome. "Our facilities are crowded, particularly since Dr. Mindes and his engineers have arrived and—and others. Still, I imagine you will find it welcome to have an opportunity to refresh yourselves and to sleep, perhaps. You will wish for food, I am sure, and it will be sent to you. Tomorrow will be time enough for you to meet us all socially, and for us to find out your purpose in coming here. For myself, the fact that the Council of Science vouches for you is sufficient. We will have a kind of banquet in your honor."

The corridor level was sinking as they walked, and they were burrowing into Mercury's vitals toward the residential level of the Dome.

Lucky said, "You are very kind. Perhaps I will also have the opportunity to inspect the Observatory."

Peverale seemed delighted at that. "I will be at your service in the matter, and I am sure you will not regret time spent in such an inspection. Our major equipment is mounted on a movable platform designed to move with the advancing or receding Terminator. In that fashion, a particular portion of the Sun can be kept continually in view despite Mercury's motions."

"Wonderful! But now, Dr. Peverale, one question. What is your opinion of Dr. Mindes? I'd appreciate a frank answer without any consideration for such things as diplomacy."

Peverale frowned. "Are you a sub-temporal engineer too?"

"Not quite," said Lucky, "but I was asking about Dr. Mindes."

"Exactly. Well"—and the astronomer looked thoughtful—"he is a pleasant young man, quite competent, I should think, but nervous, very nervous. He is easily offended, too easily offended. It has shown up as time has gone on and things have not been quite right with his project, and it is making him a little difficult to get along with. A pity, for as I say, he is a pleasant young man, otherwise. I am his superior, of course, while he is here at the Dome, but I don't really interfere with him. His project has no connection with our Observatory work."

"And your opinion of Jonathan Urteil?"

The old astronomer stopped walking on the instant. "What about him?"

"How does he get along here?"

"I am not interested in discussing the man," said Peverale.

They walked on in silence for a short while. The astronomer's face was lowering.

Lucky said, "Are there any other outsiders at the Dome? There are you and your men, Mindes and his men, and Urteil. Anyone else?"

"The doctor, of course. Dr. Gardoma."

"You do not consider him one of your own men?"

"Well, he's a doctor and not an astronomer. He supplies the one service the Dome must have and can't use machinery for. He cares for our health. He's new here."

"How new?"

"He replaced our old doctor after the latter's one-year shift. Dr. Gardoma arrived on the same ship that carried Mindes's group, as a matter of fact."

"One-year shift? Is that common for doctors here?"

"And most of the men. It makes it difficult to keep up continuity, and it is hard to train a man and have him leave; but then, Mercury is not an easy place to remain, and our men must be replaced frequently."

"Then in the last six months how many new men have you received here?"

"Perhaps twenty. The exact figures are in our records, but twenty is about it."

"Surely you yourself have been here quite a while."

The astronomer laughed. "Many years. I hate to think how many. And Dr. Cook, my assistant director, has been here for six years. Of course we take vacations frequently. . . . Well, here are your quarters, gentlemen. If there is anything you should wish, do not hesitate to inform me."

Bigman looked about him. The room was a small one, but it held two beds that could fold up into a wall recess when not in use; two chairs of which the same was true; a one-piece desk-chair combination; a small closet; and an adjoining wash room.

"Hey," he said, "a lot better than the ship, anyway, huh?"

"Not bad," said Lucky. "This is probably one of their better rooms."

"Why not?" said Bigman. "I guess he knows who *you* are."

"I guess not, Bigman," said Lucky. "He thought I

might be a sub-temporal engineer. All he knows is that the Council sent me."

"Everyone else knows who you are," said Bigman.

"Not everyone. Mindes, Gardoma, and Urteil. . . . Look, Bigman, why don't you use the washroom? I'll have some food sent up and have them bring in the general utility kit from the *Shooting Starr.*"

"Suits me," said Bigman cheerily.

Bigman sang loudly through the shower. As usual on a waterless world, the bath water was strictly rationed, with stern warnings on the wall as to the amount it was permissible to use. But Bigman had been born and bred on Mars. He had a huge respect for water and would no more think of splashing idly in it than in beef stew. So he used detergent copiously and water carefully and sang loudly.

He stepped in front of the forced-hot-air dryer which tingled his skin with its jets of bone-dry air and slapped his body with his hands to enhance the effect.

"Hey, Lucky," he yelled, "is there food on the table? I'm hungry."

He heard Lucky's voice speaking softly but could make out no words.

"Hey, Lucky," he repeated, and stepped out of the washroom. The desk had two steaming platters of roast beef and potatoes on it. (A slight sharpness in the aroma indicated the meat, at least, to be really a yeast imitation from the sub-sea gardens of Venus.) Lucky, however, was not eating, but sat on the bed and spoke into the room's Talkie.

Dr. Peverale's face was gazing out of the receiving plate.

Lucky said, "Well, then, was it general knowledge that this was to be our room?"

"Not general knowledge, but I gave the order to prepare your room over an open hookup. There was no reason for secrecy as far as I could see. I suppose anyone might have overheard. Furthermore, your room is one of a few such that are reserved for distinguished guests. There is no secret about it."

"I see. Thank you, sir."

"Is anything wrong?"

"Not at all," said Lucky, smiling, and broke connection. His smile disappeared and he looked thoughtful.

"Nothing wrong, my foot," exploded Bigman. "What's up, Lucky? Don't tell *me* there isn't anything wrong."

"Something is wrong, yes. I've been looking at the equipment here. These are special insulated suits for use on the Sun-side, I imagine."

Bigman lifted one of the suits hanging in a special wall recess. It was amazingly light for its bulk, nor could that be attributed to Mercurian gravity, since gravity here in the Dome was maintained at Earth-normal.

He shook his head. As usual, if he had to use a suit supplied him out of stock rather than one built to specifications, he would have to reduce all fittings to the minimum and even so find it inconvenient to use. He sighed resignedly. It was the penalty he paid for not being exactly tall. He always thought of it that way: "not exactly tall." He never thought of his five foot two as being actually "short."

He said, "Sands of Mars, they've got everything here for us, all set and waiting. Bed. Bath. Food. Suits."

"And something else too," said Lucky gravely. "Death is waiting in this room. See here."

Lucky lifted one arm of the larger suit. The ball joint at the shoulder moved easily, but where it joined the shaft of the shoulder there was a tiny, all but unnoticeable gap. It would have been completely unnoticeable if Lucky's fingers had not spread it apart.

It was a slash! Man-made, obviously! Insulation showed.

"On the inner surface," said Lucky, "there's a similar slash. This suit would have lasted just long enough to get me out on the Sun-side, and then it would have killed me neatly."

4

Over the Banquet Table

"Urteil!" cried Bigman at once, with a ferocity that stiffened every muscle of his small body. "That dirty cobber———"

"Why Urteil?" asked Lucky softly.

"He warned us to watch our suits, Lucky. Remember?"

"Of course. And it's exactly what I did."

"Sure. He set it up for us. We find a slashed suit and we think he's a great guy. Then we're cold meat for him next time around. Don't fall for that, Lucky. He's a———"

"Now wait, Bigman, wait! Don't make your mind up so fast. Look at it this way. Urteil said Mindes had tried to kill him, too. Suppose we believe him. Suppose Mindes had tried to gimmick Urteil's suit and Urteil had spotted it in time. Urteil would warn us to watch out for the same trick. Maybe Mindes did this."

"Sands of Mars, Lucky, that can't be. This guy, Mindes, is ladled full of sleeping pills, and before that he wasn't out of our sight from the minute we got onto this miserable rock."

"All right. How do we know Mindes is asleep and under medication?" asked Lucky.

"Gardoma says————" began Bigman, and fell silent.

"Exactly. Gardoma says! We haven't seen Mindes, though. We only know what Dr. Gardoma said, and Dr. Gardoma is a great friend of Mindes's."

"The two of them are in it together," said Bigman, with instant conviction. "Jumping comets————"

"Wait, wait, don't *you* jump so. Great Galaxy, Bigman, I'm just trying to straighten out my thoughts, and you take me up on everything." His tone was as disapproving as it could ever be with respect to his small friend. He went on, "Now you've complained a dozen times that I don't tell you everything on my mind until everything's done with. This is why, you blaster-happy nitwit. As soon as I advance a theory, you're off on a charge, all your weapons cocked and ready."

"I'm sorry, Lucky," said Bigman. "Go ahead."

"All right. Now Urteil is easy to suspect. Nobody likes him. Even Dr. Peverale doesn't. You saw how he reacted just to the mention of his name. We've met him only once and you dislike him————"

"I'll say," muttered Bigman.

"—while I don't exactly like him, either. Anyone can slash this suit and hope that suspicion will fall on Urteil if it should happen to be discovered, and it would be surely discovered after it's killed someone, if not before."

"I see all that, Lucky."

"On the other hand," went on Lucky smoothly, "Mindes has already tried to get rid of me with a blaster. If that were a serious attempt, he doesn't seem the type to do anything as indirect as suit-slashing. As for Dr. Gardoma, I don't see him involving himself in the murder of a Councilman just out of friendship for Mindes."

"Then what's the decision?" cried Bigman impatiently.

"There isn't any so far," said Lucky, "except maybe that we go to sleep." He turned down the bed sheets and stepped into the washroom.

Bigman looked after him and shrugged his shoulders.

Scott Mindes was sitting up in bed when Lucky and Bigman entered his quarters the next morning. He was pale and looked tired.

"Hello," he said. "Karl Gardoma told me what happened. You don't know how sorry I am."

Lucky passed it off with a shrug. "How do you feel?"

"Wrung out but all right, if you know what I mean. I'll be at the dinner party old Peverale is giving tonight."

"Is that wise?"

"I won't leave Urteil there holding the fort," said Mindes, hatred suddenly flooding his face with momentary color, "telling everyone I'm crazy. Or Dr. Peverale, either, for that matter."

"Dr. Peverale doubts your sanity?" asked Lucky softly.

"Well——— Look, Starr, I've been scouting the Sunside in a small rocket-scooter ever since the accidents started getting bad. I had to do it. It's my project. Twice, now, I—I've seen something."

Mindes paused and Lucky prodded him. "Seen what, Dr. Mindes?"

"I wish I could say for sure. I saw it only from a distance each time. Something moving. Something that looked human. Something in a space-suit. Not one of our inso-suits, our special insulated jobs, you know. It looked more like an ordinary space-suit. Ordinary metal, you know."

"Did you try to get closer?"

"Yes, and I lost it. And the photographs showed nothing either. Just spots of light and dark that might have been something, or nothing. But it was something, all right. Something that moved under the Sun as though it didn't care a thing for the heat and radiation. It would even stand still in the Sun for minutes at a time. That's what got me."

"Is that strange? Standing still, I mean?"

Mindes laughed shortly. "On the Mercury Sun-side? It sure is. Nobody stands still. Insulated suit and all, you go about your business as fast as you can and get out from under as fast as you can. This near the Terminator the heat isn't so bad. It's the radiation, though. It's just good practice to take as little of it as possible. The inso-suits aren't complete protection against gamma rays. If you must stand still, you move into the shade of a rock."

"What's your explanation of it all?"

Mindes's voice fell to an almost shamed whisper. "I don't think it's a man."

"You're not going to say it's a two-legged ghost, are you?" said Bigman suddenly, before Lucky could nudge him into silence.

But Mindes only shook his head. "Did I use that phrase on the surface? I seem to remember——— No, I think it's a Mercurian."

"What?" cried Bigman, sounding as if he thought that were worse.

"How else could it endure the Sun's radiation and heat so?"

"Why would it need a space-suit then?" asked Lucky.

"Well, I don't know." Mindes's eyes flashed, and a restless wildness settled upon them. "But it's *something*. When I got back to the Dome, every man and every suit could be accounted for each time. Dr. Peverale won't authorize an expedition to make a real search. He says we're not equipped for it."

"Have you told him what you told me?"

"He thinks I'm crazy. I'm sure of it. He thinks I'm seeing reflections and building men out of them in my imagination. But that's not so, Starr!"

Lucky said, "Have you contacted the Council of Science?"

"How can I? Dr. Peverale wouldn't back me. Urteil would say I was mad and they would listen to *him*. Who would listen to me?"

"I would," said Lucky.

Mindes sat up in bed with a jerk. His hand shot out as though it were ready to grasp the other's sleeve but then held back. He said, in a choked voice, "Then you'll investigate it?"

"In my way," promised Lucky, "I will."

The others were already at the banquet table that evening when Lucky and Bigman arrived. Above the hum of greeting that rose as they entered and the beginning of the introductions, there were obvious signs that the gathering was not entirely a pleasant one.

Dr. Peverale sat at the head of the table, his thin lips set and his sunken cheeks quivering, the picture of dignity maintained under difficulty. At his left was the broad-shouldered figure of Urteil, lounging back in his chair, thick fingers playing delicately with the rim of a drinking glass.

Toward the foot of the table was Scott Mindes, looking painfully young and tired as he stared with angry frustration at Urteil. Next to him was Dr. Gardoma, watching with an anxious and thoughtful eye as though ready to interfere in case Mindes grew rash.

The remaining seats, except for two empty ones at Dr. Peverale's right, were occupied by several of the senior men of the Observatory. One in particular, Hanley Cook, second in command at the Dome, leaned his tall, lean body forward and took Lucky's hand firmly in his own.

Lucky and Bigman took their seats and the salads were served.

Urteil said at once in a harsh voice that effectively took over the conversation, "We were wondering just before you came in whether young Mindes ought not to tell you of the great wonders in store for Earth as a result of his experiments."

"No such thing," snapped Mindes, "and I'll do my own talking if you don't mind."

"Oh, come on, Scott," said Urteil, grinning broadly, "don't be bashful. Well, then, look here, *I'll* tell the man."

Dr. Gardoma's hand fell, as though by accident, on Mindes's shoulder, and the young engineer swallowed a cry of indignation and remained silent.

Urteil said, "Now I warn you, Starr, this is going to be good. It———"

Lucky interrupted, "I know something of the experiments. The grand result of an air-conditioned planet is quite possible, I think."

Urteil scowled. "That so? I'm glad you're optimistic. Poor Scott can't even make the pilot experiment work. Or at least he says he can't, don't you, Scott?"

Mindes half rose, but again Dr. Gardoma's hand was on his shoulder.

Bigman's eyes traveled from speaker to speaker, resting on Urteil with black distaste. He said nothing.

The arrival of the main course stopped the conversation momentarily, and Dr. Peverale tried desperately to turn it into less explosive channels. For a while he succeeded, but then Urteil, with the last of his helping of roast beef impaled on his fork, leaned toward Lucky and said, "So you go for the project Mindes is running, do you?"

"I think it's a reasonable one."

"You have to think that, being a member of the Council of Science. But what if I told you that the experiments here were phony; they could be run on Earth for one per cent of the cost if the Council were only interested enough in the taxpayers' money to save a little of it. What would you say if I told you that?"

"The same thing I would say if you told me anything at all," retorted Lucky composedly. "I would say, Mr. Urteil, that the chances are that you're lying. It's your greatest talent and, I believe, pleasure."

Instantly a great silence fell on the banqueters, even on Urteil. His thick cheeks seemed to sag in surprise and his eyes to bulge. With sudden passion, he leaned directly across Dr. Peverale's place, rising from his seat and bringing his right hand down hard and flat just short of Lucky's platter.

"No Council lackey—" he began in a roar.

And as he did that, Bigman moved, too. No eye at the table saw the details of that move, since it flashed with the speed of a striking snake, but Urteil's roar ended in a shout of dismay.

Urteil's hand, which had come down with such hard finality, now showed the carved metallic haft of a force-knife growing out of it.

Dr. Peverale scraped his chair back suddenly, and there was a cry or an exclamation from every man there but Bigman himself. Even Lucky seemed startled.

Bigman's tenor voice rose in delight. "Spread your fingers, you tub of mineral oil. Spread them and then grease back down into your seat."

Urteil stared at his small tormenter without understanding for a moment and then very slowly spread his fingers. His hand was not hurt, not a sliver of skin had been removed. The force-knife stood quivering in the hard plastic table top, an inch of its waveringly luminescent force-blade (it wasn't matter, merely a thin field of immaterial force) in sight. The knife had entered the table, working its way neatly and unerringly between the second and third finger of Urteil's hand.

Urteil snatched his hand away as though it were suddenly in flames.

Bigman crowed with delight and said, "And next time you reach a hand in Lucky's direction or in mine, you cobber, I chop it right off. What would you say if I told you that? And whatever you say, say it politely." He reached out for the force-knife, deactivating the blade as he seized the haft, and returned it to its inconspicuous holster on his belt.

Lucky said, with a light frown, "I wasn't aware that my friend was armed. I'm sure he's sorry for having disturbed the meal, but I believe Mr. Urteil may take this incident to heart."

Someone laughed and there was a tight smile on Mindes's face.

Urteil looked with hot eyes from face to face. He said, "I won't forget this treatment. It's obvious to me that the senator is receiving little co-operation, and he'll hear of that. And meanwhile, I'm staying right here." He folded his arms as though daring anyone to make him leave.

Little by little the conversation grew general.

Lucky said to Dr. Peverale, "You know, sir, it seems to me that your face is familiar."

"Is it?" The astronomer smiled in a strained fashion. "I don't think I ever met you before."

"Well, were you ever on Ceres?"

"Ceres?" The old astronomer looked at Lucky with some surprise. He had obviously not yet recovered from the force-knife episode. "The largest observatory in the Solar System is on that asteroid. I worked there as a young man, and I frequently visit it even now."

"Then I wonder if I didn't perhaps see you there."

Lucky couldn't help thinking, as he spoke, of those exciting days when the chase was on for Captain Anton and the pirates who were making their lair in the asteroids. And particularly the day when the pirate ships raided the very heart of Council territory, onto the surface of Ceres itself, winning out temporarily by the very daring of their undertaking.

But Dr. Peverale was shaking his head in gentle good humor. "I would have been certain, sir, had I had the pleasure of seeing you there. I am sure I did not."

"Too bad," said Lucky.

"The loss is mine, I assure you. But then it was my season for loss. As a result of an intestinal ailment, I missed all the excitement in connection with the pirate raid. I knew of it only through the conversations I overheard among my nurses."

Dr. Peverale looked about the table now, his good humor restored. The dessert was being served by the mechanical tray-carrier. He said, "Gentlemen, there has been some discussion of Project Light."

He paused to smile benignly, then went on. "It isn't exactly a happy subject under the circumstances, but I have been thinking a good deal about the accidents that have disturbed so many of us. It seems it would be a good time for me to give you all my thoughts on the matter. After all, Dr. Mindes is here. We have had a good meal. And, finally, I have something interesting to say."

Urteil broke a long silence to ask grimly, "*You,* Dr. Peverale?"

The astronomer said mildly, "Why not? I have had

interesting things to say many times in my life. And I *will* say what's on my mind now." There was a sudden gravity about him. "I believe I know the whole truth, the exact truth. I know who is causing the destruction in connection with Project Light and why."

5

The Direction of Danger

The old astronomer's gentle face seemed pleased as he looked about the table, perhaps at having gained so absolutely the attention of all. Lucky looked about the table too. He caught the expressions that greeted Dr. Peverale's statement. There was contempt on Urteil's broad features, a puzzled frown on Dr. Gardoma's face, a sulkier one on that of Mindes. The others were held in various attitudes of curiosity and interest.

One man caught Lucky's attention particularly. It was Hanley Cook, Dr. Peverale's second in command. He stared at his finger ends, and there was something like weary disgust about him. When he looked up, his expression had changed and settled into a cautious blankness.

Nevertheless Lucky thought: "I'll have to talk to the man."

And then his attention shifted back to Dr. Peverale.

Dr. Peverale was saying, "The saboteur can't be one of us, of course. Dr. Mindes tells me that he has investigated and is sure of that. Even without investigation, I am sure that none of us is capable of such criminal action. Yet the saboteur must be intelligent, since the destruction is too purposeful, too exclusively directed against Project Light, to be the result of chance or of anything nonintelligent. Therefore————"

Bigman interrupted excitedly. "Hey, you mean Mercury has native life? It's Mercurians doing this?"

There was a sudden buzz of confused comment and some laughter, at which Bigman reddened. "Well," said the small Martian, "isn't that what Dr. Peverale is saying?"

"Not quite," said Dr. Peverale gently.

"There is no life of any kind native to Mercury," said one of the astronomers with emphasis. "That's one thing we're sure of."

Lucky interposed, "How sure? Has anyone looked?"

The astronomer who had spoken seemed taken aback. He said, "There have been exploring parties. Certainly."

Lucky smiled. He had met intelligent beings on Mars that no other man knew of. He had discovered semi-intelligent beings on Venus where none had been thought to exist. He, for one, was not ready to admit that any planet lacked life, or even intelligence.

He said, "How many exploring parties? How thorough was each exploration? Has every square mile been searched?"

The astronomer did not answer. He looked away, raising his eyebrows as though to say: What's the use?

Bigman grinned, his little face wrinkling into a caricature of gnomish good humor.

Dr. Peverale said, "My dear Starr, explorations have uncovered nothing. While we grant that the possibility of Mercurian life is not completely excluded, the probability of its existence is very low. Suppose we assume that the only intelligent life in the Galaxy is the human race. Certainly, it's the only one we know of."

With the Martian mind-beings in his memory, Lucky

did not agree with that, but he kept silent and let the old man continue.

It was Urteil, little by little having recovered his self-possession, who intervened. "What do you think you're getting at," he asked, and it was characteristic of the man that he could not resist adding, "if anything?"

Dr. Peverale did not answer Urteil directly. He looked from face to face, deliberately ignoring the Congressional investigator. He said, "The point is, there are humans elsewhere than on Earth. There are humans in many star systems." A queer change came across the astronomer's face. It pinched in, grew white, and his nostrils flared as though he were suddenly overpowered with anger. "For instance, there are humans on the planets of Sirius. What if they are the saboteurs?"

"Why should they be?" asked Lucky at once.

"Why not? They have committed aggression against Earth before."

So much was true. Lucky Starr himself had helped, not too long before, to repel a Sirian invasion flotilla that had landed on Ganymede, but in that case they had left the Solar System without pushing matters to a showdown. Yet, on the other hand, it was a common thing for many Earthmen to blame Sirians for anything that went wrong.

Dr. Peverale was saying with energy, "I've *been* there. I've *been* to Sirius only five months ago. It took a great deal of red tape because Sirius welcomes neither immigrants nor visitors, but it was a matter of an interstellar astronomical convention, and I managed to get a visa. I was determined to see for myself, and I must say I wasn't disappointed.

"The planets of Sirius are thinly populated and they are extremely decentralized. They live in isolated individual family units, each with its own energy source and services. Each has its group of mechanical slaves—there's no other word possible—slaves in the shape of positronic robots, which do the labor. The Sirian humans maintain themselves as a fighting aristocracy. Every one of them can handle a space-cruiser. They'll never rest till they destroy the Earth."

Bigman shifted restlessly in his seat. "Sands of Mars, let them try. Let them try, is all I say."

"They will when they are quite ready," said Dr. Peverale, "and, unless we do something quickly to meet the danger, they will win. What have we got to oppose them? A population in the billions, true, but how many can handle themselves in space? We are six billion rabbits and they are one million wolves. Earth is helpless and grows more helpless every year. We are fed by grain from Mars and yeast from Venus. We get our minerals from the asteroids, and we used to get them from Mercury, too, when the mines here were working.

"Why, Starr, if Project Light succeeds, Earth will be dependent on space stations for the manner in which it gets its very sunshine. Don't you see how vulnerable that makes us? A Sirian raiding party, by attacking the outposts of the System, could panic and starve Earth without ever having to fight us directly.

"And can we do anything to them in return? No matter how many of them we kill, the remaining Sirians are always self-contained and self-sufficient. Any of them could continue the war."

The old man was almost breathless with passion. There was no questioning his sincerity. It was as though he were getting something out of himself that had been stifling him.

Lucky's eye wandered back to Dr. Peverale's second, Hanley Cook. The man was resting his forehead on the bony knuckles of one large hand. His face was flushed, but to Lucky it did not seem like a flush of either anger or indignation. Rather, it seemed one of embarrassment.

Scott Mindes spoke up skeptically. "What would be the point, Dr. Peverale? If they're getting along on Sirius, why should they come to Earth? What would they get out of us? Even supposing they conquer Earth, they would only have to support us———"

"Nonsense!" rapped out the senior astronomer. "Why should they? They would want Earth's resources, not Earth's population. Get that through your head. They'd let us starve. It would be part of their policy."

"Oh, come," said Gardoma. "That's unbelievable."

"Not out of cruelty," said Dr. Peverale, "out of policy. They despise us. They consider us scarcely more than animals. The Sirians themselves are very race-conscious. Since Earthmen first colonized Sirius, they have been breeding themselves carefully until they are free of diseases and of various characteristics which they consider undesirable.

"They are of uniform appearance, while Earthmen are of all shapes, sizes, colors, varieties. The Sirians consider us inferior. That's why they won't let us emigrate to Sirius. They wouldn't let me attend the convention till the government pulled every string possible. Astronomers from other systems were all welcome but not from Earth.

"And human life, any kind of human life, doesn't mean much to them, anyway. They're machine-centered. I've watched them with their metal men. They're more considerate of a Sirian robot, almost, than of a Sirian man. They would regard a robot as worth a hundred men of Earth. They pamper those robots. They love them. Nothing's too good for them."

Lucky murmured, "Robots are expensive. They have to be treated carefully."

"Maybe so," said Dr. Peverale, "but men who become

accustomed to worrying about the needs of machines become callous about the needs of men."

Lucky Starr leaned forward, elbows on the table, dark eyes serious and the smooth vertical lines of his handsome, still subtly boyish face set gravely. He said, "Dr. Peverale, if the Sirians are race-conscious and are breeding themselves into uniformity, they will defeat themselves in the long run. It is variety in the human race that brings about progress. It is Earth and not Sirius that is in the forefront of scientific research. Earthmen settled Sirius in the first place, and it is we, not our Sirian cousins, who are advancing in new directions every year. Even the positronic robots you mention were invented and developed on Earth by Earthmen."

"Yes," said the astronomer, "but Earthmen don't make use of the robot. It would upset our economy, and we place the comfort and security of today above the safety of tomorrow. We use our scientific advance to make ourselves weaker. Sirius uses its to make itself stronger. That's the difference and that's the danger."

Dr. Peverale threw himself back in his chair, looking grim. The mechanical tray-carrier cleared the table.

Lucky pointed at it. "That's a sort of a robot, if you like," he said.

The mechanical tray-carrier went quietly about its task. It was a flat-surfaced thing moving smoothly on a diamagnetic field, so that its gently curved base never actually touched the floor. Its limber tentacles removed dishes with careful delicacy, placing some on its upper surface, others within a cabinet in its side.

"That's a simple automaton," snorted Dr. Peverale. "It has no positronic brain. It cannot adapt itself to any change in its task."

"Well, then," said Lucky, "are you saying that the Sirians are sabotaging Project Light?"

"Yes. I am."

"Why should they?"

Dr. Peverale shrugged. "Perhaps it's just part of a larger plan. I don't know what trouble there is elsewhere in the Solar System. These may be the first random probings to prepare for ultimate invasion and conquest. Project Light in itself means nothing, the Sirian danger everything. I wish I could rouse the Council of Science and the government and the people to that truth."

Hanley Cook coughed, then spoke for the first time. "The Sirians are human like the rest of us. If they're on the planet, *where* are they?"

Dr. Peverale said coldly, "That's for an exploring expedition to find out. A well-prepared, well-equipped expedition."

"Wait a minute," said Mindes, his eyes glinting with excitement, "I've been out on the Sun-side, and I'll swear———"

"A well-prepared, well-equipped expedition," repeated the old astronomer firmly. "Your one-man flights mean nothing, Mindes."

The engineer stuttered a moment and slumped into an embarrassed silence.

Lucky said suddenly, "You seem to be unhappy about this, Urteil. What is your opinion of Dr. Peverale's view?"

The investigator lifted his eyes and met those of Lucky for a long moment in hatred and open defiance. It was obvious he had not forgotten, nor would forget, the earlier exchange at this table.

He said, "I'm keeping my opinion to myself. But I will say this, I'm not fooled by anything that's going on here tonight."

His mouth clamped shut and Lucky, having waited a moment for further remarks, turned to Peverale and said, "I wonder if we do need a complete expedition, sir. If we suppose that the Sirians are here on Mercury, can we perhaps deduce where they might be?"

"Go ahead, Lucky," crowed Bigman at once. "Show them how."

Dr. Peverale said, "How do you mean?"

"Well, what would be the best for the Sirians? If they've been sabotaging Project Light at frequent intervals over a period of months, it would be most convenient for them to have a base near the project. Yet at the same time, the base must not be easily detected. They've certainly been successful in the second requirement, anyway. Now where could such a handy, but secret, base be?

"Let's divide up Mercury into two parts, Sun-side and dark-side. It seems to me that they would be foolish to set up a base on Sun-side. Too hot, too much radiation, too inhospitable."

Cook grunted. "No more inhospitable than the dark-side."

"No, no," said Lucky at once, "you're wrong there. The Sun-side presents an environment which is quite unusual. Humans aren't accustomed to it at all. The dark-side is something very familiar. It is simply ground which is exposed to space, and the conditions of space are very familiar. The dark-side is cold but no colder than space. It is dark and airless but no darker than any portion of space not in direct sunlight and certainly no more airless. Men have learned to live comfortably in space, and they can live on the dark-side."

"Go on," said Dr. Peverale, his old eyes gleaming with interest. "Go on, Mr. Starr."

"But establishing a base that would serve over a period of months is not a simple thing. They must have a ship or ships to get back to Sirius someday. Or if they're to be picked up by a ship from outside they must still have ample stores of food and water, as well as an energy source. All this takes up room, and yet they must be certain they will not be detected. It leaves only one place where they can be."

"Where, Lucky?" asked Bigman, nearly jumping up and down in his eagerness. He, at least, had no doubts that whatever Lucky said was so. "Where?"

"Well," said Lucky, "when I first arrived here, Dr. Mindes made mention of mines on Mercury which had failed. Just a few moments ago, Dr. Peverale spoke of mines on Mercury that were once working. From that I gather that there must be empty mine shafts and corridors on the planet, and they must be either here or at the South Pole, since the polar regions are the only places where the temperature extremes are not too great. Am I right?"

Cook faltered. "Yes, there are mines here. Before the Observatory was established, the Dome was the mining center."

"Then we're sitting on top of a large empty hole in Mercury. If the Sirians are successfully hiding a large base, where else would it be? *There* is the direction of danger."

A murmur of appreciation passed around the table, but it was shattered abruptly by Urteil's guttural tones.

"All very pretty," he said, "but what does it all come to? What are you going to do about it?"

"Bigman and I," said Lucky, "intend to enter the mines just as soon as we can get ready. If there's anything there, we'll find it."

6

Preparations

Dr. Gardoma said sharply, "Do you intend to go alone?"

"Why not?" interposed Urteil. "The heroics are cheap enough. Of course they'll go alone. There's nothing and nobody there, and they know it."

"Care to join us?" asked Bigman. "If you leave your big mouth behind you can fit into a suit."

"You wouldn't crowd one even with yours," snarled Urteil.

Dr. Gardoma said again, "There's no point in going alone if———"

"A preliminary investigation," said Lucky, "will do no harm. Actually, Urteil may be right. There may be no one there. At the worst, we'll keep in touch with you at the Dome and hope that we can handle any Sirians we meet. Bigman and I are used to handling tight situations."

"Besides which," added Bigman, his gnomish face puckering into a grin, "Lucky and I like tight situations."

Lucky smiled and rose to his feet. "If we may be excused———"

Urteil at once rose, turned, and stamped away. Lucky's eyes followed him thoughtfully.

Lucky stopped Hanley Cook as the latter passed him. He touched his elbow gently.

Cook looked up, his eyes all concern. "Yes. What is it, sir?"

Lucky said quietly, "May I see you in our quarters as soon as possible?"

"I'll be there in fifteen minutes. Is that all right?"

"Fine."

Cook was very little later than that. He stepped into their quarters softly, wearing the look of concern that seemed a constant part of him. He was a man in his late forties with an angular face and light brown hair that was beginning to be touched with gray.

Lucky said, "I had forgotten to tell you where our quarters were. I'm sorry."

Cook looked surprised. "I knew where you were assigned."

"Well, good. Thank you for coming at our request."

"Oh," Cook paused. Then he said hurriedly, "Glad to. Glad to."

Lucky said, "There's a small matter of the insulation suits in this room. The ones intended for use on the Sunside."

"The inso-suits? We didn't forget the instruction film, did we?"

"No, no. I viewed that. It's quite another thing."

Cook said, "Something wrong?"

"Something wrong?" crowed Bigman. "Look for yourself." He spread the arms in order to display the slashes.

Cook looked blank, then flushed slowly and grew round-eyed with horror. "I don't see——— It's impossible——— Here at the Dome!"

Lucky said, "The main thing is to get it replaced."

"But who would do such a thing? We must find out."

"No use disturbing Dr. Peverale."

"No, no," said Cook, at once, as though he had not thought of it before.

"We'll find out the details in due time. Meanwhile I would like to get it replaced."

"Certainly. I'll attend to it promptly. No wonder you wanted to see me. Great Space————" He got to his feet in a kind of speechlessness and made as though to go.

But Lucky stopped him. "Wait, this is a minor thing. There are other things we must discuss. By the way, before we get to that—I take it you did not agree with Dr. Peverale's views on the Sirians."

Cook frowned. "I'd rather not discuss that."

"I watched you as he was speaking. You disapproved, I think."

Cook sat down again. His bony fingers clutched one another in a tight clasp and he said, "He's an old man. He's been all mixed up about the Sirians for years. Psychopathic, almost. He sees them under his bed. He blames them for everything. If our plates are overexposed, he blames them. Since he's been back from Sirius he's worse than ever, because of what he claims he went through."

"What was it he went through?"

"Nothing terrible, I suppose. But they quarantined him. They assigned him a separate building. They were too polite sometimes. They were too rude other times. There was no way of suiting him, I suppose. Then they forced a positronic robot on him to take care of personal services."

"Did he object to that too?"

"He claims it was because they wouldn't come near him themselves. That's what I mean. He took *everything* as an insult."

"Were you with him?"

Cook shook his head. "Sirius would only accept one man, and he's senior. I ought to have gone. He's too old, really—too old."

Cook was talking in a brooding sort of way. He looked up suddenly. "This is all confidential, by the way."

"Completely," Lucky assured him.

"What about your friend?" said Cook uncertainly. "I mean, I know he's honorable, but he's a little, uh, hotheaded."

"Hey," began Bigman, stiffening.

Lucky's affectionate hand came down on the little fellow's head and brushed his hair down on his forehead. "He's hotheaded, all right," he said, "as you saw at the banquet table. I can't always stop him in time and sometimes, when he's riled, he uses his tongue and his fist instead of his head. That's something I always have to keep in mind. Still, when I ask him specifically to keep quiet about something, he is quiet, and that's all there is to it."

"Thank you," said Cook.

Lucky went on. "To get back to my original question: Do you agree with Dr. Peverale concerning the Sirians in this present case?"

"I don't. How would they know about Project Light, and why should they care? I don't see them sending ships and men and risking trouble with the Solar System just so they can break a few cables. Of course, I tell you this, Dr. Peverale has been feeling hurt for quite a while now————"

"In what way?"

"Well, Mindes and his group were established here while he was at Sirius. He came back and found them here. He knew they were coming eventually. It's been planned for years. Still, coming back and actually finding them here was a shock."

"Has he tried to get rid of Mindes?"

"Oh no, nothing like that. He's even been friendly. It's just that it makes him feel that someday he'll be replaced altogether, maybe someday soon, and I suppose he hates the thought. So it's pleasant for him to take charge and start a big affair about Sirians. That's *his* baby, you see."

Lucky nodded, then said, "Tell me, have you ever been on Ceres?"

Cook looked surprised at the change in subject but said, "Occasionally. Why?"

"With Dr. Peverale? Alone?"

"With him, usually. He goes more frequently than I do."

Lucky grinned. "Were you there at the time the pirates made their raid on Ceres last year?"

Cook smiled too. "No, but the old man was. We've heard the story several times. He was very angry about it. He's practically never sick, and this one time he was just completely out. He missed everything."

"Well, that's the way it goes. . . . And, now, I think we'd better get to the main business. I didn't like to bother Dr. Peverale. As you say, he's an old man. You're his second and quite a bit younger————" Lucky smiled.

"Yes, of course. What can I do?"

"It's about the mines. I assume that somewhere at the Dome there are records, maps, charts, something which will tell us the arrangements of the main shafts and so on. Obviously, we can't wander at random."

"I'm sure there are," agreed Cook.

"And you can get them and perhaps go over them with us?"

"Yes, of course."

"Now as far as you know, Dr. Cook, the mines are in good shape, I hope. I mean, there's no danger of collapse or anything like that?"

"Oh no, I'm sure there's nothing of the sort possible. We're built right over some of the shafts, and we had to look into the engineering when the Observatory was first being set up. The shafts are well-buttressed and completely safe, particularly in Mercury's gravity."

"How come," asked Bigman, "the mines were shut down, if they're in such good shape?"

"A good question," said Cook, and a small smile broke through his expression of settled melancholy. "Do you want the true explanation or the interesting one?"

"Both," said Bigman at once.

Cook offered smokes to the others which were refused, then lit a cigarette after tamping it on the back of one hand in an abstracted manner. "The truth is this. Mercury is quite dense, and there were hopes that it would be a rich source of the heavy metals: lead, silver, mercury, platinum. It was, too; not as rich as might be, perhaps, but rich enough. Unfortunately, it was uneconomic. Supporting the mines here and transporting the ore back to Earth or even the Moon for processing raised the price too high.

"As for the interesting explanation, that's another thing completely. When the Observatory was first set up fifty years ago, the mines were still a going concern, though they were already closing down some of the shafts. The original astronomers heard stories from the miners and passed it on to the newcomers. It's part of the Mercurian legendry."

"What are the stories?" asked Bigman.

"It seems miners died in the shafts."

"Sands of Mars!" cried Bigman testily. "They die anywhere. You think anybody lives forever?"

"These were frozen to death."

"So?"

"It was a mysterious freezing. The shafts were fairly

well heated in those days, and their suit power units were in operation. The stories accumulate embroidery, you know, and, eventually miners wouldn't go into the main shafts in anything but gangs, wouldn't go into the side shafts at all, and the mines shut down."

Lucky nodded. He said, "You'll get the plans for the mines?"

"Right off. And replacements for that inso-suit too."

Preparations proceeded as though for a major expedition. A new inso-suit, replacing the one that had been slashed, was brought and tested, then laid to one side. After all, it would be ordinary space-suits for the darkside.

The charts were brought and studied. Together with Cook, Lucky sketched out a possible route of exploration, following the main shafts.

Lucky left Bigman to take care of packing the adjunct-units with homogenized food and with water (which could be swallowed while still in the suit), make sure of the charge of the power units and the pressure on the oxygen tanks, inspect the working efficiency of the waste disposal unit and the moisture recirculator.

He himself made a short trip to their ship, the *Shooting Starr*. He made the trip via the surface, carrying a field pack, the contents of which he did not discuss with Bigman. He returned without it but carrying two small objects that looked like thick belt buckles, slightly curved, in dull-steel finish and centered by a rectangle in glassy red.

"What's that?" asked Bigman.

"Microergometers," said Lucky. "Experimental. You know, like the ergometers on board ship except that those are bolted to the floor."

"What can these things detect?"

"Nothing at a couple of hundred thousand miles like a

ship's ergometer, but it can detect atomic power sources at ten miles, maybe. Look, Bigman, you activate it here. See?"

Lucky's thumbnail exerted pressure against a small slit in one side of the mechanism. A sliver of metal moved in, then out, and instantly the red patch on the surface glowed brightly. Lucky turned the small ergometer in this direction and that. In one particular position, the red patch glowed with the energy of a nova.

"That," said Lucky, "is probably the direction of the Dome's power plant. We can adjust the mechanism to zero that out. It's a little tricky." He worked painstakingly on the adjustment of two small controls so smoothly inset as nearly to be invisible.

He smiled as he worked, his engagingly youthful face lighting with pleasure. "You know, Bigman, there isn't a time I visit Uncle Hector but that he doesn't load me up with the Council's latest gadgets. He claims that with the chances you and I are always taking (you know the way he talks) we need them. Sometimes, though, I think he just wants us to act as field-testers for the gadgets. This one, though, may be useful."

"How, Lucky?"

"For one thing, Bigman, if there are Sirians in the mines, they'll have a small atomic power plant. They'll have to. They'll need power for heat, for electrolyzing water, and so on. This ergometer should detect that at ample distance. And for another thing————"

He fell silent, and Bigman's lips compressed in chagrin. He knew what that silence meant. Lucky had thoughts which later he would claim had been too vague to talk about.

"Is one of the ergometers for me?" he asked.

"You bet," said Lucky, tossing one of the ergometers toward him. Bigman snatched it out of the air.

• • •

Hanley Cook was waiting for them when they stepped out
of their quarters, wearing their suits but with headpieces
tucked under their arms.

He said, "I thought I'd lead you as far as the nearest
entrance to the shafts."

"Thank you," said Lucky.

It was the tail end of the sleeping period in the Dome.
Human beings always established an Earth-like alternation of waking and sleeping, even where there was no day
and night to guide them. Lucky had chosen this time on
purpose, since he did not want to enter the mines at the
head of a curious procession. In this Dr. Peverale had co-
operated.

The corridors of the Dome were empty. The lighting
was dimmed. And as they walked, a heavy silence seemed
to fall about them while the clank of their footsteps
sounded even louder.

Cook stopped. "This is Entry Two."

Lucky nodded. "All right. I hope we'll be seeing one
another again soon."

"Right."

Cook operated the lock with his usual gloomy gravity,
while Lucky and Bigman put on their headpieces, clamp-
ing them firmly along the paramagnetic seams. Lucky
took his first breath of canned air with what was almost
pleasure, he was so accustomed to it.

Lucky first, then Bigman, stepped into the air lock.
The wall closed behind them.

Lucky said, "Ready, Bigman?"

"You bet, Lucky." His words rang in Lucky's radio
receiver, and his small form was a shadow in the extremely dim light of the lock.

Then the opposing wall opened. They could feel the

puff of air escaping into vacuum, and they stepped for-ward through the opening once again.

A touch at the outer controls and the wall closed be-hind them again. This time, light was shut off altogether.

Standing in absolute darkness, they found themselves inside the silent and empty mines of Mercury.

The Mines of Mercury

They flicked on their suit-lights and the darkness was alleviated over a little space. They lit a tunnel that stretched out before them, dimly and more dimly and ending in darkness. The light beam had the usual sharp edge inevitable in a vacuum. Everything outside the direct beam remained completely black.

The tall man from Earth and his short companion from Mars faced that darkness and marched forward into the bowels of Mercury.

In the radiance of their suit-lights, Bigman looked curiously about at the tunnel, which resembled those he had seen on the Moon. Rounded out smoothly by the use of blasters and disintegrating procedures, it stretched out straight and even. The walls were curved and merged into the rocky ceiling. The oval cross section, slightly flattened above and quite flattened below, made for the greatest structural strength.

Bigman could hear his own steps through the air in his suit. He could sense Lucky's steps only as a small shock of vibration along rock. It was not quite sound, but to a person who had passed as much of his life in vacuum and near-vacuum as had Bigman it was almost as meaningful. He could "hear" the vibration of solid material much as ordinary Earthmen could hear the vibration of air which is called "sound."

Periodically they passed columns of rock which had been left unblasted and which served as buttresses for the layers of rock between the tunnel and the surface. Again this was like the mines on the Moon, except that the buttresses were both thicker and more numerous here, which was reasonable, since Mercury's gravity, small as it was, was two and a half times that of the Moon.

Tunnels branched off the main shaft along which they traveled. Lucky, who seemed in no hurry, paused at each opening in order to compare matters with the chart he carried.

To Bigman, the most melancholy aspect of the mines was the vestiges of one-time human occupancy: the bolts where illumo-plates must once have been attached to keep the corridors blazing with the light of day, the faint markings where paramagnetic relays must once have afforded traction for ore cars, occasional side pockets where rooms or laboratories must have existed, where miners might pause to eat at field kitchens or where samples of ore might be assayed.

All dismantled now, all torn down, only bare rock left.

But Bigman was not the man to brood overlong on such matters. Rather, he grew concerned at the lack of action. He had not come out here merely for the walk.

He said, "Lucky, the ergometer doesn't show a thing."

"I know, Bigman. Cover."

He said it quietly, with no special emphasis, but Bigman knew what it meant. He shoved his radio control to the particular notch which activated a shield for the carrier wave and scrambled the message. It was not regulation equipment on a space-suit, but it was routine for

Lucky and Bigman. Bigman had added the scrambler to the radio controls when preparing the suits almost without giving the matter a conscious thought.

Bigman's heart was beating a little faster. When Lucky called for a tight, scrambled beam between the two of them, danger was near. Nearer, at any rate. He said, "What's up, Lucky?"

"It's time to talk." Lucky's voice had a faintly far-off sound, as though it was coming indeterminately from all directions. That was due to the inevitable lack of perfection of the part of the receiving unscrambler, which always left a small fraction of "noise."

Lucky said, "This is Tunnel 7a, according to the chart. It leads back by a fairly simple route to one of the vertical shafts leading to the surface. I'll be going there."

Bigman said, amazed, "You will? Why, Lucky?"

"To get to the surface," and Lucky laughed lightly. "Why else?"

"What for?"

"In order to travel along the surface to the hangar and the *Shooting Starr*. When I went to the ship last time, I took the new inso-suit with me."

Bigman chewed that over and said slowly, "Does that mean you'll be heading for Sun-side?"

"Right. I'll be heading for the big Sun. I can't get lost, at least, since I need only follow the coronal glow on the horizon. It makes it very simple."

"Come off it, Lucky, will you? I thought it was the mines that have the Sirians in them. Didn't you prove that at the banquet?"

"No, Bigman, I didn't prove it. I just fast-talked it into sounding as though it were proven."

"Then why didn't you say so to me?"

"Because we've argued this out before, I don't want to go into it. I can't risk your losing your temper at the wrong time. If I had told you our coming down here was part of a deeper plan and if, for any reason, Cook had irritated you, you might have blurted it right out."

"I would not, Lucky. It's just that you hate to say anything at all till you're all ready."

"There's that too," admitted Lucky. "Anyway, that's the situation. I wanted everyone to think I was going into the mines. I wanted everyone to think I hadn't the foggiest notion of heading for Sun-side. The safest way of seeing to it was to make sure nobody, but nobody, not even you, Bigman, thought any differently."

"Can you tell me why, Lucky? Or is that still all a big secret?"

"I can tell you this. I have a strong notion that someone at the Dome is behind the sabotage. I don't believe in the Sirian theory."

Bigman was disappointed. "You mean there's nothing down here in the mines?"

"I could be wrong. But I agree with Dr. Cook. It is just too unlikely that Sirius would put all the effort that would be involved in setting up a secret base on Mercury just to achieve a bit of sabotage. It would be much more likely that, if they wanted to do such a thing, they would bribe an Earthman to do it. After all, who slashed the inso-suit? That, at least, can't be blamed on Sirians. Even Dr. Peverale hasn't suggested there are Sirians inside the Dome."

"Then you're looking for a traitor, Lucky?"

"I'm looking for the saboteur. He may be a traitor in the pay of Sirius, or he may be working for reasons of his own. I hope the answer is on the Sun-side. And I hope, furthermore, that my smoke screen concerning an invasion of the mines will keep the guilty person from having time to cover up or from preparing an uncomfortable reception for me."

"What answer do you expect?"

"I'll know when I find it."

"Okay," said Bigman. "I'm sold, Lucky. On our way. Let's go."

"Hold on, there," cried Lucky in honest perturbation. "Great Galaxy, boy! I said *I'm* going. There's only one inso-suit. You'll stay here."

For the first time, the significance of the pronouns Lucky had used sank into Bigman's consciousness. Lucky had said "I," "I." Not once had he said "we." And yet Bigman, with the easy confidence of long association, had assumed that "I" meant "we."

"Lucky!" he cried, torn between outrage and dismay. "Why do I have to stay?"

"Because I want the men at the Dome to be sure that we're here. You keep the chart and follow the route we talked about or something like it. Report back to Cook every hour. Tell them where you are, what you see, tell the truth; you don't have to make anything up—except that you say I'm with you."

Bigman considered that. "Well, what if they want to talk to you?"

"Tell them I'm busy. Yell that you think you've just seen a Sirian. Say you've got to cut off. Make up something, but keep them thinking I'm here. See?"

"All right. Sands of Mars, you'll go to Sun-side and have all the fun, and I'll just wander around in the dark playing games on the suit radio."

"Cheer up, Bigman, there *may* be something in the mines. I'm not always right."

"I'll bet you are this time. There's *nothing* down here."

Lucky couldn't resist a joke. "There's the freezing death Cook spoke about. You could investigate that."

Bigman didn't see the humor. He said, "Aw, shut up."

There was a short pause. Then Lucky placed his hand on the other's shoulder. "All right, that wasn't funny, Bigman, and I'm sorry. Now cheer up, really. We'll be together again in no time. You know that."

Bigman pushed Lucky's arm to one side. "All right. Drop the soft soap. You say I've got to do it, so I'll do it. Only you'll probably get sunstroke without me there keeping an eye on you, you big ox."

Lucky laughed. "I'll try to be careful." He turned down tunnel 7a but had not taken two steps when Bigman called out.

"Lucky!"

Lucky stopped. "What?"

Bigman cleared his throat. "Listen. Don't take stupid chances, will you? I mean, I'm not going to be around to drag you out of trouble."

Lucky said, "Now you sound like Uncle Hector. Suppose you take some of your own advice, eh?"

It was as close as they ever got to expressing their real affection for one another. Lucky waved his hand and stood glimmering for a moment in Bigman's suit-light. Then he turned and went off.

Bigman looked after him, following his figure as it gradually melted into the surrounding shadows until it turned about a curve in the tunnel and was lost to him.

He felt the silence, and the loneliness doubled. If he had not been John Bigman Jones, he might have weakened with the sense of loss, been overwhelmed at finding himself alone.

But he was John Bigman Jones, and he set his jaw and clamped his teeth and marched farther down the main shaft with unshaken tread.

Bigman made his first call to the Dome fifteen minutes later. He was miserable.

How could he have believed that Lucky seriously expected adventure in the mines? Would Lucky have arranged to make radio calls for the Sirians to pick up and keep tabs on?

Sure, it was a tight beam, but the messages weren't scrambled, and no beam was so tight that it couldn't be tapped with patience.

He wondered why Cook allowed such an arrangement, and almost at once the thought occurred to him that Cook disbelieved in the Sirians too. Only Bigman had believed. Big-brain!

At the moment, he could have chewed through a spaceship hull.

He gathered in Cook and used the agreed-upon signal for all clear.

Cook's voice at once shot back. "All clear?"

"Sands of Mars! Yes. Lucky's up ahead twenty feet, but there's no sign of anything. Look, if I've buzzed all clear, take my word for it next time."

"Let me talk to Lucky Starr."

"What for?" Bigman kept it casual with an effort. "Get him next time."

Cook hesitated, then said, "All right."

Bigman nodded to himself grimly. There'd be no next time. He'd buzz all clear and that would be all. . . . Only how long was he supposed to wander about in the darkness before he heard from Lucky? An hour? Two? Six? Suppose six hours went by and there was no word? How long should he stay? How long *could* he stay?

And what if Cook demanded specific information? Lucky had said to describe things, but what if Bigman accidentally failed to keep up the act? What if he tipped the boat and let slip the fact that Lucky had gone into the Sun-side? Lucky would never trust him again! With anything!

He put the thought aside. It would do him no good to concentrate on it.

If there were only something to distract him. Something besides darkness and vacuum, besides the faint vibration of his own footsteps and the sound of his own breath.

He stopped to check his position in the main shaft. The side passages had letters and numbers ground sharply into their walls, and time had done nothing to dull their sharpness. Checking wasn't difficult.

However, the low temperature made the chart brittle and difficult to handle, and that didn't sweeten his mood. He turned his suit-light on his chest controls in order that he might adjust the dehumidifier. The inner surface of his face-plate was beginning to mist over faintly from the moisture in his breath, probably because the temperature within rose with his temper, he told himself.

He had just completed the adjustment when he moved his head sharply to one side as though he were suddenly cocking an ear to listen.

It was exactly what he was doing. He strained to sense the rhythm of faint vibration that he "heard" now only because his own steps had ceased.

He held his breath, remained as motionless as the rocky wall of the tunnel.

"Lucky?" he breathed into the transmitter. "Lucky?" The fingers of his right hand had adjusted the controls. The carrier wave was scrambled. No one else would make sense out of that light whisper. But Lucky would, and soon his voice would come in answer. Bigman was ashamed to admit to himself how welcome that voice would be.

"Lucky?" he said again.

The vibration continued. There was no answer.

Bigman's breathing quickened, first with tension, then

with the savage joy born of excitement that always came over him when danger was in the offing.

There was someone else in the mines of Mercury with him. Someone other than Lucky.

Who, then? A Sirian? Had Lucky been right after all though he had thought he was merely putting up a smoke screen?

Maybe.

Bigman drew his blaster and put out his suit-light.

Did they know he was there? Were they coming to get him?

The vibrations weren't the blurred nonrhythmic "sound" of many people, or even two or three. To Bigman's keen ear, the distinctly separated "thrum-thrum" of vibration was the "sound" of one man's legs, rhythmically advancing.

And Bigman would meet any one man, anywhere, under any conditions.

Quietly, he put out his hand, touching the nearer wall. The vibrations sharpened noticeably. The other was in that direction then.

He moved forward quietly in the pitch-dark, his hand keeping a light touch on the wall. The vibrations being set up by the other were too intense, too careless. Either the other believed himself alone in the mines (as Bigman himself had until a moment before) or, if he were following Bigman, he wasn't wise in the ways of the vacuum.

Bigman's own footsteps had died to a murmur as he advanced catlike, yet the other's vibrations showed no change. Again, if the other had been following Bigman by sound, the sudden change in Bigman's progress should have been reflected in a change in the other's. It wasn't. The same conclusion, then as before.

He turned right at the next side-tunnel entrance and

continued. His hand on the wall at once kept him along the way and guided him toward the other.

And then there was the blinding flash of a suit-light far ahead in the darkness as the motion of another's body whipped the beam across him. Bigman froze against the wall.

The light vanished. The other had passed across the tunnel Bigman was on. He was not advancing along it. Bigman hurried forward lightly. He would find that cross tunnel and then he would be behind the other.

They would meet then. He, Bigman, representing Earth and the Council of Science, and the enemy representing—whom?

8

The Enemy in the Mines

Bigman had calculated correctly. The other's light was bobbing along ahead of him, as he found the opening. Its owner was unaware of him. He *must* be.

Bigman's blaster was ready. He might have shot unerringly, but a blaster would not have left much behind. Dead men tell no tales and dead enemies explain no mysteries.

He pursued with catlike patience, cutting down the distance between them, following the light, trying to estimate the nature of the enemy.

His blaster always ready, Bigman moved to make first contact. First, radio! His fingers set the controls quickly for general local transmission. The enemy might have no equipment to receive that on the wave lengths Bigman could deliver. Unlikely, but possible! Very unlikely and barely possible!

Yet it didn't matter. There was always the alternative of a light blaster bolt against the wall. It would make his point clearly enough. A blaster carried authority and had a plain way of speaking that was understood in any language anywhere.

He said, his tenor voice carrying all the force it could muster, "Stop, you! Stop where you are and don't turn around! There's a blaster beaded in on you!"

Bigman flashed on his suit-light, and in its glare the enemy froze. Nor did he make any effort to turn around, which was proof enough for Bigman that he had received the message.

Bigman said, "Now turn around. Slowly!"

The figure turned. Bigman kept his right hand in the path of his suit-light. Its metal sheath was clamped tightly about the large-caliber blaster. In the glow of the light, its outline was comfortingly clear.

Bigman said, "This blaster is fully charged. I've killed men with it before, and I'm a dead shot."

The enemy obviously had radio. He was obviously receiving, for he glanced at the blaster and made a motion as though to raise a hand to block off the blaster's force.

Bigman studied what he could see of the enemy's suit. It looked quite conventional (did the Sirians use such familiar models?).

Bigman said curtly, "Are you keyed in for radio transmission?"

There was sudden sound in his ears and he jumped. The voice was a familiar one, even under the disguising distortion of the radio; it said, "It's Peewee, isn't it?"

Never in his life had Bigman needed greater self-control to keep from using his blaster.

As it was, the weapon leaped convulsively in his hand and the figure facing him leaned quickly to one side.

"Urteil!" yelled Bigman.

His surprise turned to disappointment. No Sirian! Only Urteil!

Then the sharp thought: What was Urteil doing here?

Urteil said, "It's Urteil all right. So put away the bean-shooter."

"That gets put away when I feel like it," said Bigman. "What are you doing here?"

"The mines of Mercury are not your private property, I think."

"While I have the blaster they are, you fat-faced cobber." Bigman was thinking hard and, to a certain extent, futilely. What was there to do with this poisonous skunk? To take him back to the Dome would reveal the fact that Lucky was no longer in the mines. Bigman could tell them that Lucky had lingered behind, but then they would become either suspicious or concerned when Lucky failed to report. And of what crime could he accuse Urteil? The mines were free to all, at that.

On the other hand, he could not remain indefinitely pointing a blaster at the man.

If Lucky were here, he would know—

And as though a telepathic spark had crossed the vacuum between the two men, Urteil suddenly said, "And where's Starr, anyway?"

"That," said Bigman, "is nothing you have to worry about." Then, with sudden conviction, "You were following us, weren't you?" and he shoved his blaster forward a little as though encouraging the other to talk.

In the glare of Bigman's suit-light, the other's glassite-hidden face turned downward slightly as though to follow the blaster. He said, "What if I were?"

Again there was the impasse.

Bigman said, "You were going along a side passage. You were going to swing in behind us."

"I said——— What if I were?" Urteil's voice had almost a lazy quality about it, as though its owner were thoroughly relaxed, as though he enjoyed having a blaster pointed at him.

Urteil went on. "But where's your friend? Near here?"

"I know where he is. No need for you to worry."

"I insist on worrying. Call him. Your radio is on local transmission or I wouldn't hear you so well. . . . Do you mind if I turn on my fluid jet? I'm thirsty." His hand moved slowly.

"Careful," said Bigman.

"Just a drink."

Bigman watched tensely. He did not expect a weapon to be activated by chest control, but the suit-light could be suddenly raised to blinding intensity, or—or——— Well, anything.

But Urteil's fingers finished their motion while Bigman stood irresolute, and there was only the sound of swallowing.

"Scare you?" asked Urteil calmly.

Bigman could find nothing to say.

Urteil's voice grew sharp. "Well, call the man. Call Starr!"

Under the impact of the order, Bigman's hand began a movement and stopped.

Urteil laughed. "You almost adjusted radio controls, didn't you? You needed distance transmission. He's nowhere near here, is he?"

"No such thing," cried Bigman hotly. He was burning with mortification. The large and poisonous Urteil was clever. There he stood, the target of a blaster, yet winning the battle, proving himself master of the situation, while with every passing second Bigman's own position, in which he could neither shoot nor lower his blaster, leave nor stay, grew more untenable.

Wildly the thought gnawed at him: Why not shoot?

But he knew he could not. He would be able to advance no reason. And even if he could, the violent death of Senator Swenson's man would make tremendous trouble for the Council of Science. And for Lucky!

If only Lucky were here———

Partly because he wished that so ardently, his heart leaped as Urteil's light lifted slightly and focused beyond him, and he heard Urteil say, "No, I'm wrong after all and you're right. Here he comes."

Bigman whirled. "Lucky————"

In his right mind, Bigman would have waited calmly enough for Lucky to reach them, for Lucky's arm to be on his shoulder, but Bigman was not quite in his right mind. His position was impossible, his desire for a way out overwhelming.

He had time only for that one cry of "Lucky" before going down under the impact of a body fully twice as massive as his own.

For a few moments he retained the grip on his blaster, but another arm was tearing at his hand, strong fingers were wrenching and twisting his. Bigman's breath was knocked out of him, his brain was whirling with the suddenness of the attack, and his blaster went flying.

The weight lifted from him, and when he turned to struggle to his feet Urteil was towering over him and Bigman was staring into the muzzle of his own blaster.

"I have one of my own," said Urteil, grimly, "but I think I'd rather use yours. Don't move. Stay that way. On hands and knees. That's right."

Never in his life had Bigman so hated himself. To be tricked and hoodwinked this way. He almost deserved death. He would almost rather die than ever have to face Lucky and say, "He looked behind me and said you were coming so I turned————"

He said in a strangled voice, "Shoot, if you have the nerve for it. Shoot, and Lucky will track you down and see to it that you spend the rest of your life chained to the smallest, coldest asteroid ever used as a prison."

"Lucky will do that? Where is he?"

"Find him."

"I will because you'll tell me where he is. And tell me, too, why he came down to the mines in the first place. What's he doing here?"

"To find Sirians. You heard him."

"To find comet gas," growled Urteil. "That senile fool, Peverale, may talk Sirians, but your friend never believed any of it. Not even if he only has the brains you do. He came down for another reason. You tell me."

"Why should I?"

"To save your miserable life."

"That's not enough reason for me," said Bigman, and he rose to his feet and took a step forward.

Urteil moved backward till he was leaning against the wall of the tunnel. "One more motion and I'll blast you with pleasure. I don't need your information very badly. It will save time, but not much. If I spend more than five minutes with you, it's a waste.

"Now let me tell you exactly what I think. Maybe it will teach you that you and your tin hero, Starr, are fooling nobody. Neither one of you is good for anything more than tricks with force-knives against an unarmed man."

Bigman thought gloomily: *That's* what's griping the cobber. I made him look like a jackass in front of the boys, and he's waiting for me to crawl.

"If you're going to do all that talking," he said, squeezing as much contempt into his voice as he could manage, "you might as well shoot. I'd rather be blasted than talked to death."

"Don't race for it, little fellow, don't race for it. In the first place, Senator Swenson is breaking the Council of Science. You're just an item, a tiny one. Your friend Starr is just another item, and not a much bigger one. I'm the one who's going to do the breaking. We've got the Council where we want it. The people of Earth know it's riddled with corruption, that its officers waste the taxpayers' money and line their own pockets————"

"That's a filthy lie," broke in Bigman.

"We'll let the people decide that. Once we puncture the phony propaganda the Council puts out, we'll see what the people think."

"You try that. Go ahead and try!"

"We intend to. We'll succeed too. And this will be exhibit number one: you two in the mines. I know why you're here. The Sirians! Huh! Starr either put Peverale up to telling the story, or he just took advantage of it. I'll tell you what you two are doing down here. You're faking the Sirians. You're setting up a Sirian camp to show people.

" 'I chased them off singlehanded,' Starr will say. 'I, Lucky Starr, big hero.' The sub-etherics make a big deal out of it and the Council calls off its Project Light on the sly. They've milked it for all it's worth, and they're getting out with their skins. . . . Except that they won't be because I'll catch Starr in the act and he'll be so much mud under shoe and so will the Council."

Bigman was sick with fury. He longed to tear at the other with his bare hands, but somehow he managed to hold himself in leash. He knew why Urteil was talking as he was. It was because the man *didn't* know as much as he pretended. He was trying to get more out of Bigman by making him blind-mad.

In a low voice, Bigman tried to turn the tables. "You know, you putrid cobber, if anyone ever punctured you and let out the comet gas, your peanut-sized soul would show itself clear. Once they let the rot out of you, you'd collapse to nothing but a loose sack of dirty skin."

Urteil shouted, "That's enough————"

But Bigman shouted over him, his high-pitched voice ringing. "Shoot, you yellow pirate. You showed yellow at the dinner table. Stand up to me, man to man, with bare fists and you'll show yellow again, bloated as you are."

Bigman was tense now. Let Urteil act in rash haste now. Let Urteil aim on impulse and Bigman would jump. Death was probable, but there would be a chance———

But Urteil seemed only to stiffen and grow colder.

"If you don't talk, I'll kill you. And nothing will happen to me. I'll claim self-defense and make it stick."

"Not with Lucky, you won't."

"He'll have his own troubles. When I'm through with him, his opinions won't mean a thing." The blaster in Urteil's hand was steady. "Are you going to try to run for it?"

"From you?" Bigman said.

"It's up to you," said Urteil coldly.

Bigman waited, waited without saying a word while Urteil's arm grew stiff and Urteil's headpiece dropped slightly as though he were taking aim, though at point-blank range he could not miss.

Bigman counted the moments, trying to choose the one in which to make his desperate jump for life as Lucky had when Mindes had similarly aimed at him. But here there was no second party to tackle Urteil as Bigman had tackled Mindes on that occasion. And Urteil was no pan-icky, mind-sick Mindes. He would laugh and aim again.

Bigman's muscles tensed for that final jump. He did not expect to live for more than five more seconds, perhaps.

9

Dark and Light

But with his body taut, his leg muscles almost vibrating in the first part-instant of contraction, there was a sudden hoarse cry of utter surprise in Bigman's ears.

They were standing there, both of them, in a gray, dark world in which their beams of light etched one another out. Outside the beams of light, nothing, so that the sudden blob of motion that flashed across the line of sight made no sense at first.

His first reaction, his first thought was: Lucky! Had Lucky returned? Had he somehow mastered the situation, turned the tables?

But there was motion again, and the thought of Lucky faded away.

It was as though a fragment of the rocky wall of the shaft had worked itself loose and was drifting downward in the lazy fall that was characteristic of Mercury's low gravity.

A rope of rock that was somehow flexible, that struck Urteil's shoulder and—clung. One such encircled his waist already. Another moved slowly, bringing itself down and around as though it were part of an unreal world of slowed motion. But as its edge circled Urteil's arm and touched the metal covering Urteil's chest, arm and chest closed upon one another. It was as though the sluggish and seemingly brittle rock contained the irresistible strength of a boa constrictor.

If Urteil's first reaction had been one of surprise, there was now nothing but complete terror in his voice.

"Cold," he croaked harshly. "They're cold."

Bigman's whirling mind was having trouble encompassing the new situation. A piece of that rock had encircled Urteil's lower arm and wrist. The butt of the blaster was clamped in place.

A final rope came floating down. They were so rocklike in appearance that they were invisible until one actually detached itself from the wall.

The ropes were connected one with another as a single organism, but there was no nucleus, no "body." It was like a stony octopus consisting of nothing but tentacles.

Bigman had a kind of explosion of thought.

He thought of rock developing life through the long ages of Mercurian evolution. A completely different form of life from anything Earth knew. A life that lived on scraps of heat alone.

Why not? The tentacles might crawl from place to place, seeking any bit of heat that might exist. Bigman could see them drifting toward Mercury's North Pole when mankind was first established there. First the mines and then the Observatory Dome supplied them with unending trickles of heat.

Man could be their prey too. Why not? A human being was a source of heat. Occasionally an isolated miner might have been trapped. Paralyzed with sudden cold and terror, he would be unable to call for help. Minutes later his power unit would be too low to make a radio call possible in any case. Still later, he would be dead, a frozen relic.

Cook's mad story of the deaths in the mines made sense.

All this passed through Bigman's mind almost in one flash while he remained unmoving, still struggling with a sense of stunned amazement at the sudden new turn of events.

Urteil's voice was somewhere between a moan and a harsh gasp. "I—can't——— Help me—help———It's cold—cold———"

Bigman yelled, "Hold on. I'm coming."

Gone in a moment was any thought that this man was an enemy, that moments before he had been on the point of killing Bigman in cold blood. The little Martian recognized but one thing; here was a man, helpless in the grip of something nonhuman.

Since man had first left Earth and ventured into the dangers and mysteries of outer space, there had grown up a stern, unwritten law. Human feuds must be forgotten when man faced the common enemy, the nonhuman and inhuman forces of the other worlds.

It might be that not everyone adhered to that law, but Bigman did.

He was at Urteil's side in a bound, tearing at his arm.

Urteil mumbled, "Help me———"

Bigman grasped at the blaster Urteil still held, trying to avoid the tentacle that encircled Urteil's clutching fist. Bigman noted absently that the tentacle didn't curve smoothly like a snake would. It bent in sections as though arranged in numerous stiff segments hinged together.

Bigman's other hand, groping for purchase on Urteil's suit, made momentary contact with one of the tentacles and sprang away reflectively. The cold was an icy shaft, penetrating and burning his hand.

Whatever method the creatures had of withdrawing heat, it was like nothing he had ever heard of.

Bigman yanked desperately at the blaster, heaving and wrenching. He did not notice at first the alien touch on his back, then—iciness lay over him and did not go away. When he tried to jump away he found he could not. A tentacle had reached out for him and embraced him.

The two men might have grown together, so firmly were they bound.

The physical pain of the cold grew, and Bigman wrenched at the blaster like a man possessed. Was it giving?

Urteil's voice startled him as it murmured, "No use————"

Urteil staggered and then, slowly, under the weak pull of Mercury's gravity, he toppled over to one side, carrying Bigman with him.

Bigman's body was numb. It was losing sensation. He could scarcely tell whether he was still holding the muzzle of the blaster or not. If he was, was it yielding to his wild, sidewise wrenches, or was it a last gasp of wishful thinking?

His suit-light was dimming as his power-unit drained much of its energy into the voracious power-sucking ropes.

Death by freezing could not be far away.

Lucky, having left Bigman in the mines of Mercury, and having changed to an inso-suit in the quiet of the hangared *Shooting Starr,* stepped out onto the surface of Mercury and turned his face toward the "white ghost of the Sun."

For long minutes he stood motionless, taking in once again the milky luminescence of the Sun's corona.

Absently, as he watched, he flexed his smoothly-muscled limbs one at a time. The inso-suit worked more smoothly than an ordinary space-suit. That, combined with its lightness, lent it an unusual sensation of not being there altogether. In an environment obviously airless, it was disconcerting, but Lucky brushed aside any feeling of uneasiness he might have had and surveyed the sky.

The stars were as numerous and brilliant as in open space, and he paid them little attention. It was something else he wanted to see. It was two days now, standard Earth time, since he had last seen these skies. In two days, Mercury had moved one forty-fourth of the way along its orbit around the Sun. That meant over eight degrees of sky had appeared in the east and over eight degrees had disappeared in the west. That meant new stars could be seen.

New planets too. Venus and Earth ought both to have risen above the horizon in the interval.

And there they were. Venus was the higher of the two, a diamond-bright bit of white light, much more brilliant than it ever appeared to be on Earth. From Earth, Venus was seen at a disadvantage. It was between Earth and the Sun, so that when Venus was closest, Earth could see only its dark side. On Mercury, Venus could be seen at the full.

At the moment, Venus was thirty-three million miles from Mercury. At the closest, however, it could approach to within almost twenty million miles, and then keen eyes could actually see it as a tiny disk.

Even as it was, its light almost rivaled that of the corona, and, staring at the ground, Lucky thought he could make out a double shadow extending from his feet, one cast by the corona (a fuzzy one) and one by Venus (a sharp one). He wondered if, under ideal circumstances, there might not be a triple shadow, the third being cast by Earth itself.

He found Earth, too, without difficulty. It was quite

near the horizon, and, though it was brighter than any star or planet in its own skies, it was pale in comparison to the glorious Venus. It was less brightly lit by its more distant Sun; it was less cloudy and therefore reflected less of the light it did give. Furthermore, it was twice as far from Mercury as Venus was.

Yet in one respect it was incomparably more interesting. Where Venus's light was a pure white, Earth's light was a blue-green glow.

And more than that, there was near it, just skirting the horizon, the smaller yellow light of Earth's Moon. Together, Earth and Moon made a unique sight in the skies of the other planets inside the orbit of Jupiter. A double planet, traveling majestically across the skies in each other's company, the smaller circling the larger in a motion which, against the sky, looked like a slow wobble from side to side.

Lucky stared at the sight perhaps longer than he should have, yet he could not help it. The conditions of his life took him far from his home planet on occasion, and that made it all the dearer to him. All the quadrillions of human beings throughout the Galaxy had originated on Earth. Through almost all of man's history, Earth had been his only home, in fact. What man could look on Earth's speck of light without emotion?

Lucky tore his eyes away, shaking his head. There was work to be done.

He set out with firm stride toward the coronal glow, skimming close to the surface as was proper in low gravity, keeping his suit-light on and his gaze fixed at the ground before him in order to guard against its rough unevenness.

He had an idea of what he might find, but it was purely a notion, backed as yet by no definite fact. Lucky had a horror of discussing such notions, which were sometimes nothing more than intuitions. He even disliked lingering on them in his own mind. There was too great a danger of growing used to the idea, of beginning to depend upon it as truth, of closing the mind unintentionally to alternate possibilities.

He had seen this happen to the ebullient, ready-to-believe, ready-to-act Bigman. He had watched vague possibilities become firm convictions in Bigman's mind more than once———

He smiled gently at the thought of the little bantam. Injudicious he might be, levelheaded never, but he was loyal and ablaze with fearlessness. Lucky would rather have Bigman at his side than a fleet of armored spacecruisers manned by giants.

He missed the gnome-faced Martian now, as he leaped flatly along the Mercurian terrain, and it was partly to wipe out that uncomfortable sensation that Lucky returned to thoughts of the problem at hand.

The trouble was that there were so many crosscurrents.

First, there was Mindes himself, nervous, unstable, unsure of himself. It had never been entirely settled, really, how far his attack on Lucky had been momentary madness and how far settled calculation. There was Gardoma, who was Mindes's friend. Was he a dedicated idealist caught up in the dream of Project Light, or was he with Mindes for purely practical reasons? If so, what were they?

Urteil, himself, was a main focus of disturbance. He was intent on ruining the Council, and the object of his main attack was Mindes. Yet his arrogance naturally spread hate of himself wherever he went. Mindes hated him, of course, and so did Gardoma. Dr. Peverale hated him in a much more restrained fashion. He would not even discuss the man with Lucky.

At the banquet, Cook had seemed to shrink from talking to Urteil, never let his eyes as much as move in his direction. Was this simply because Cook was anxious to avoid the sharp, flailing edge of Urteil's tongue, or were there more specific reasons?

Cook thought little of Peverale too. He was ashamed of the old man's preoccupation with Sirius.

And there was one question that remained to be answered aside from all these things. Who had slashed Lucky's inso-suit?

There were too many factors. Lucky had a line of thought that threaded through them, but as yet that line was weak. Again he avoided concentrating on that line. He must retain an open mind.

The ground was sloping upward and he had adjusted his stride to suit it automatically. So preoccupied was he with his thoughts that the sight that caught his eyes as he topped that rise found him unprepared and struck him with amazement.

The extreme upper edge of the Sun was above the broken horizon, yet not the Sun itself. Only the prominences that edged the Sun showed, a small segment of them.

The prominences were brilliant red in color, and one, in the very center of those visible, was made up of blazing streamers moving upward and outward with inching slowness.

Sharp and bright against the rock of Mercury, undimmed by atmosphere, unhazed by dust, it was a sight of incredible beauty. The tongue of flame seemed to be growing out of Mercury's dark crust as though the planet's horizon were on fire or a volcano of more than giant size had suddenly erupted and been trapped in midblaze.

Yet those prominences were incomparably more than

anything that could have appeared on Mercury. The one he watched, Lucky knew, was large enough to swallow a hundred Earths whole, or five thousand Mercuries. And there it burned in atomic fire, lighting up Lucky and all his surroundings.

He turned off his suit-light to see.

Those surfaces of the rocks that faced directly toward the prominences were awash with ruddy light, all other surfaces were black as coal. It was as though someone had painted a bottomless pit with streaks of red. Truly it was the "red ghost of the Sun."

The shadow of Lucky's hand on his chest made a patch of black. The ground ahead was more treacherous, since the patches of light that caught every fragment of unevenness fooled the eye into a false estimate of the nature of the surface.

Lucky turned on his suit-light once again and moved forward toward the prominences along the curve of Mercury, the Sun rising six minutes of arc for every mile he went.

That meant that in less than a mile, the body of the Sun would be visible and he would be on Mercury's Sun-side.

Lucky had no way of knowing then that at that moment Bigman was facing death by freezing. His thought as he faced the Sun-side was only this: There lies the danger and the crux of the problem, and there lies the solution too.

10

The Sun-Side

More of the prominences were now visible. Their redness brightened. The corona did not vanish (there was no atmosphere to scatter the prominence light and wash out dimmer glows), but it seemed less important now. The stars were still out and would stay out, Lucky knew, even when Mercury's sun was full in the sky, but who could pay attention to them now?

Lucky ran forward eagerly in the steady stride which he could maintain for hours without feeling unduly tired. Under the circumstances, he felt he could have maintained such a stride even under Earth's gravity.

And then, with no warning, no premonitory glow in the sky, no hint from any atmosphere, *there was the Sun!*

Rather, there was a hairline that was the Sun. It was an unbearable line of light edging a notch of broken rock on the horizon, as though some celestial painter had outlined the gray stone in brilliant white.

Lucky looked backward. Across the uneven ground that lay behind him there were the splotches of prominence-red. But now, just at his feet, there was a wash of white, catching crystal formations in glinting highlights.

He moved onward again, and the line of light became first a small splotch and then a larger one.

The boundary of the Sun was clearly visible, lifting a bit above the horizon in its center, curving gently down on each side. The curve was awesomely flat to one whose eyes were accustomed to the curvature of Earth's Sun.

Nor did the Sun's blaze drown out the prominences which crawled along its edge like flaming red snake-hair. The prominences were all over the Sun, of course, but only at the edge could they be seen. On the Sun's face, they were lost amid the glare below.

And over all was the corona.

Lucky marveled, even as he watched, at the manner in which the inso-suit had been adapted to its purpose.

A glance at the edge of Mercury's Sun would have been blinding to unprotected eyes, blinding forever. The visible light was bad enough in its intensity, but it was the hard ultra-violet, unfiltered by atmosphere, that would have meant death to vision . . . and to life itself, eventually.

Yet the glass of the inso-suit's face-plate was so arranged molecularly as to grow less transparent in direct proportion to the brightness of the light that fell upon it. Only a small fraction of a percent of the Solar blaze penetrated the plate, and he could stare at the Sun without danger, almost without discomfort. Yet at the same time, the light of the corona and the stars come through undiminished.

The inso-suit protected him in other ways. It was impregnated with lead and bismuth, not enough so as to raise its weight unduly, but enough to block out ultraviolet and x-radiation from the Sun. The suit carried a positive charge to deflect most of the cosmic rays to one side. Mercury's magnetic field was weak, but Mercury was close to the Sun and the cosmic ray density was large.

Still, cosmic rays are composed of positively-charged protons, and like charges repel like.

And, of course, the suit protected him against the heat, not only by its insulating composition but by its mirrorlike reflecting surface, a pseudo-liquid molecular layer that could be activated by a touch on the controls.

In fact, Lucky reflected, when the advantages of the inso-suit were considered, it seemed a pity that it was not standard protection under all conditions. Unfortunately, he realized, its structural weakness, as a result of lacking metal in real quantity, made it impractical for use except where protection against heat and radiation were paramount considerations.

Lucky was a mile into the Sun-side now and not conscious of undue heat.

This did not surprise him. To stay-at-homes who confined their knowledge of space to the sub-etheric thriller shows, the Sun-side of any airless planet was simply a solid mass of undeviating heat.

This was an oversimplification. It depended on how high the Sun was in the sky. From this point on Mercury, for instance, with only a portion of the Sun above the horizon, comparatively little heat reached the surface, and that little was spread over a lot of ground as the radiation struck almost horizontally.

The "weather" changed as one went deeper into the Sun-side and finally, when one reached that portion where the Sun was high in the sky, it was everything the sub-etherics said it was.

And besides, there were always the shadows. In the absence of air, light and heat traveled in a straight line. Neither could reach within the shadow except for small fractions which were reflected or radiated into it from neighboring sunlit portions. The shadows were therefore frosty cold and carbon black though the Sun was ever so hot and bright.

Lucky was growing more aware of these shadows. At first, after the upper line of Sun had appeared, the ground had been almost all shadow with only occasional patches of light. Now, as the Sun rose higher and higher, the light spread and coalesced until the shadows were distinct things hovering behind boulders and hills.

At one time Lucky deliberately plunged into the shadow of a rise of rock a hundred yards across, and it was as though for a long minute he were back on the dark-side. The heat of the Sun, which he had scarcely noticed while it beat upon him, became evident by its decrease in the shadow. All around the shadow the ground glimmered brightly in sunlight, but within the shadow his suit-light was necessary to guide his steps.

He could not help noticing the difference in the surfaces that were in the shadow from those in the light. For on the Sun-side, at least, Mercury did have a kind of atmosphere. Not one in the Earthly sense, no nitrogen, oxygen, carbon dioxide, or water vapor, nothing like that. On the Sun-side, however, mercury would boil in places. Sulfur would be liquid and so would a number of volatile compounds. Traces of the vapor of such substances would cling to Mercury's superheated surface. These vapors froze out in the shadows.

This was brought forcibly to Lucky's mind when his insulated fingers brushed over the dark surface of one outcropping and came away smeared with a frozen hoar of mercury, glittering in his suit-light. It changed quickly into clinging liquid droplets as he emerged into the Sun and then, more slowly, evaporated away.

Slowly, the Sun seemed to be getting hotter. That did not worry Lucky. Even if it grew uncomfortably hot, he could always dodge into a shadow to cool off when necessary.

Short-wave radiation was perhaps a more important consideration. Lucky doubted even that was serious in this short-term exposure. Workers on Mercury had a horror of radiation, because they were continually exposed to small amounts. Lucky recalled Mindes's emphasis on the fact that the saboteur he had seen had remained standing in the Sun. It was natural that Mindes should be disturbed at that. When exposure was chronic any lengthening of the time of exposure was foolish. In Lucky's own case, however, exposure would be short-term—he hoped.

He ran across patches of blackish ground that stood out somberly against Mercury's more general reddish gray. The reddish gray was familiar enough. It resembled the soil of Mars, a mixture of silicates with the addition of iron oxide, which gave it that ruddy tinge.

The black was more puzzling. Wherever it was, the ground was definitely hotter, since black absorbed more of the Sun's heat.

He bent as he ran and found the black areas crumbly rather than gritty. Some of it came up on the palm of his gauntlet. He looked at it. It might be graphite, it might be iron or copper sulfide. It might be any of a number of things, but he would have bet on its being some variety of impure iron sulfide.

He paused in the shadow of a rock, finally, and took stock. In an hour and a half, he estimated he had traveled some fifteen miles, judging from the fact that the Sun was just about entirely above the horizon now. (At the moment, he was more interested in sipping sparingly at the suit's supply of liquid nutrient mixture than in estimating distance, however.)

Somewhere to the left of him were cables of Mindes's Project Light. Somewhere to the right of him were others.

Their exact location did not matter. They covered hundreds of square miles, and to wander aimlessly among them in search of a saboteur would have been foolish.

Mindes had tried it, hit or miss, and had failed. If the object or objects he had seen had indeed been the saboteur, there might have been a warning from inside the Dome. Mindes had made no secret of the fact that he was heading out to Sun-side.

Lucky had, however. There would be no warning, he hoped.

And he had a form of help Mindes had not had. He flipped his small ergometer out of the pouch he had placed it in. He held it before him in cupped palm, his suit-light playing full on it.

Once activated, its red signal-patch blazed with incredible fury when held out in the sunlight. Lucky smiled tightly and adjusted it. There was short-wave radiation from the Sun.

The flame died.

Patiently, then, Lucky stepped out into the sunlight and scanned the horizon in every direction. Where, if anywhere, was there a source of atomic power other than the Sun? He found an indication of the Dome, of course, but the light due to that region increased as he dipped the ergometer downward. The Dome's power plant was nearly a mile underground, and a twenty degree downward dip was required for maximum power where he stood.

He turned slowly, the ergometer held gingerly between the two forefingers of each hand in order that the opaque material of the suit should not block off the telltale radiation. Around a second time and a third.

It seemed to him that in one particular direction there had been the briefest of flashes—scarcely enough to see against the sunlight, really. Perhaps no more than the product of wishful thinking.

He tried again.

No mistake now!

Lucky sighted along the direction in which that glow had appeared and moved in that direction. He did not conceal from himself the fact that he might only be tracking down a patch of radioactive ore.

He caught his first glimpse of one of Mindes's cables nearly a mile farther on.

It was not a single cable at all, rather a web of cables, lying half buried in the ground. He followed it some hundreds of yards and came upon a square metal plate, about four feet on a side and polished to a high gloss. It reflected the stars as though it were a clear pool of water.

No doubt, thought Lucky, if he placed himself in the proper position he would find himself staring into the reflection of the Sun. He became aware that the plate was changing its angle of elevation, becoming less horizontal, more vertical. He looked away to see if it were shifting in such a way as to catch the Sun.

When he looked back he was amazed. The clear square was no longer clear. Instead, it was a dull black, so dull that not all the light of Mercury's Sun seemed to be able to brighten it.

Then, as he watched, that dullness trembled, broke, and fragmented.

It was bright again.

He watched it through three more cycles as the angle of elevation made it more and more vertical. First, incredible reflection; then, complete dullness. During the dullness, Lucky realized, light would be absorbed; during the glossiness, it would be reflected. The alternation in phase might be perfectly regular, or there might be a deliberate, irregular pattern. He could not linger to find out and, if he did, it was doubtful whether his knowledge of hyperoptics would be enough to enable him to understand the purpose of it all.

Presumably hundreds or even thousands of such squares, all connected by a network of cables and all powered from an atomic micropile inside the Dome, were absorbing and reflecting light in a set way at different angles to the Sun. Presumably, this, in some way, could force light energy through hyperspace in a controlled manner.

And, presumably, torn cables and smashed plates prevented the over-all pattern from being properly completed.

Lucky tried his ergometer again. It was much brighter now, and again he followed in the indicated direction.

Brighter, brighter! Whatever it was he was following, it was something that was changing its position. The source of gamma rays was not a fixed point on Mercury's surface.

And *that* meant it was not merely an outcropping of radioactive ore. It was something portable, and to Lucky that meant it was man or something belonging to man.

Lucky saw the figure first as a moving speck, black against the fire-lit ground. The sight came after a long spell in the open Sun, at a time when he had been about to find himself a shadow in which to let the slowly accumulating heat drain away.

Instead, he accelerated his pace now. He estimated the temperature outside his suit to be at not quite the boiling point of water. Inside, fortunately, it was considerably lower.

He thought grimly: If the Sun were overhead and not at the horizon, even these suits would be of no use.

The figure paid no attention to him. It continued on its own path, its gait showing it far from as expert in handling low gravity as was Lucky. Indeed its motion might almost be described as lumbering. Yet it managed to devour space. It covered the ground.

It wore no inso-suit. Even at long distance, the surface exposed to Lucky's gaze was obviously one of metal.

Lucky paused briefly in the shade of a rock but forced himself into the open again before there was time for much cooling.

The figure seemed unbothered by the heat. At least, in the time Lucky watched him he made no move to enter shadows, though he passed within a few feet of some.

Lucky nodded thoughtfully. It all fit well.

He sped on. The heat was beginning to feel like something he could touch and squeeze. But it would only be a few moments now.

He had abandoned his low-slung lope now. Every bit of his muscular power was being put into giant strides of up to fifteen feet each.

He shouted, "You! You there! Turn around!"

He said it peremptorily, with all the authority he could produce, hoping that the other could receive his radio signal and that he would not be reduced to sign language.

Slowly the figure turned, and Lucky's nostrils flared in a kind of cold satisfaction. So far, at least, it was as he thought, for the figure was no man—nothing human at all!

11

Saboteur!

The figure was tall, taller even than Lucky. It was nearly seven feet tall, in fact, and broad in proportion. All of the figure that met the eye was gleaming metal, brilliant where it caught the Sun's rays, black with shadow where it did not.

But underneath that metal was no flesh and blood, only more metal, gears, tubes, a micropile which powered the figure with nuclear energy and produced the gamma rays that Lucky had detected with his pocket ergometer.

The limbs of the creature were monstrous and its legs were straddled far apart as it stood there facing Lucky. What passed for its eyes were two photoelectric cells that gleamed a deep red. Its mouth was a slash across the metal on the lower part of its face.

It was a mechanical man, a robot, and it took Lucky no more than one glance to know that it was no robot of Earth's manufacture. Earth had invented the positronic robot, but it had never built any model like this.

The robot's mouth opened and closed in irregular movements as though it were speaking.

Lucky said, "I cannot hear sound in a vacuum, robot."

He said it sternly, knowing that it was essential to establish himself as a man and therefore a master at once. "Switch to radio."

And now the robot's mouth remained motionless but a voice sounded in Lucky's receiver, harsh and uneven, with the words unnaturally spaced. It said, "What is your business, sir? Why are you here?"

"Do not question me," said Lucky. "Why are *you* here?"

A robot could only be truthful. It said, "I have been instructed to destroy certain objects at intervals."

"By whom?"

"I have been instructed not to answer that question."

"Are you of Sirian manufacture?"

"I was constructed on one of the planets of the Sirian Confederation."

Lucky frowned. The creature's voice was quite unpleasant. The few robots of Earth manufacture that Lucky had had occasion to see in experimental laboratories had been outfitted with voices boxes which, by direct sound or by radio, seemed as pleasant and natural as a well-cultivated human voice. Surely the Sirians would have improved on that.

Lucky's mind shifted to a more immediate problem. He said, "I must find a shadowed area. Come with me."

The robot said at once, "I will direct you to the nearest shade." It set off at a trot, its metal legs moving with a certain irregularity.

Lucky followed the creature. He needed no direction to reach the shade, but he lagged behind to watch the robot's gait.

What had seemed to Lucky, from a distance, to be a lumbering or a clumsy pace, turned out, at close hand, to be a pronounced limp. A limp and a harsh voice. Two imperfections in this robot whose outer appearance was that of a magnificent mechanical marvel.

It struck him forcibly that the robot might not be adjusted to the heat and radiation of Mercury. Exposure had damaged it, probably. Lucky was scientist enough to feel a twinge of regret at that. It was too beautiful to have to endure such damage.

He regarded the machine with admiration. Underneath that massive skull of chrome-steel was a delicate ovoid of sponge platinum-iridium about the size of a human brain. Within it, quadrillions of quadrillions of positrons came into being and vanished in millionths of a second. As they came into being and vanished they traced precalculated paths which duplicated, in a simplified way, the thinking cells of the human brain.

Engineers had calculated out those positronic paths to suit humanity, and into them they had designed the "Three Laws of Robotics."

The First Law was that a robot could not harm a human being or let one come to harm. Nothing came ahead of that. Nothing could substitute for it.

The Second Law was that a robot must obey orders except those that would break the First Law.

The Third Law allowed a robot to protect itself, provided the First and Second Laws weren't broken.

Lucky came out of his short reverie when the robot stumbled and almost fell. There was no unevenness in the ground that Lucky could see, no trifling ridge that might have caught his toe. If there had been, a line of black shadow would have revealed it.

The ground was table-smooth at that point. The robot's stride had simply broken for no reason and thrown him to one side. The robot recovered after threshing about wildly. Having done that, it resumed its stride toward the shade as though nothing had happened.

Lucky thought: It's definitely in poor working order.

They entered the shadow together, and Lucky turned on his suit-light.

He said, "You do wrong to destroy necessary equipment. You are doing harm to men."

There was no emotion in the robot's face; there could be none. Nor was there emotion in its voice. It said, "I am obeying orders."

"That is the Second Law," said Lucky severely. "Still, you may not obey orders that harm human beings. That would be to violate the First Law."

"I have not seen any men. I have harmed no one."

"You have harmed men you did not see. I tell you that."

"I have harmed no man," said the robot stubbornly, and Lucky frowned at the unthinking repetition. Despite its polished appearance, perhaps it was not a very advanced model.

The robot went on. "I have been instructed to avoid men. I have been warned when men were coming, but I was not warned about you."

Lucky stared out past the shadow at the glittering Mercurian landscape, ruddy and gray for the most part but blotched with a large area of the crumbly black material which seemed so common in this part of Mercury. He thought of Mindes spotting the robot twice (his story made sense now) and losing it when he tried to get closer. His own secret invasion of the Sun-side, combined with the use of an ergometer, had turned the trick, fortunately.

He said suddenly and forcefully, "*Who* warned you to avoid men?"

Lucky didn't really expect to catch the robot. A robot's mind is machinery, he thought. It cannot be tricked or fooled, any more than you can trick a suit-light into going on by jumping at the switch and pretending to close contact.

The robot said, "I have been instructed not to answer that question." Then slowly, creakily, as though the words were coming out against its will, it said, "I do not wish you to ask such questions any longer. They are disturbing."

Lucky thought: To break the First Law would be more disturbing still.

Deliberately he stepped out of the shadow into the sunlight.

He said to the robot, who followed, "What is your serial number?"

"RL-726."

"Very well, RL-726, you understand I am a man?"

"Yes."

"I am not equipped to withstand the heat of Mercury's Sun."

"Nor am I," said the robot.

"I realize that," said Lucky, thinking of the robot's near-fall a few minutes earlier. "Nevertheless, a man is much less equipped for it than is a robot. Do you understand that?"

"Yes."

"Now, then, listen. I want you to stop your destructive activities, and I want you to tell me who ordered you to destroy equipment."

"I am instructed——"

"If you do not obey me," said Lucky loudly, "I will remain here in the Sun until I am killed and you will have broken the First Law, since you would have allowed me to be killed when you could have stopped it."

Lucky waited grimly. A robot's statement could not be accepted as evidence, of course, in any court, but it would assure him that he was on the right track if it were to say what he expected it to.

But the robot said nothing. It swayed. One eye blinked out suddenly (more imperfection!), then came to life. Its voice sounded in a wordless squawk, then it said in an almost drunken mumble, "I will carry you to safety."

"I would resist," said Lucky, "and you would have to harm me. If you answer my question, I will return to the shade of my own accord, and you will have saved my life without any damage to me at all."

Silence.

Lucky said, "Will you tell me who ordered you to destroy equipment?"

And suddenly the robot lunged forward, coming to within two feet of Lucky before stopping. "I told you not to ask that question."

Its hands moved forward as though to seize Lucky but did not complete the motion.

Lucky watched grimly and without concern. A robot could not harm a human being.

But then the robot lifted one of those mighty hands and put it to its head, for all the world as though it were a man with a headache.

Headache!

A sudden thought stabbed at Lucky. Great Galaxy! He'd been blind, stupidly, criminally blind!

It wasn't the robot's legs that were out of order, nor its voice, nor its eyes. How could the heat affect them? It was—it had to be—the positronic brain itself that was affected; the delicate positronic brain subjected to the direct heat and radiation of the Mercurian Sun for how long? Months?

That brain must be partially broken down already.

If the robot had been human, one would say he was in

one of the stages of mental breakdown. One might say he was on the road to insanity.

A mad robot! Driven mad by heat and radiation!

How far would the Three Laws hold in a broken-down positronic brain?

And now Lucky Starr stood there, threatening a robot with his own death, while that same robot, nearly mad, advanced toward him, arms outstretched.

The very dilemma in which Lucky had placed the robot might be adding to that madness.

Cautiously, Lucky retreated. He said, "Do you feel well?"

The robot said nothing. Its steps quickened.

Lucky thought: If it's ready to break the First Law, it must be on the point of complete dissolution. A positronic brain would have to be in pieces to be capable of that.

Yet, on the other hand, the robot had endured for months. It might endure for months more.

He talked in a desperate attempt to delay matters and allow time for more thought.

He said, "Does your head ache?"

"Ache?" said the robot. "I do not understand the meaning of the word."

Lucky said, "I am growing warm. We had better retire to the shadow."

No more talk of heating himself to death. He retreated at a half-run now.

The robot's voice rumbled. "I have been told to prevent any interference with the orders given me."

Lucky reached for his blaster and he sighed. It would be unfortunate if he were forced to destroy the robot. It was a magnificent work of man, and the Council could investigate its workings with profit. And to destroy it without even having obtained the desired information was repugnant to him.

Lucky said, "Stop where you are."

The robot's arms moved jerkily as it lunged, and Lucky escaped by a hair as he floated away in a sidewise twist, taking the fullest advantage of Mercury's gravity.

If he could maneuver his way into the shadow; if the robot followed him there——

The coolness might calm those disordered positronic paths. It might become tamer, more reasonable, and Lucky might be spared the necessity of its destruction.

Lucky dodged again, and again the robot rushed past, its metal legs kicking up spurts of black grit that settled back to Mercury promptly and cleanly since there was no atmosphere to keep it in suspension. It was an eerie chase, the tread of man and robot hushed and silent in the vacuum.

Lucky's confidence grew somewhat. The robot's movements had grown jerkier. Its control of the gears and relays that manipulated its limbs was imperfect and growing more so.

Yet the robot was making an obvious attempt to head him off from the shadow. It was definitely and beyond any doubt trying to kill him.

And still Lucky could not bring himself to use the blaster.

He stopped short. The robot stopped too. They were face to face, five feet apart, standing on the black patch of iron sulfide. The blackness seemed to make the heat all the greater and Lucky felt a gathering faintness. The robot stood grimly between Lucky and the shade.

Lucky said, "Out of my way." Talking was difficult.

The robot said, "I have been told to prevent any interference with the orders given me. You have been interfering."

Lucky no longer had a choice. He had miscalculated. It had never occurred to him to doubt the validity of the

Three Laws under all circumstances. The truth had come to him too late, and his miscalculation had brought him to this: the danger of his own life and the necessity of destroying a robot.

He raised his blaster sadly.

And almost at once he realized that he had made a second miscalculation. He had waited too long, and the accumulation of heat and weariness had made his body as imperfect a machine as was the robot's. His arm lifted sluggishly, and the robot seemed to be twice life-sized to his own reeling mind and sight.

The robot was a blur of motion, and this time Lucky's tired body could not be driven into quick enough movement. The blaster was struck from Lucky's hand and went flying. Lucky's arm was clamped tight in the grip of one metal hand, and his waist was embraced by a metal arm.

Under the best of circumstances, Lucky could not have withstood the steel muscles of the mechanical man. No human being could have. Now he felt all capacity for resistance vanish. He felt only the heat.

The robot tightened its grip, bending Lucky backward as though he were a rag doll. Lucky thought dizzily of the structural weakness of the inso-suit. An ordinary spacesuit might have protected him even against a robot's strength. An inso-suit could not. Any moment, a section of it might buckle and give.

Lucky's free arm flailed helplessly, his fingers dragging into the black grit below.

One thought flicked through his mind. Desperately he tried to drive his muscles into one last attempt to fend off what seemed inevitable death at the hands of a mad robot.

12

Prelude to a Duel

Lucky's predicament was a duplicate in reverse of that
which had faced Bigman some hours previously.
Bigman had been threatened not by heat but by growing
cold. He was held in the grip of the stony "ropes" as
firmly as Lucky in the grip of the metal robot. In one
respect, though, Bigman's position held hope. His numb-
ing grasp held desperately on the blaster pinned in
Urteil's hand.

And the blaster was coming loose. In fact, it came free
so suddenly that Bigman's numbed fingers nearly
dropped it.

"Sands of Mars!" he muttered, and held on.

If he had known where in the tentacles a vulnerable
spot might be, if he could have blasted any part of those
tentacles without killing either Urteil or himself, his problem would have been simple. As it was, there was only
one gamble, not a good one either, open to him.

His thumb worked clumsily on the intensity control,
pushing it down and down. He was getting drowsy, which
was a bad sign. It had been minutes since he had heard
any sign of life from Urteil.

He had intensity at minimum now. One more thing; he must reach the activator with his forefinger without dropping the blaster.

Space! He mustn't drop it.

The forefinger touched the proper spot and pushed against it.

The blaster grew warm. He could see that in the dull red glow of the grid across the muzzle. That was bad for the grid since a blaster was not designed to be used as a heat ray, but to deep Space with that.

With what strength was left him, Bigman tossed the blaster as far as he could.

It seemed to him then as though reality wavered for a moment, as though he were on the edge of unconsciousness.

Then he felt the first glow of warmth, a tiny leakage of heat entering his body from the laboring power-unit, and he shouted in weak joy. That heat was enough to show that power was no longer being drained directly into the voracious bodies of the heat-sucking tentacles.

He moved his arms. He lifted a leg. They were free. The tentacles were gone.

His suit-light had brightened, and he could see clearly the spot where the blaster had been thrown. The spot, but not the blaster. Where the blaster should be was a sluggishly moving mass of gray, intertwining tentacles.

With shaky motions, Bigman snatched at Urteil's own blaster, setting it to minimum and tossing it past the position of the first. That would hold the creature if the energy of the first gave out.

Bigman said urgently, "Hey, Urteil. Can you hear me?"

There was no answer.

With what strength he could muster he pulled the space-suited figure away with him. Urteil's suit-light glimmered, and his power-unit gauge showed itself as not quite empty. The temperature inside his suit should return to normal quickly.

Bigman called the Dome. There was no other decision possible now. In their weakened condition, with their power supply low, another encounter with Mercurian life would kill them. And he would manage to protect Lucky's position somehow.

It was remarkable how quickly men reached them.

With two cups of coffee and a hot meal inside him and the Dome's light and heat all about him, Bigman's resilient mind and body put the recent horror into proper perspective. It was already only an unpleasant memory.

Dr. Peverale hovered about him with an air partly like that of an anxious mother, partly like that of a nervous old man. His iron-gray hair was in disarray. "You're sure you're all right, Bigman. No ill effects?"

"I feel fine. Never better," insisted Bigman. "The question is, Doc, how's Urteil?"

"Apparently he'll be all right." The astronomer's voice grew cold. "Dr. Gardoma has examined him and reported favorably on his condition."

"Good," said Bigman almost gloatingly.

Dr. Peverale said with some surprise, "Are you concerned for him?"

"You bet, Doc. I've plans for him."

Dr. Hanley Cook entered now, almost trembling with excitement. "We've sent men into the mines to see if we can round up any of the creatures. They're taking heating pads with them. Like bait to a fish, you know." He turned to Bigman. "Lucky you got away."

Bigman's voice rose in pitch and he looked outraged, "It wasn't luck, it was brains. I figured they were after straight heat most of all. I figured it was their favorite kind of energy. So I gave it to them."

Dr. Peverale left after that, but Cook remained behind, talking of the creatures, walking back and forth, bubbling with speculation. "Imagine! The old stories about the freezing death in the mines were true. Really true! Think of it! Just rocky tentacles acting as heat sponges, absorbing energy wherever they can make contact. You're sure of the description, Bigman?"

"Of course I'm sure. When you catch one, see for yourself."

"What a discovery."

"How come they were never discovered before?" asked Bigman.

"According to you, they blend into their environment. Protective mimicry. Then, too, they attack only isolated men. Maybe," his words grew quicker, more animated, and his long fingers intertwined and twisted with one another, "there is some instinct there, some rudimentary intelligence that kept them hidden and out of sight. I'm sure of it. It's a kind of intelligence that kept them out of our way. They knew their only safety was in obscurity, so they attack only single, isolated men. Then for thirty years or more no men appeared in the mines. Their precious kernels of unusual heat were gone, and yet they never succumbed to the temptation to invade the Dome itself. But when men finally appeared once more in the mines, *that* temptation was too great and one of the creatures attacked, even though there were two men there and not one. For them, that was fatal. They have been discovered."

"Why don't they go to the Sun-side if they want energy and they're all that intelligent?" demanded Bigman.

"Maybe that's too hot," said Cook at once.

"They took the blaster. It was red hot."

"The Sun-side may be too full of hard radiation. They may not be adapted to that. Or maybe there is another breed of such creature on the Sun-side. How can we know? Maybe the dark-side ones live on radioactive ores and on the coronal glow."

Bigman shrugged. He found such speculation unprofitable.

And Cook's line of thought seemed to change too. He stared speculatively at Bigman, one finger rubbing his chin rhythmically. "So you saved Urteil's life."

"That's right."

"Well, maybe it's a good thing. If Urteil had died, they would have blamed you. Senator Swenson could have made it darned hot for you and for Starr *and* for the Council. No matter what explanation you gave, you would have been there when Urteil died, and that would have been enough for Swenson."

"Listen," said Bigman, moving about uneasily, "when do I get to see Urteil?"

"Whenever Dr. Gardoma says you may."

"Get him on the wire and tell him to say I can, then."

Cook's gaze remained fastened thoughtfully on the small Martian. "What's on your mind?"

And because Bigman had to make arrangements about the gravity, he explained some of his plan to Cook.

Dr. Gardoma opened the door and nodded to Bigman to enter. "You can have him, Bigman," he whispered. "I don't want him."

He stepped out, and Bigman and Urteil were alone with one another once again.

Jonathan Urteil was a little pallid where stubble didn't darken his face, but that was the only sign of his ordeal. He bared his lips to a savage grin. "I'm in one piece, if that's what you've come to see."

"That's what I've come to see. Also to ask you a question. Are you still full of that drivel about Lucky Starr setting up a fake Sirian base in the mines?"

"I intend to prove it."

"Look, you cobber, you know it's a lie, and you're going to fake proof if you can. *Fake* it! Now I'm not expecting you to get on your knees to thank me for saving your life————"

"Wait!" Slowly Urteil's face flushed. "All I remember is that that thing got me first by surprise. That was an accident. After that, I don't know what happened. What *you* say means nothing to me."

Bigman shrieked with outrage. "You smudge of space dust, you yelled for help."

"Where's your witness? I don't remember a thing."

"How do you suppose you got out?"

"I'm not supposing anything. Maybe the thing crawled away on its own. Maybe there was no thing at all. Maybe a rockfall hit me and knocked me out. Now if you came here expecting me to cry on your shoulders and promise to lay off your grafting friend, you're going to be disappointed. If you have nothing else to say, good-by."

Bigman said, "There's something you're forgetting. You tried to kill me."

"Where's your witness? Now if you don't get out, I'll pucker up and blow you out, midget."

Bigman remained heroically calm. "I'll make a deal with you, Urteil. You've made every threat you can think of because you're half an inch taller than I am and half a pound heavier, but you crawled the only time I made a pass at you."

"With a force-knife and myself unarmed. Don't forget that."

"I say you're yellow. Meet me rough and tumble, *now*. No weapons. Or are you too weak?"

"Too weak for you? Two years in the hospital and I wouldn't be too weak for you!"

"Then fight. Before witnesses! We can use the space in the power room. I've made arrangements with Hanley Cook."

"Cook must hate you. What about Peverale?"

"Nobody asked him. And Cook doesn't hate me."

"He seems anxious to get you killed. But I don't think I'll give him the satisfaction. Why should I fight a half-pint of skin and wind?"

"Yellow?"

"I said, why? You said you were making a deal."

"Right. You win, I don't say a word about what happened in the mines, what really happened. I win, you lay off the Council."

"Some deal. Why should I worry about anything you can say about me?"

"You're not afraid of losing, are you?"

"Space!" The exclamation was enough.

Bigman said, "Well, then?"

"You must think I'm a fool. If I fight with you before witnesses I'll be indicted for murder. If I lean a finger on you, you're squashed. Go find yourself another way to commit suicide."

"All right. How much do you outweigh me?"

"A hundred pounds," said Urteil contemptuously.

"A hundred pounds of fat," squeaked Bigman, his gnomish face screwed into a ferocious scowl. "Tell you what. Let's fight under Mercurian gravity. That makes your advantage forty pounds. And you keep your inertia advantage. Fair enough?"

Urteil said, "Space, I'd like to give you one smash, just to plaster your big mouth over your miserable little face."

"You've got your chance. Is it a deal?"

"By Earth, it's a deal. I'll try not to kill you, but that's as far as I'll go. You've asked for this, you've begged for it."

"Right. Now let's go. Let's go." And Bigman was so anxious that he hopped about as he talked, sparring a little with rapid birdlike motions of his fists. In fact, such was his eagerness for this duel that not once did he give a specific thought to Lucky nor suffer any presentiment of disaster. He had no way of telling that, some time before, Lucky had fought a more deadly duel than the one Bigman now proposed.

The power-level had its tremendous generators and heavy equipment, but it also had its broad level space suitable for gatherings of personnel. It was the oldest part of the Dome. In the first days, before even a single mine shaft had been blasted into Mercurian soil, the original construction engineers had slept on cots in that space between the generators. Even now it was still occasionally used for trifilm entertainment.

Now it served as a ring, and Cook, together with half a dozen or so technicians, remained dubiously on the side lines.

"Is this all?" demanded Bigman.

Cook said, "Mindes and his men are out Sun-side. There are ten men in the mines looking for your ropes, and the rest are mostly at their instruments." He looked apprehensively at Urteil and said, "Are you sure you know what you're doing, Bigman?"

Urteil was stripped to the waist. He had a thick growth of hair over his chest and shoulders, and he moved his muscles with an athletic joy.

Bigman looked in Urteil's direction indifferently. "All set with the gravity?"

"We'll have it off at the signal. I've rigged the controls

so the rest of the Dome won't be affected. Has Urteil agreed?"

"Sure." Bigman smiled. "It's all right, pal."

"I hope so," said Cook fervently.

Urteil called out, "When do we get started?" Then looking about the small group of spectators, he asked, "Anyone care to bet on the monkey?"

One of the technicians looked at Bigman with an uneasy grin. Bigman, now also stripped to his waist, looked surprisingly wiry, but the difference in size gave the match a grotesque appearance.

"No bet here," said the technician.

"Are we ready?" called Cook.

"I am," said Urteil.

Cook licked his pale lips and flicked the master switch. There was a change in the pitch of the subdued droning of the generators.

Bigman swayed with the sudden loss of weight. So did all the rest. Urteil stumbled but recovered rapidly and advanced gingerly into the middle of the clear space. He did not bother to lift his arms but stood waiting in a posture of complete relaxation.

"Start something, bug," he said.

13

Results of a Duel

For his part, Bigman advanced with gentle movements of his legs that translated themselves into slow and graceful steps, almost as though he were on springs.

In a way he was. Mercurian surface gravity was almost precisely equal to Martian surface gravity, and it was something he was at home with thoroughly. His cool, gray eyes, watching sharply, noticed every sway in Urteil's body, every knotting of a sudden muscle as he worked to keep erect.

Small misjudgments even in merely keeping one's balance were inevitable when working in a gravity to which one was unaccustomed.

Bigman moved in suddenly, springing from foot to foot and side to side in a broken motion that was at once amusingly dancelike and completely confusing.

"What is this?" growled Urteil in exasperation. "A Martian waltz?"

"Kind of," said Bigman. His arm lunged outward, and his bare knuckles slammed into Urteil's side with a resounding thwack, staggering the big fellow.

There was a gasp from the audience and one yell of "Hey, *boy!*"

Bigman stood there, arms akimbo, waiting for Urteil to recover his balance.

Urteil did so in a matter of five seconds, but now there was an angry red splotch on his side and a similar and angrier one on each cheekbone.

His own arm shot out powerfully, his right palm half open as though a slap would be sufficient to fling this stinging insect out of his way forever.

But the blow continued, dragging Urteil about. Bigman had ducked, leaving a fraction of an inch to spare, with the sure judgment of a perfectly co-ordinated body. Urteil's efforts to stop his follow-through left him teetering wildly, back to Bigman.

Bigman placed his foot on the seat of Urteil's pants and shoved gently. The recoil sent him hopping easily backward on the other foot, but Urteil went slowly forward on his face in grotesque slow motion.

There was sudden laughter from the side lines.

One of the spectators called out, "Changed my mind, Urteil. I'm betting."

Urteil made no gesture of hearing this. He was facing Bigman again, and from the corner of his thick lips a viscid drop of saliva made its way down the corner of his chin.

"Up the gravity!" he roared hoarsely. "Get it to normal!"

"What's the matter, tubbo?" mocked Bigman. "Isn't forty pounds in your favor enough?"

"I'll kill you. I'll kill you," Urteil shouted.

"Go ahead!" Bigman spread his arms in mock invitation.

But Urteil was not entirely beyond reason. He circled Bigman, hopping a little in ungainly fashion. He said, "I'll get my gravity legs, bug, and once I grab you anywhere, that piece gets torn off you."

"Grab away."

But there was an uneasy silence among the men who watched now. Urteil was a stooping barrel, his arms sweeping out and wide, his legs spread. He was keeping his balance, catching the rhythm of the gravity.

Bigman was a slender stalk in comparison. He might be as graceful and self-assured as a dancer, yet he looked pitifully small.

Bigman seemed unworried. He hopped forward with a sudden stamp of his feet that sent him shooting high in the air, and when Urteil lunged at the rising figure, Bigman lifted his feet and went down behind his adversary before the other could turn around.

There was loud applause, and Bigman grinned.

He performed what was almost a pirouette as he ducked under one of the great arms that threatened him, reaching out and bringing the side of his hand sharply down against the biceps.

Urteil restrained a cry and whirled again.

Urteil maintained a dreadful calm to all these grandstanding provocations now. Bigman, on the other hand, tried in every way he could to taunt and sting Urteil into a wild motion that would send him shooting off balance.

Forward and away; quick, sharp blows, which for all their flicking qualities carried a sting.

But a new respect for Urteil was growing in the small Martian's mind. The cobber was taking it. He was maintaining his ground like a bear warding off the attack of a hunting dog. And Bigman was the hunting dog which could only hover at the outskirts, snap, snarl, and keep out of the reach of the bear's paws.

Urteil even looked like a bear with his large, hairy body, his small, bloodshot eyes, and his jowly, bristly face.

"Fight, cobber," jeered Bigman. "I'm the only one giving the customers a show."

Urteil shook his head slowly. "Come closer," he said.

"Sure," said Bigman lightly, dashing in. With flashing movements, he caught Urteil on the side of the jaw and was under his arm and away in almost the same movement.

Urteil's arm half moved, but it was too late and the motion wasn't completed. He swayed a little. "Try it again," he said.

Bigman tried it again, twisting and diving under his other arm this time and finishing with a little bow to accept the roars of approval.

"Try it again," said Urteil thickly.

"Sure," said Bigman. And he dashed.

This time Urteil was thoroughly prepared. He moved neither head nor arms, but his right foot shot forward.

Bigman doubled, or tried to, in mid-air and didn't quite make it. His ankle was caught and pinned brutally for a moment by Urteil's shoe. Bigman yelped at the pressure.

Urteil's rapid movement carried him forward, and Bigman, with a quick, desperate shove at the other's back, accelerated that movement.

This time Urteil, more accustomed to the gravity, was not thrown forward as far and recovered more quickly, while Bigman, with his ankle on fire, moved about with a frightening clumsiness.

With a wild shout Urteil charged and Bigman, pivoting on his good foot, was not fast enough. His right shoulder was caught in one hamlike fist. His right elbow was caught in the other. They went down together.

A groan went up almost in concert from the spectators and Cook, watching ashen-faced, cried out, "Stop the fight" in a croaking voice that went completely unheeded.

Urteil got to his feet, his grip firm on Bigman, lifting

the Martian as though he were a feather. Bigman, face twisted in pain, writhed to get a footing of his own.

Urteil muttered into the little fellow's ear. "You thought you were wise, tricking me into fighting under low gravity. Do you still think so?"

Bigman wasted no time in thought. He would have to get at least one foot on the floor. . . . Or on Urteil's kneecap, for his right foot rested momentarily on Urteil's knee and that would have to do.

Bigman pushed down hard and lunged his body backward.

Urteil swayed forward. That was not dangerous for Urteil in itself, but his balancing muscles overshot the mark in the low gravity, and in righting himself he swayed backward. And as he did so, Bigman, expecting that, shifted his weight and pushed hard forward.

Urteil went down so suddenly that the spectators could not see how it was accomplished. Bigman wrenched half free.

He was on his feet like a cat, with his right arm still pinned. Bigman brought his left arm down on Urteil's wrist and brought up his knee sharply against the other's elbow.

Urteil howled and his grip on Bigman loosened as he shifted position to keep his own arm from being broken.

Bigman took his chance with the quickness of a jet's ignition. He wrenched his pinned hand completely loose while maintaining his grip on Urteil's wrist. His freed hand came down upon Urteil's arm above the elbow. He had a two-handed grip now on Urteil's left arm.

Urteil was scrabbling to his feet, and as he did so, Bigman's body bowed and his back muscles went down hard with effort. He lifted along the line of Urteil's own motion of rising.

Bigman's muscles, combined with the action of

Urteil's lift, carried that large body free of the ground in a slow motion, impressive display of what could be done in a low gravity field.

With his muscles near to cracking, Bigman whipped Urteil's torso still farther upward, then let go, watching it as it went flailing in a parabolic arc that seemed grotesquely slow by Earth standards.

They all watched and were all caught in the sudden change of gravity. Earth's full gravity snapped on with the force and speed of a blaster bolt, and Bigman went to his knees with a painful wrench on his twisted ankle. The spectators also went down in a chorus of confused cries of pain and astonishment.

Bigman caught only the merest glimpse of what happened to Urteil. The change in gravity had caught him almost at the high point of the parabola, snapping him downward with sharp acceleration. His head struck a protecting stanchion of one of the generators a sharp, cracking blow.

Bigman, rising painfully to his feet, tried to shake sense into his addled brains. He staggered and was aware of Urteil sprawled limply, of Cook kneeling at Urteil's side.

"What happened?" cried Bigman. "What happened to the gravity?"

The others echoed the question. As nearly as Bigman could tell, Cook was the only one on his feet, the only one who seemed to be thinking.

Cook was saying, "Never mind the gravity. It's Urteil."

"Is he hurt?" cried someone.

"Not any more," said Cook, getting up from his kneeling position. "I'm pretty sure he's dead."

They made an uneasy circle about the body.

Bigman said, "Better get Dr. Gardoma." He scarcely heard himself say it. A great thought had come to him.

"There's going to be trouble," said Cook. "You killed him, Bigman."

"The change in gravity did that," said Bigman.

"That'll be hard to explain. You threw him."

Bigman said, "I'll face any trouble. Don't worry."

Cook licked his lips and looked away. "I'll call Gardoma."

Gardoma arrived five minutes later, and the shortness of his examination was proof enough that Cook had been correct.

The physician rose to his feet, wiping his hands on a pocket handkerchief. He said gravely, "Dead. Fractured skull. How did it happen?"

Several spoke at once, but Cook waved them down. He said, "A grudge fight between Bigman and Ur-teil————"

"Between Bigman and Urteil!" exploded Dr. Gardoma. "Who allowed that? Are you crazy, expecting Bigman to stand up————"

"Easy there," said Bigman. "*I'm* in one piece."

Cook said in angry self-defense, "That's right, Gardoma, it's Urteil that's dead. And it was Bigman who insisted on the fight. You admit that, don't you?"

"I admit it all right," said Bigman. "I also said it was to be under Mercurian gravity."

Dr. Gardoma's eyes opened wide. "Mercurian gravity? Here?" He looked down at his feet as though wondering if his senses were playing him tricks and he were really lighter than he felt.

"It isn't Mercurian gravity any more," said Bigman, "because the pseudo-grav field snapped to full Earth gravity at a crucial time. Bam! Like that! That's what killed Urteil, not yours truly."

"What made the pseudo-grav snap to Earth levels?" asked Gardoma.

There was silence.

Cook said feebly, "It might have been a short————"

"Nuts," said Bigman, "the level is pulled up. It didn't do that by itself."

There was a new silence and an uneasy one.

One of the technicians cleared his throat and said, "Maybe in the excitement of the fight someone was moving around and shoved it up with his shoulder without even realizing it."

The others agreed eagerly. One of them said, "Space! It just happened!"

Cook said, "I'll have to report the entire incident. Bigman————"

"Well," said the small Martian calmly, "am I under arrest for manslaughter?"

"N—no," said Cook uncertainly. "I won't arrest you, but I have to report, and you may be arrested in the end."

"Uh huh. Well, thanks for the warning." For the first time since returning from the mines, Bigman found himself thinking of Lucky. This, he thought, is a fine peck of trouble for Lucky to find waiting for him when he comes back.

And yet there was an odd stir of excitement in the little Martian, too, for he was sure he could get out of the trouble . . . and show Lucky a thing or two in the process.

A new voice broke in. "Bigman!"

Everyone looked up. It was Peverale, stepping down the ramp that led from the upper levels. "Great Space, Bigman, are you down there? And Cook?" Then almost pettishly, "What's going on?"

No one seemed to be able to say anything at all. The old astronomer's eyes fell on the prone body of Urteil, and he said with mild surprise, "Is he dead?"

To Bigman's astonishment, Peverale seemed to lose interest in that. He didn't even wait for his question to be answered before turning to Bigman once more.

He said, "Where's Lucky Starr?"

Bigman opened his mouth but nothing came out. Finally, he managed to say weakly, "Why do you ask?"

"Is he still in the mines?"

"Well———"

"Or is he on Sun-side?"

"Well———"

"Great Space, man, is he on Sun-side?"

Bigman said, "I want to know why you're asking."

"Mindes," said Peverale impatiently, "is out in his flitter, patrolling the area covered by his cables. He does that sometimes."

"So?"

"So he's either mad or he's correct in saying he's seen Lucky Starr out there."

"Where?" cried Bigman at once.

Dr. Peverale's mouth compressed in disapproval. "Then he *is* out there. That's plain enough. Well, your friend Lucky Starr was apparently in some trouble with a mechanical man, a robot———"

"A robot!"

"And according to Mindes, who has not landed but who is waiting for a party to be sent out, Lucky Starr is dead!"

14

Prelude to a Trial

During the moment in which Lucky lay bent in the inexorable grip of the robot, he expected momentary death, and when it did not come at once a weak hope flared up within him.

Could it be that the robot, having the impossibility of killing a human being ingrained in its tortured mind, found itself incapable of the actual act now that it was face to face with it?

And then he thought that couldn't be, for it seemed to him the pressure of the robot's grip was increasing in smooth stages.

He cried with what force he could muster, "Release me!" and brought up his one free hand from where it had dragged, trailing in the black grime. There was one last chance, one last, miserably weak chance.

He lifted his hand to the robot's head. He could not turn his head to see, crushed as that was against the robot's chest. His hand slipped along the smooth metal surface of the robot's skull two times, three times, four times. He took his hand away.

There was nothing more he could do.

Then————Was it his imagination, or did the robot's grip seem to loosen? Was Mercury's big Sun on his side at last?

"Robot!" he cried.

The robot made a sound, but it was only like gears scraping rustily together.

Its grip *was* loosening. Now was the time to reinforce events by calling what might be left of the Laws of Robotics into play.

Lucky panted, "You may not hurt a human being."

The robot said, "I may not————" haltingly, and without warning fell to the ground.

Its grip was constant, as though rigid in death.

Lucky said, "Robot! Let go!"

Jerkily, the robot loosened his hold. Not entirely, but Lucky's legs came free and his head could move.

He said, "Who ordered you to destroy equipment?"

He no longer feared the robot's wild reaction to that question. He knew that he himself had brought that positronic mind to full disintegration. But in the last stages before final dissolution, perhaps some ragged remnant of the Second Law might hold. He repeated, "Who ordered you to destroy equipment?"

The robot made a blurred sound. "Er—Er————" Then, maddeningly, radio contact broke off, and the robot's mouth opened and closed twice as though, in the ultimate extremity, it were trying to talk by ordinary sound.

After that, nothing.

The robot was dead.

Lucky's own mind, now that the immediate emergency of near-death was over, was wavering and blurred. He lacked the strength to unwind the robot's limbs entirely from his body. His radio controls had been smashed in the robot's hug.

He knew that he must first regain his strength. To do that meant he must get out of the direct radiation of Mercury's big Sun and quickly. That meant reaching the shadow of the near-by ridge, the shadow he had failed to reach during the duel with the robot.

Painfully he doubled his feet beneath him. Painfully he inched his body toward the shadow of the ridge, dragging the robot's weight with him. Again. Again. The process seemed to last forever and the universe shimmered about him.

Again. Again.

There seemed to be no strength or feeling in his legs, and the robot seemed to weigh a thousand pounds.

Even with Mercury's low gravity, the task seemed beyond his weakening strength, and it was sheer will that drove him on.

His head entered the shadow first. Light blanked out. He waited, panting, and then, with an effort that seemed to crack his thigh muscles, he pushed himself along the ground once more and even once more.

He was in the shadow. One of the robot's legs was still in the sun, blazing reflections in all directions. Lucky looked over his shoulder and noted that dizzily. Then, almost gratefully, he let go of consciousness.

There were intervals later when sense perception crawled back.

Then, much later, he lay quietly, conscious of a soft bed under him, trying to bring those intervals back to mind. There were fragmentary pictures in his memory of people approaching, a vague impression of motion in a jet vehicle, of Bigman's voice, shrill and anxious. Then, a trifle more clearly, a physician's ministrations.

After that, a blank again, followed by a sharp memory of Dr. Peverale's courtly voice asking him gentle questions. Lucky remembered answering in connected fashion, so the worst of his ordeal must have been over by then. He opened his eyes.

Dr. Gardoma was looking at him somberly, a hypodermic still in his hand. "How do you feel?" he asked.

Lucky smiled. "How should I feel?"

"Dead, I should think, after what you've gone through. But you have a remarkable constitution, so you'll live."

Bigman, who had been hovering anxiously at the outskirts of Lucky's vision, entered it full now. "No thanks to Mindes for that. Why didn't that mud-brain go down and get Lucky out of there after he spotted the robot's leg? What was he waiting for? He was leaving Lucky to die?"

Dr. Gardoma put away his hypodermic and washed his hands. With his back to Bigman, he said, "Scott Mindes was convinced Lucky was dead. His only thought was to stay away so that no one could accuse him of being the murderer. He knew he had tried to kill Lucky once before and that others would remember that."

"How could he think that this time? The robot———"

"Mindes isn't himself under pressure these days. He called for help; that was the best he could do."

Lucky said, "Take it easy, Bigman. I was in no danger. I was sleeping it off in the shade, and I'm all right now. What about the robot, Gardoma? Was it salvaged?"

"We've got it in the Dome. The brain is gone, though, quite impossible to study."

"Too bad," said Lucky.

The physician raised his voice. "All right, Bigman, come on. Let him sleep."

"Hey———" began Bigman indignantly.

Lucky at once added, "That's all right, Gardoma. As a matter of fact, I want to speak to him privately."

Dr. Gardoma hesitated, then shrugged. "You need sleep, but I'll give you half an hour. Then he must go."

"He'll go."

As soon as they were alone, Bigman seized Lucky's shoulder and shook it violently. He said in a strangled kind of voice, "You stupid ape. If the heat hadn't got that robot in time—like in the sub-etherics————"

Lucky smiled mirthlessly. "It wasn't coincidence, Bigman," he said. "If I had waited for a sub-etheric ending, I'd be dead. I had to gimmick the robot."

"How?"

"Its brain case was highly polished. It reflected a large part of the sun's radiation. That meant the temperature of the positronic brain was high enough to ruin its sanity but not high enough to stop it completely. Fortunately, a good part of Mercurian soil about here is made up of a loose black substance. I managed to smear some on its head."

"What did that do?"

"Black absorbs heat, Bigman. It doesn't reflect it. The temperature of the robot's brain went up quickly and it died almost at once. It was close, though. . . . Still, never mind that. What happened at this end while I was gone? Anything?"

"*Anything?* Wow! You listen!" And as Bigman talked, Lucky did listen, with an expression that grew continually graver as the story unfolded.

By the time it drew to a conclusion he was frowning angrily. "Why did you fight Urteil, anyway? That was foolish."

"Lucky," said Bigman in outrage, "it was *strategy!* You always say I just bull right ahead and can't be trusted to do the shrewd thing. This was *shrewd.* I knew I could lick him at low gravity————"

"It seems as though you almost didn't. Your ankle is taped."

"I slipped. Accident. Besides, I *did* win. A deal was involved. He could do a lot of damage to the Council with his lies, but if I won he'd get off our backs."

"Could you take his word for that?"

"Well———" began Bigman, troubled.

Lucky drove on. "You saved his life, you said. He must have known that, and yet that didn't persuade him to abandon his purpose. Did you think he was likely to do so as a result of a fist fight?"

"Well———" said Bigman, again.

"Especially if he lost and would therefore be raging at the humiliation of a public beating. . . . I tell you what, Bigman. You did it because you wanted to beat him and get revenge for making fun of you. Your talk about making a deal was just an excuse to give you an opportunity for the beating. Isn't that right?"

"Aw, Lucky! Sands of Mars———"

"Well, am I wrong?"

"I wanted to make the deal———"

"But mainly you wanted to fight, and now look at the mess."

Bigman's eyes dropped. "I'm sorry."

Lucky relented at once. "Oh, Great Galaxy, Bigman, I'm not angry at you. I'm angry at myself, really. I misjudged that robot and nearly got myself killed because I wasn't thinking. I could see it was out of order and never tied it up with the effect of heat on its positronic brain till it was nearly too late. . . . Well, the past has a lesson for the future, but otherwise, let's forget it. The question is what to do about the Urteil situation."

Bigman's spirits bounced back at once. "Anyway," he said, "the cobber is off our backs."

"*He* is," said Lucky, "but what about Senator Swenson?"

"Hmm."

"How do we explain things? The Council of Science is being investigated, and as a result of a fight instigated by someone close to the Council, someone who's almost a member, the investigator dies. That won't look good."

"It was an accident. The pseudo-grav field——"

"That won't help us. I'll have to talk to Peverale and————"

Bigman reddened and said hastily, "He's just an old guy. He's not paying any attention to this."

Lucky hitched himself to one elbow. "What do you mean, he's not paying any attention?"

"He isn't," said Bigman vehemently. "He came in with Urteil lying dead on the ground and thought nothing of it. He said, 'Is he dead?' and that's all."

"That's all?"

"That's all. Then he asked about where you were and said Mindes had called and said a robot had killed you."

Lucky's level glance held Bigman. "That's all?"

"That was all," said Bigman uneasily.

"What's happened since then? Come on, Bigman. You don't want me to talk to Peverale. Why not?"

Bigman looked away.

"Come *on*, Bigman."

"Well, I'm being tried or something."

"*Tried!*"

"Peverale says it's murder and it'll raise a smell back on Earth. He says we've got to fix responsibility."

"All right. When is the trial?"

"Aw, Lucky, I didn't want to tell you. Dr. Gardoma said you weren't to be excited."

"Don't act like a mother hen, Bigman. When is the trial?"

"Tomorrow at two P.M., System Standard Time. But there's nothing to worry about, Lucky."

Lucky said, "Call in Gardoma."

"Why?"

"Do as I say."

Bigman stepped to the door, and when he returned, Dr. Gardoma was with him.

Lucky said, "There's no reason I can't get out of bed by two P.M. tomorrow, is there?"

Dr. Gardoma hesitated. "I'd rather you took more time."

"I don't care what you'd rather. It won't kill me, will it?"

"It wouldn't kill you to get out of bed right now, Mr. Starr," said Dr. Gardoma, offended. "But it's not advisable."

"All right, then. Now you tell Dr. Peverale that I'll be at the trial of Bigman. You know about that, I suppose?"

"I do."

"Everyone does except myself. Is that it?"

"You were in no condition————"

"You tell Dr. Peverale I'll be at that trial and it isn't to start without me."

"I'll tell him," said Gardoma, "and you'd better go to sleep now. Come with me, Bigman."

Bigman squealed. "Just one second." He stepped rapidly to the side of Lucky's bed and said, "Look, Lucky, don't get upset. I've got the whole situation under control."

Lucky's eyebrows lifted.

Bigman, almost bursting with self-importance, said, "I wanted to surprise you, darn it. I can prove I had nothing to do with Urteil breaking his neck. I've solved the case." He pounded his chest. "*I* have. *Me!* Bigman! I know who's responsible for everything."

Lucky said, "Who?"

But Bigman cried instantly, "No! I'm not saying. I want to show you I have more on my mind than fist fights.

I'll run the show this time and you watch me, that's all. You'll find out at the trial."

The little Martian wrinkled his face into a delighted grin, executed a small dance step, and followed Dr. Gardoma out of the room, wearing a look of gay triumph.

15

The Trial

Lucky strode into Dr. Peverale's office shortly before 2 P.M. the next day.

The others had already gathered. Dr. Peverale, sitting behind an old and crowded desk, nodded pleasantly at him, and Lucky responded with a grave, "Good afternoon, sir."

It was much like the evening of the banquet. Cook was there, of course, looking as always, nervous and, somehow, gaunt. He sat in a large armchair at Dr. Peverale's right, and Bigman's small body squirmed and was nearly lost in an equally large armchair at the left.

Mindes was there, his thin face twisted glumly and his intertwining fingers separating occasionally to drum on his pants leg. Dr. Gardoma sat next to him, stolid, his heavy eyelids lifting to glance disapprovingly at Lucky as he entered. The department heads among the astronomers were there.

In fact, the only man who had been present at the banquet but was absent now was Urteil.

Dr. Peverale began at once in his gentle way, "We can start now. And first, a few words for Mr. Starr. I understand that Bigman described this proceeding to you as a trial. Please be assured that it is nothing of the sort. If there is to be a trial, and I hope not, it will take place on Earth with qualified judges and legal counsel. What we are trying to do here is merely to assemble a report for transmission to the Council of Science."

Dr. Peverale arranged some of the helter-skelter of objects on his desk and said, "Let me explain why a full report is necessary. In the first place, as a result of Mr. Starr's daring penetration of the Sun-side, the saboteur who has been upsetting Dr. Mindes's project has been stopped. It turned out to be a robot of Sirian manufacture, which is now no longer functional. Mr. Starr————"

"Yes?" said Lucky.

"The importance of the matter was such that I took the liberty of questioning you when you were first brought in and when your state was one of only half-consciousness."

"I remember that," said Lucky, "quite well."

"Would you confirm some of the answers now, for the record?"

"I will."

"In the first place, are there any other robots involved?"

"The robot did not say, but I do not believe there were others."

"However, it did not say specifically that it was the only robot on Mercury?"

"It did not."

"Then there might be many others."

"I don't think so."

"That's only your own opinion, though. The robot didn't say there were no others."

"It did not."

"Very well, then. How many Sirians were involved?"

"The robot would not say. It had been instructed not to."

"Did it locate the base of the Sirian invaders?"

"It said nothing concerning that. It made no mention of Sirians at all."

"But the robot was of Sirian manufacture, wasn't it?"

"It admitted that."

"Ah." Dr. Peverale smiled humorlessly. "Then it is obvious, I think, that there are Sirians on Mercury and that they are active against us. The Council of Science must be made aware of this. There must be an organized search of Mercury and, if the Sirians evade us and leave the planet, there must at least be an increased awareness of the Sirian danger."

Cook interposed uneasily. "There is also the question of the native Mercurian life-forms, Dr. Peverale. The Council will have to be informed of that, too." He turned to address the gathering at large. "One of the creatures was captured yesterday and———"

The old astronomer interrupted with some annoyance. "Yes, Dr. Cook, the Council shall assuredly be informed. Nevertheless, the Sirian question is what must be kept foremost. Other matters must be sacrificed to the immediate danger. For instance, I suggest that Dr. Mindes abandon his project until Mercury be made safe for Earthmen."

"Hold on, now," cried Mindes quickly. "There's a lot of money and time and effort invested here———"

"I said, until Mercury was safe. I do not imply permanent abandonment of Project Light. And because it is necessary to put the Mercurian danger foremost, it is necessary to make sure that Urteil's protector, Senator Swenson, be prevented from setting up obstructions over side issues."

Lucky said, "You mean you want to present the sena-

tor with a scapegoat in the form of Bigman, neatly tick-
eted and bound hand and foot. Then while he's worrying
and clawing at Bigman, the chase for Sirians can proceed
on Mercury without interference."

The astronomer lifted his white eyebrows. "A scapegoat, Mr. Starr? We just want the facts."

"Well, go ahead, then," said Bigman, moving restlessly
in his chair. "You'll get the facts."

"Good," said Dr. Peverale. "As the central figure, do
you care to begin? Tell everything that occurred between
you and Urteil in your own words. Tell it in your own
words, but I would appreciate brevity. And remember,
these proceedings are being recorded on sound micro-
film."

Bigman said, "Do you want me to take my oath?"

Peverale shook his head. "This is not a formal trial."

"Suit yourself." And with surprising dispassion,
Bigman told the story. Beginning with Urteil's slurs on his
height and continuing through the encounter in the
mines, he ended with the duel. He left out only Urteil's
threats of action against Lucky Starr and the Council.

Dr. Gardoma followed, verifying what had occurred
on the occasion of the first meeting between Urteil and
Bigman and also describing, for the record, the scene at
the banquet table. He went on to describe his treatment
of Urteil after the return from the mines.

He said, "He recovered quickly from the hy-
pothermia. I didn't ask him for details, and he didn't offer
any. However, he asked after Bigman, and, from his expression when I said Bigman was entirely well, I should
judge that his dislike for Bigman was as great as ever. He
didn't act as though Bigman had saved his life. Just the
same, I must say that from my observation of the man I
should say Urteil was not subject to attacks of gratitude."

"That is only an opinion," interposed Dr. Peverale

hastily, "and I recommend that we not confuse the record by such statements."

Dr. Cook came next. He concentrated on the duel. He said, "Bigman insisted on the fight. That's all there was to that. It seemed to me that if I arranged one under low gravity as Bigman suggested, with witnesses, no harm would be done. We could intervene if things grew serious. I was afraid that, if I refused, a fight between them might result without witnesses and that there might be serious results. Of course, the results could scarcely be more serious than they have turned out to be, but I never anticipated that. I ought to have consulted you, Dr. Peverale, I admit that."

Dr. Peverale nodded. "You certainly ought to have. But the fact is now that Bigman insisted on the duel and insisted on low gravity, didn't he?"

"That's right."

"And he assured you that he would kill Urteil under those conditions."

"His exact words were that he would 'murder the cobber.' I think he was only speaking figuratively. I'm sure he didn't plan actual murder."

Dr. Peverale turned to Bigman. "Have you any comments in that connection?"

"Yes, I do. And since Dr. Cook is on the stand, I want to cross-examine."

Dr. Peverale looked surprised. "This isn't a trial."

"Listen," said Bigman heatedly. "Urteil's death was no accident. It was murder, and I want a chance to prove that."

The silence that fell at that statement lasted a moment and no more. It was succeeded by a confused babbling.

Bigman's voice rose to a piercing squeal. "I'm set to cross-examine Dr. Hanley Cook."

Lucky Starr said coldly, "I suggest you allow Bigman to go through with this, Dr. Peverale."

The old astronomer was the picture of confusion. "Really, I don't————Bigman can't————" He stammered himself into silence.

Bigman said, "First, Dr. Cook, how did Urteil come to know the route Lucky and I were taking in the mines?"

Cook reddened. "I didn't know he knew the route."

"He didn't follow us directly. He took a parallel route as though he were intending to catch up and fall behind us well within the mines, after we had convinced ourselves that we were alone and unfollowed. To do that, he would have to be certain of the route we were planning to take. Now Lucky and I planned that route with you and with no one else. Lucky didn't tell Urteil and neither did I. Who did?"

Cook looked wildly about as though for help. "I don't know."

"Isn't it obvious you did?"

"*No.* Maybe he overheard."

"He couldn't overhear marks on a map, Dr. Cook. . . . Let's pass on, now. I fought Urteil, and if gravity had stayed at Mercurian normal, he would still be alive. But it didn't stay there. It was suddenly hopped up to Earth-levels at just the moment where it helped to kill him. Who did that?"

"I don't know."

"You were the first one at Urteil's side. What were you doing? Making sure he was dead?"

"I resent that. Dr. Peverale————" Cook turned a flaming face toward his chief.

Dr. Peverale said with agitation, "Are you accusing Dr. Cook of having murdered Urteil?"

Bigman said, "Look. The sudden change in gravity pulled me to the ground. When I got to my feet, everyone else was either getting to their feet, too, or was still on the ground. When 75 to 150 pounds fall on your back without warning, you don't get to your feet in a hurry. But Cook had. He was not only on his feet, he had gotten to Urteil's side and was bending over him."

"What does that prove?" demanded Cook.

"It proves you didn't go down when the gravity went up, or you couldn't have gotten there in time. And *why* didn't you go down when the gravity went up? Because you *expected* it to go up and were braced for it. And *why* did you expect it to go up? Because *you* tripped the lever."

Cook turned to Dr. Peverale. "This is persecution. It's madness."

But Dr. Peverale looked at his second in stricken horror.

Bigman said, "Let me reconstruct the business. Cook was working with Urteil. That's the only way Urteil could have learned our route in the mines. But he was working with Urteil out of fear. Maybe Urteil was blackmailing him. Anyway, the only way Cook could get out from under was to kill Urteil. When I said I could murder the cobber if we fought under low gravity, I must have put an idea into his head, and when we had the fight he stood there waiting at the lever. That's all."

"Wait," cried Cook urgently, almost choked, "this is all —this is all———"

"You don't have to go by me," said Bigman. "If my theory is right, and I'm sure it is, then Urteil must have something in writing or on recording or on film that he can hold over Cook's head. Otherwise, Cook wouldn't have felt trapped to the point of murder. So search Urteil's effects. You'll find something and that will be it."

"I agree with Bigman," said Lucky.

Dr. Peverale said in bewilderment, "I suppose it's the only way of settling the matter, though how————"

And the air seemed to go out of Dr. Hanley Cook, leaving him pale, shaken, and helpless. "Wait," he said weakly, "I'll explain."

And all faces turned toward him.

Hanley Cook's lean cheeks were bathed in perspiration. His hands as he raised them, almost in supplication, trembled badly. He said, "Urteil came to me shortly after he arrived on Mercury. He said he was investigating the Observatory. He said Senator Swenson had evidence of inefficiency and waste. He said it was obvious that Dr. Peverale ought to be retired; that he was an old man and incapable of bearing up under the responsibility. He said I might make a logical replacement."

Dr. Peverale, who listened to this with an air of stunned surprise, cried out. *"Cook!"*

"I agreed with him," said Cook sullenly. "You *are* too old. I'm running the place anyway while you occupy yourself with your Sirius mania." He turned again to Lucky. "Urteil said that if I helped him in his investigation he would see to it that I would be the next director. I believed him; everyone knows Senator Swenson is a powerful man.

"I gave him a great deal of information. Some of it was in writing and signed. He said he needed it for legal proceedings afterward.

"And then—and then he began holding that written information over my head. It turned out that he was a lot more interested in Project Light and the Council of Science. He wanted me to use my position to become a kind of personal spy for him. He made it quite plain that he would go to Dr. Peverale with evidence of what I had done if I refused. That would have meant the end of my career, of everything.

"I *had* to spy for him. I had to give information concerning the route Starr and Bigman were to take in the mines. I kept him up to date on everything Mindes did. Every time I surrendered a bit more to him I was more helplessly in his power. And after a while I knew that someday he would break me, no matter how much I helped him. He was that kind of man. I began to feel that the only way I could escape was to kill him. If only I knew how———

"Then Bigman came to me with his plan to fight Urteil under low gravity. He was so confident that he could toss Urteil about. I thought then I might———The chances would be one in a hundred, maybe one in a thousand, but I thought, what was there to lose? So I stood at the pseudo-grav controls and waited my chance. It came and Urteil died. It worked perfectly. I thought it would go down as an accident. Even if Bigman were in trouble, then the Council could get him out of it. No one would be hurt except Urteil, and he deserved it a hundred times over. Anyway, that's it."

In the awed silence that followed, Dr. Peverale said huskily, "Under the circumstances, Cook, you will of course consider yourself relieved of all duty and under ar———"

"Hey, hold it, *hold it,*" cried Bigman. "The confession isn't complete yet. Look here, Cook, that was the second time you tried to kill Urteil, wasn't it?"

"The second time?" Cook's tragic eyes lifted.

"What about the gimmicked inso-suit? Urteil said for us to watch out for one, so he must have had experience with it. He made out Mindes was doing it, but that Urteil was a lying cobber and nothing he says has to be believed. What I say is that you tried to kill Urteil that way, but he caught the suit and forced you to transfer it to our room when we came. Then he warned us about it just to get us thinking he was on our side and make trouble for Mindes. Isn't that so?"

"No," shouted Cook. "No! I had nothing to do with that inso-suit. Nothing."

"Come on," began Bigman. "We're not going to believe————"

But now Lucky Starr got to his feet. "It's all right, Bigman. Cook had nothing to do with the inso-suit. You can believe him. The man responsible for the slashed inso-suit is the man responsible for the robot."

Bigman stared at his tall friend incredulously. "You mean the Sirians, Lucky?"

"No Sirians," said Lucky. "There are no Sirians on Mercury. There never have been."

16

Results of the Trial

Dr. Peverale's deep voice was hoarse with dismay. "No Sirians? Do you know what you're saying, Starr?"

"Perfectly." Lucky Starr moved up to Dr. Peverale's desk, sat down on one corner of it, and faced the assemblage. "Dr. Peverale will bear me out on that, I'm sure, when I've explained the reasoning."

"*I'll* bear you out? No fear of that, I assure you," huffed the old astronomer, his face set in an attitude of bitter disapproval. "It is scarcely worth discussing. . . . By the way, we'll have to place Cook under arrest." He half rose.

Lucky urged him gently back into his seat. "It's all right, sir. Bigman will make sure that Cook will remain under control."

"I won't make any trouble," said the despairing Cook in a muffled tone. Bigman pulled his armchair close to Cook's nevertheless.

Lucky said, "Think back, Dr. Peverale, on the night of the banquet and of your own words concerning the Sirian robots. . . . By the way, Dr. Peverale, you've known for a long time there was a robot on the planet, haven't you?"

The astronomer said uneasily, "What do you mean?"

"Dr. Mindes came to you with stories of having sighted moving manlike figures in what seemed like metal space-suits who also seemed to endure solar radiation better than one would expect humans to."

"I certainly did," interposed Mindes, "and I should have known I was seeing a robot."

"You didn't have the experience with robots that Dr. Peverale did," said Lucky. He turned to the old astronomer again. "I'm sure that you suspected the existence of Sirian-designed robots on the planet as soon as Mindes reported what he had seen. His description fit them perfectly."

The astronomer nodded slowly.

"I, myself," Lucky went on, "did not suspect robots when Mindes told me his story any more than he himself did. After the banquet, however, when, Dr. Peverale, you discussed Sirius and its robots, the thought occurred to me very forcefully that here was the explanation. You must have thought so too."

Dr. Peverale nodded slowly again. He said, "I realized that we ourselves could do nothing against a Sirian incursion. That is why I discouraged Mindes."

(Mindes turned pale at this point and muttered savagely to himself.)

Lucky said, "You never reported to the Council of Science?"

Dr. Peverale hesitated. "I was afraid they wouldn't believe me and that I would only succeed in getting myself replaced. Frankly, I didn't know what to do. It was obvious that I could make no use of Urteil. He was interested only in his own plans. When you came, Starr," his voice grew deeper, more flowing, "I felt I might have an ally at last, and for the first time I felt able to talk about Sirius, its dangers, and its robots."

"Yes," said Lucky, "and do you remember how you described the Sirian affection for their robots? You used the word 'love.' You said the Sirians pampered their robots; they loved them; nothing was too good for them. You said they would regard a robot as worth a hundred Earthmen."

"Of course," said Dr. Peverale. "That's true."

"Then if they loved their robots so much, would they send one of them to Mercury, uninsulated, unadapted to Solar radiation? Would they condemn one of their robots to a slow, torturing death by the Sun?"

Dr. Peverale fell silent, his lower lip trembling.

Lucky said, "I, myself, could scarcely think of blasting the robot even though it endangered my life, and I am no Sirian. Could a Sirian have been so cruel to a robot, then?"

"The importance of the mission————" began Dr. Peverale.

"Granted," said Lucky. "I don't say a Sirian wouldn't send a robot to Mercury for purposes of sabotage, but, Great Galaxy, they would have insulated its brain first. Even leaving their love for robots out of account, it's only good sense. They could get more service out of it."

There was a murmur of approval and agreement from the assemblage.

"But," stammered Dr. Peverale, "if not the Sirians then who————"

"Well," said Lucky, "let's see what leads we have. Number one. Twice Mindes spotted the robot, and twice it vanished when Mindes tried to draw close. The robot later informed me that it had been instructed to avoid people. Obviously, it had been warned that Mindes was out searching for the saboteur. Obviously, too, it must have been warned by someone inside the Dome. It wasn't warned against me, because I announced that I was going into the mines.

"Lead number two. As the robot lay dying, I asked once more who had given it its instructions. It could only say, 'Er—er———' Then its radio blanked out, but its mouth moved as though it were making two syllables."

Bigman shouted suddenly, his pale red hair standing on end with passion, "Urteil! The robot was trying to say Urteil! That filthy cobber was the saboteur all the time. It fits in! It fits———"

"Maybe," said Lucky, "maybe! We'll see. It struck me as a possibility that the robot was trying to say, 'Earthman.'"

"And maybe," said Peverale dryly, "it was only a vague sound made by a dying robot and it meant nothing at all."

"Maybe," agreed Lucky. "But now we come to lead number three and it is instantly conclusive. That is this: The robot was of Sirian manufacture, and what human here at the Dome could possibly have had a chance to gain possession of a Sirian robot? Have any of us been on the Sirian planets?"

Dr. Peverale's eyes narrowed. "I have."

"Exactly," said Lucky Starr, "and no one else. That's your answer."

Mad confusion followed and Lucky called for silence. His voice was authoritative and his face stern. "As a Councilman of Science," he said, "I declare this observatory to be in my charge from this moment on. Dr. Peverale is replaced as director. I have been in communication with Council Headquarters on Earth, and a ship is on its way now. Appropriate action will be taken."

"I demand to be heard," cried Dr. Peverale.

"You will be," said Lucky, "but first listen to the case against you. You are the only man here who had the opportunity to steal a Sirian robot. Dr. Cook told us that you were awarded a robot for personal service during your stay on Sirius. Is that correct?"

"Yes, but————"

"You directed him into your own ship when you were through with him. Somehow you managed to evade the Sirians. Probably they never dreamed anyone could commit so horrible a crime, to them, as robot-stealing. They took no precautions against it for that reason, perhaps.

"What's more, it makes sense to suppose the robot was trying to say, 'Earthman' when I asked him who had given it instructions. You were the one Earthman on Sirius. You would be spoken of as 'Earthman' when the robot was first placed in your service, probably. It would think of you as 'Earthman.'

"Finally, who would know better when anyone might be exploring the Sun-side? Who would better inform the robot by radio when it might be safe and when it ought to go into hiding?"

"I deny everything," said Dr. Peverale tightly.

"There's no point in denying it," said Lucky. "If you insist on your innocence, the Council will have to send to Sirius for information. The robot gave me its serial number as RL-726. If the Sirian authorities say that the robot assigned to you during your stay on Sirius was RL-726 and that it disappeared about the time you left Sirius, that will condemn you.

"Furthermore, your crime of robot-stealing was committed on Sirius, and because we have an extradition treaty with the Sirian planets we may be forced to release you into their custody. I would advise you, Dr. Peverale, to confess and let Earth's justice take its course, rather than to maintain innocence and risk what Sirius might do for your crime of having stolen one of their beloved robots and tortured it to death."

Dr. Peverale stared pitifully at the assemblage with unseeing eyes. Slowly, joint by joint, he collapsed and dropped to the floor.

Dr. Gardoma rushed to his side and felt for his heart. "He's alive," he said, "but I think he'd better be moved to bed."

Two hours later, with Dr. Gardoma and Lucky Starr at his bedside and with Council Headquarters in subetheric contact, Dr. Lance Peverale dictated his confession.

With Mercury falling rapidly behind and the sure knowledge that Council emissaries now had the situation in hand, relieving him of any feeling of responsibility, Lucky still felt tension. His expression was brooding and thoughtful.

Bigman, face puckered anxiously, said, "What's the matter, Lucky?"

"I'm sorry for old Peverale," said Lucky. "He meant well in his way. The Sirians *are* a danger, if not quite as immediate as he thought."

"The Council wouldn't have turned him over to Sirius, would it?"

"Probably not, but his fears of Sirius were sufficiently great to force his confession. It was a cruel trick, but necessary. However patriotic his motives, he had been forced into attempted murder. Cook, too, was goaded into his crime, yet it was none the less a crime, however little we think of Urteil."

Bigman said, "What did the old guy have against Project Light anyway, Lucky?"

"Peverale made that clear at the banquet," said Lucky grimly. "Everything was made clear that night. You remember, he complained that Earth was weakening itself by depending on imported food and resources. He said Project Light would make Earth dependent on space stations for the very manner in which it got its sunlight. He wanted Earth to be self-sufficient so that it could better resist the Sirian danger.

"In his slightly unbalanced mind, he must have thought he would help that self-sufficiency along by trying to sabotage Project Light. Perhaps he originally brought back the robot just as a dramatic demonstration of Sirian power. Finding Project Light in progress when he returned, he turned the robot into a saboteur instead.

"When Urteil arrived he must have been afraid at first that Urteil was going to investigate the Project Light affair and expose him. So he planted a slashed inso-suit in Urteil's room, but Urteil spotted it. Maybe Urteil really believed Mindes had been responsible."

Bigman said, "Sure, come to think of it. The first time we met the old guy he wouldn't even talk about Urteil, he was so mad about him."

"Exactly," said Lucky, "and there was no obvious reason why that should be, as in Mindes's case, for instance. I thought there might be some reason I knew nothing about."

"Is that what put you on to him first, Lucky?"

"No, it was something else. It was the slashed inso-suit in our own room. The man with the best opportunity to do that was obviously Peverale himself. He also would be in the best position to dispose of the suit after it had killed its man. He best knew our assigned room, and he could assign an inso-suit too. What bothered me, though, was the motive? Why should he want to kill me?

"My name apparently meant nothing to him. He asked if I were a sub-temporal engineer like Mindes the first time we met. Now Mindes had recognized my name and tried to get me to help him. Dr. Gardoma had heard of me in connection with the poisonings on Mars. Urteil knew all about me, of course. I wondered if Dr. Peverale might not have heard of me too.

"There was Ceres, for instance, where you and I stayed a while during the battle against the pirates. The largest observatory in the System is there. Might not Dr. Peverale have been there then? I asked him that, and he denied having met me there. He admitted that he visited Ceres, and Cook later told us the old man visited Ceres frequently. Peverale went on to explain, without any prompting from me, that he had been sick in bed during the pirate raid, and Cook later backed that statement. That was the giveaway. In his anxiety, Peverale had talked too much."

The little Martian stared. "I don't get that."

"It's simple. If Peverale had been on Ceres a number of times, how was it he felt it necessary to alibi that particular time when the pirates had attacked? Why that time and not another? Obviously, he knew on which occasion I had been on Ceres and was trying to alibi that one. Obviously, again, he knew who I was.

"If he knew me, why should he try to kill me, and Urteil too? Both of us suffered from slashed inso-suits, you know. We were both investigators. What was it Peverale feared?

"Then he began to talk about Sirians and robots at the banquet table, and things began to drop into place. Mindes's story suddenly made sense, and I knew at once that the only ones who could have brought a robot to Mercury were either Sirians or Dr. Peverale. To me it seemed that Peverale was the answer, that he was talking about Sirians now as a kind of insurance. If the robot were found and the sabotage stopped, it would serve as a smoke screen to hide his own part and, furthermore, it would make good anti-Sirian propaganda.

"I needed proof. Otherwise, Senator Swenson would shout *we* were setting up a smoke screen to cover the Council's own incompetence and extravagance. I needed good proof. With Urteil right on the ground, I dared not talk about the matter to anyone, Bigman, not even to you."

Bigman groaned in disgust. "When are you going to trust me, Lucky?"

"When I can count on you to avoid tricks like rough-and-tumbles with men twice your size," said Lucky with a smile that robbed the statement of some of its sting. "Anyway, I set out to capture the robot on the Sun-side and use him as evidence. That failed and I was forced to work a confession out of Peverale."

Lucky shook his head.

Bigman said, "What about Swenson now?"

"It's a draw, I think," said Lucky. "He can't do much with Urteil's death, since we can use Dr. Cook as a witness to show some of Urteil's dirty tactics. We can't do much against him, either, since the two top men at the Mercurian Observatory have had to be relieved of duty for felonies. It's a standoff."

"Sands of Mars!" moaned Bigman. "We'll have that cobber on our necks later on then."

But Lucky shook his head. "No, Senator Swenson is not a real cause for worry. He's ruthless and dangerous, but for that very reason he keeps the Council on its toes, keeps us from getting flabby.

"Besides," he added thoughtfully, "the Council of Science needs its critics, just as Congress and the government do. If ever the Council began to consider itself above criticism, then the time might come when it would establish a dictatorship over the Earth, and certainly I wouldn't want that to happen."

"Well, maybe," said Bigman, unsatisfied, "but I don't like that Swenson."

Lucky laughed and reached out to tousle the Martian's hair. "Nor I, but why worry about that now. Out there are the stars, and who knows where we'll be going next week, or why?"

ABOUT THE AUTHOR

Isaac Asimov was America's most prolific author, with more than 440 published books to his credit. His Foundation Trilogy was given a special Hugo Award as Best All-Time Science Fiction Series. Foundation's Edge won a Hugo Award as Best Science Fiction Novel in 1982, and Dr. Asimov was presented the Science Fiction Writers of America Grand Master Award in 1988. Dr. Asimov died in 1992.